Storm

A Sci-Fi Alien Romance

Hattie Jacks

Copyright © 2022 by Hattie Jacks

All rights reserved.

No part of this book may be reproduced in any form or by any electronic or mechanical means, including information storage and retrieval systems, without written permission from the author, except for the use of brief quotations in a book review.

Cover by Kasmit

Editing: Epona Author Solutions

Proofing: Polaris Editing

❦ Created with Vellum

Kat

"Are you sure you want to go by yourself?" Lana's voice is tinny on my phone, and the connection begins to crackle as I enter the valley.

"I'm basically already here, so, yes, I want to go by myself. I need some time for me...you know how it is..."

"I don't know, Kat." Lana sounds peevish. "What's wrong with you? I had a really good weekend planned. Billy was going to do a barbecue and everything, then you text me out of the blue and say you're going away."

She's annoyed, and she has every right to be. Apparently I blew her amazing weekend plans out for an isolated cottage in a forgotten corner of the English Lake District, and not even the nice bit where all the tourists hang out.

"I'm sorry, Lana. I didn't think you had anything special planned. Things have been difficult for me recently. I wanted some time to clear my head."

"How can making trinkets be difficult?" Lana fires at me. "It's hardly taxing playing around with pretty stones all day."

My knuckles turn white on the steering wheel at her

description of my jewelry business, and a sign flashes past. I'm sure I've missed my turning, and I jam on the brakes, making a screeching sound as I skid a short way along the road.

"What was that?" she says.

"I missed my turn. Look, it's getting dark, and I need to concentrate. I'm going to lose the signal soon anyway. I'm sorry, Lana. I'll try to make it up to you some other time." I press the end call button on my phone and drop it onto the passenger seat.

My hands shake, and it's not from the need to stop suddenly. It's because that sort of conflict is exactly the reason I needed to get away, what with customer complaints giving me flashbacks to three years ago. Things haven't been difficult. They've been awful.

I shake my head. I promised myself I'd not think about it all weekend. I've just been paid for a commission, and the cottage was dirt cheap because it's out of season and, frankly, in the middle of nowhere. This weekend is supposed to be about me getting my confidence back, doing some hiking and sketching. Just me and peace.

I don't need the conflict and the stress. I've had more than enough in the last three years. That's why I'm a thirty-five-year-old single woman heading into the hills on her own.

Because I can do this. I can adult. I can have a life again, someday.

By the time I've reversed and found my turn, darkness is really falling. The unpaved, rocky road winds up the side of a mountain toward a tiny white speck of a place, outlined in the gathering gloom. By the time I reach the whitewashed, stone cottage, it's clear that it's even smaller than it looked on the website, but I don't care. I can be on my own, eating chocolate ice cream and binging on all the downloads of silly 1980's movies I brought with me.

Definitely preferable to making small talk with Lana's husband who still can't understand why I gave up my job in the City of London. She's supposed to be my best friend, but all she ever wants to do is hook me up with Billy's awful pinstripe-suited city friends and talk me into going back.

That's never going to happen.

I pull into the yard in front of the stone cottage. Killing the engine and the headlights, I open the door to complete silence. It's dark in the yard, the kind of inky blackness you can only get somewhere where there are no humans for many miles.

Above me, the stars shine incredibly bright and beautiful. Sometimes I wonder what it would be like to float among them. I'm spellbound for a long time, staring and staring, watching the occasional satellite dotting across the sky.

Leaning back against the cold metal of the car, I allow my mind to wander, to just be in the moment and forget everything. A green glow appears behind the stone cottage, and it takes my brain a short time to process what I'm seeing.

Aurora borealis!

Surely, I'm too far south to be seeing it? I duck back into my car to grab my phone. I already know there's no signal, but I might be able to take some video. There's a scraping sound behind me that stops suddenly as soon as I'm back out.

"Hello?" I call out. I'm supposed to be the only occupant of the cottage this weekend.

The owners told me that the key would be under the doormat and to just let myself in after I told them I'd be driving up from London and wouldn't get there until late. Maybe they decided to come up and check me in after all.

"It's Kat Bolton. I'm staying here this weekend," I add as an afterthought.

The scraping comes again. Maybe it's a sheep. The Lake

District is famous for its sheep. Sheep and Beatrix Potter. Although I'm sure bunnies, kittens, and hedgehogs wouldn't make me feel like this.

My skin slowly creeps, prickling with fear.

Then I hear the growl.

Low and feral, it sends a chill down my spine. I'm sure the website said 'no dogs,' but that noise has to be from a dog and not a friendly one either.

I contemplate my options. I'm all alone and there's no phone signal. I can either get back in my car and drive an hour to the nearest hotel, which I can't afford to do, or I can see if I make it to the cottage before I'm shredded by the beast in the dark.

I take a step away from the car. The growl comes again, but this time it sounds more like a word in a language I don't understand.

"I'll call the police!" I shout out, my voice pathetically high and reedy as I hold up my useless mobile phone.

The light from the screen provides some small illumination of the yard next to the cottage and the hulking *thing* that stands only a few feet away from me.

"Fuck!" I leap back, dropping my phone and, finding that my legs are working, I scramble around the front of the car and start to run.

As I reach the edge of the yard, there's a fence and no sign of any gate. With all the grace of an elephant on roller skates, I attempt to vault it and simply end up on my face in the mud, grass, and sheep droppings.

The growling thing looms over me, and the starlight disappears as an unbelievably strong white light flicks on above us.

As it turns out, aliens are green.

They are just not little and not men.

The huge, lizard-like thing gazing down on me bares its

jaws. They drip with some sort of black substance. It reaches for me, a thin silver tube gripped in claw-like, three-fingered hands. My body has turned to ice with fear as it jabs at me.

My vision dims and I wish I'd listened to Lana.

I shouldn't have come here alone.

Strykr

"For vrex sake!" I dive into the scrum of feathers, limbs, and claws, locating the members of my unit who have decided to take on half a dozen new warriors. Reaching the usual suspects, I rip them free of the fight, flinging them to one side.

"Vrex off!" I snarl at the remainder of the mercs, the other Gryn warriors, some of which sport wounds. They don't need to be told twice, not by me.

"Jay, I expected better of you," I snarl at my youngest team member and best sniper. He sits on the floor, breathing heavily, but he appears undamaged, fortunately for him.

"Ayar..." I look over at my weapons specialist. He hasn't broken a sweat, his claws dripping with blood.

I shake my head.

"Get your stuff, we're moving out," I bellow at the rest of my team, standing on the sidelines. "We'll discuss this gakshow later."

It's not the first time I've broken up a fight between my unit and the other warriors who make up the new legion of the Gryn.

We had no option but to expand. With the defeat of the sentient AI, Proto, that used to control Ustokos, we've gained all the male warriors which were held in its internment camps. All we have to do now is rebuild our once great planet.

But it's not proving easy.

Putting all the newly liberated warriors together seemed like a good idea at the time. It was supposed to give them the opportunity to adjust. I suppose they have. It's my unit which seems to rub them all the wrong way.

It doesn't help that we're supposed to be the chosen ones. The ones hand-picked by Ryak, our governor, who reports directly to the Prime of the Gryn, Jyr.

That hasn't gone down well with many warriors.

"Commander." Mylo sidles up to me. "Don't go too hard on them."

"I don't want to hear it, Mylo." I turn my back on my combat master. "This mission is too important to be vrexed up by drunken fighting."

"Mission first, party later," Mylo mutters as he heaves a pack onto his back. "Although none of us have touched a drop, more's the pity."

I fix him with a gaze I know they all hate. It's the look that tells them any more of their gak and they'll be in the training pit later, going one to one with me.

And none of them want that. Once is always enough, even for Ayar, a warrior who fights as if every battle is his last.

With my team ready, I give the order, and we're in the air, heading out of the eyrie and towards the launch pad where our mission awaits.

Behind me, I already know my unit follows in perfect formation. They might fight hard and party hard, but they know the drill. My warriors are the best of the best. The elite. A bunch of dysfunctional specialists. And they are all mine.

Lucky me.

There hasn't been an appointment to senior within the ranks of the legion of the Gryn for three turns, not since the mighty Fyn was promoted the Prime's second in command.

I'm following in some big wing beats. But then defeating all the odds is what I've done best for a very long time.

The spacecraft, the *Perlin*, squats on the pad, steam rising from various vents around its outer hull. Angular and pockmarked with space debris, it's the only working space vessel the Gryn have access to and, regardless of looks, it's what's taking my unit into orbit today.

"Do we have to go in this heap of space junk?" Jay grumbles as we land as one. He hitches up his long silver laser rifle onto his back and squints at the ship.

"Why? You scared of being sucked off into space?" Mylo chides him, the cocky warrior immediately starting to inspect the exterior.

"He's like all of us, wondering if this tech is going to kill us when it feels like it," Ayar mutters darkly.

"I can confirm with confidence that Proto is not on the vrexing *Perlin*, Ayar." I shoulder the scarred warrior with my wing, and I hear him growl under his breath.

He knows better than to challenge me. Ayar might be vicious, but I fight dirty. He knows what I say is correct.

"Are you vrexers boarding or what?" Lyon calls from the bottom of the ramp.

"Get your gak loaded. And remember what I told you earlier. Don't touch any tech unless either the captain or myself tells you to," I order as I walk over to Lyon. The light-colored Gryn holds a vectorpad in his hands and is making his final checks. "Are we good to go, Captain?" I ask him in a low voice.

Lyon hesitates slightly. I know some of his memory has returned since he arrived on Ustokos, but much of his past remains a mystery, including how he ended up in the clutches of a species called the Drahon and kept as a slave assassin. He has his concerns about today's mission and whether it will bring us into contact with his former masters.

Our healer, Orvos, is not sure if he will ever remember a time before his incarceration. However, Lyon has proved himself invaluable in increasing our knowledge of tech, in particular how to fly this spacecraft.

"We're good, Commander." He pulls himself up to his full height, and I give him a supportive smile, knowing he's struggled to adjust to living with us in the new eyrie.

"Ayar!" I snap across at my troublesome weapons specialist. He took to the new laser weapons as if he had been born with them in his hands, meaning he has an unerring talent to both make the new tech work and make it extremely disruptive. "Get it loaded, or you're off the vrexing mission."

It's an idle threat. The last thing he wants is to be left behind, especially if there's an option to destroy something. Plus, he'd never leave Vypr, my explosive expert. The pair are inseparable. Even now, as Ayar glares at me, Vypr slings his arm over his shoulder, ruffling his claws through the feathers on the ridge of Ayar's wing, and I see the warrior visibly relax.

"It's like herding younglings," I grumble to Lyon as our kit is finally loaded onto the *Perlin* by my unit. "Speaking of which, how is your mate?"

"Due to birth any day now. So I'd appreciate it if we could complete this trip without incident." Lyon cocks a questioning eyebrow at me, wanting my reassurance. He arrived on Ustokos with his human female mate, Sara, having rescued her from another group of slavers. She's joined the other five human females on this planet in conceiving young.

Something we never thought was possible, given that Proto had taken all our Gryn females from us.

One of the other reasons we're going up today. The other thing Proto took from us was the ability to use any form of tech during its rule. With its defeat, the entire planet is at risk of invasion from anything that understands technology more than us. At this moment in time, that's basically every other sentient species out there. We have to secure whatever tech we can and get up to speed as soon as possible to avoid being prey to the slavers we already know have an interest in the Gryn.

"Everything I do is without incident, Lyon." I shake my wing feathers at him. "I am the very definition of 'without incident.'"

He stares at me and shrugs. "If you say so, Commander."

I check over the launch pad to make sure everything is ready and then follow Lyon on board, heading through the short passageways until I reach the bridge.

My team already wait for me, looking hungry for a fight, regardless of how many they've started today.

"Mission is a go. We're visiting an anomaly that has been identified in orbit around Ustokos. The powers that be think it may be another ship, and we need more ships. We are to secure it and bring it back to the planet. We are not to explode it or damage it in any way." I give Ayar and Vypr the benefit of my best stare. "Any questions?"

I glare around at my warriors. None of them say a word.

"Let's go," I say to Lyon, and he punches at a console in front of him.

The entire ship vibrates as it lifts, the engines whining to life as the rockets fire. Our first mission. The one that will cement my leadership of this unit and, if the goddess is on my side, will gain the Gryn an even bigger advantage on Ustokos.

Kat

I amble along the long stainless steel corridor. There's no hurry. There hasn't been any reason to hurry for, well, I don't know how long. Days? Weeks? I can't tell any more.

I pass a window that looks out over the planet I'm orbiting, but I don't give it a glance. I've seen it. I've stared at it for hours. It's not Earth.

Most of my early memories of being on this ship/space station/whatever are hazy. I was kept drugged for most of the time, but I know I didn't see the lizard-men again. There was just a soft voice that wanted me to be calm and cold metal pincers. And needles. And probes.

Even now, the thought of the probes makes me shudder.

None of it was pleasant, but there was something worse. Once the drugs wore off, it was the sounds.

The screams.

The other humans trapped like I was.

At the mercy of the robots.

Until the day I awakened, drug-free, shivering, and alone.

The door to my cell open and the entire place deserted. Not a single living soul to be found.

"KatKatKatKat!" A silver streak whizzes past me at shoulder height.

Except for him.

"Slow down, Ike! I'm coming!" I call at the tiny flying robot.

Ike. I've no idea where he came from, but I found him on the floor just down the corridor from my cell. Initially, I thought he was a silver snake, until I picked him up, and he sprang to life, little wings like a dragonfly's emerging from his sides. He hovered alongside me, pinpricks of blue lights flowing down his sides.

And then he never left me alone. Not that I'm complaining at all. He showed me where to find food and some extra blankets. He curls up next to me when I'm sleeping, the metal warmth of whatever engine drives him seeping into me.

Why these aliens should have something like Ike on their ship, I don't know or even profess to understand. All I do know is that without Ike, I wouldn't have survived on board the *SS Alien Disaster*. He kept me sane as I lurched from despair at my new life, the ultimate aloneness in space, to a euphoria that had to be me on the very edge of my sanity.

I wanted to be alone, but it turns out I'm not quite as good company as I thought. The empty space where my soul should be is still there. The one that was wrenched out of me by Hartford Corp, the high net worth wealth management company that took my spirit, chewed me up and left me hollow. I am as much a disaster area as the situation in which I find myself.

Yes, I am a sensitive soul. I was told that time and time again growing up by my parents, now long gone. My few friends told me the same. Why I chose corporate finance as a career given that I have the thinnest skin, god only knows. The fact I lasted as long as I did has to be a mystery, but when the crash came, it hit hard, and for a very long time, I was in a pit where I couldn't even see the light.

All of which has nothing on being abducted by aliens and left to die, alone. For a long time all I could think about was Lana, and how she might blame herself for my disappearance.

Some days, I just curled into a ball and lay, staring at nothing, despite Ike's attentions.

However, today I am resigned to my fate in this floating tin can. Today is a good day.

I follow the little streak of silver through into the small room where the rations are kept.

"What to have for breakfast?" I ask him as he perches on the edge of the counter next to the cubbyhole where the food is produced from a dispenser. "Shall we have flavorless porridge or flavorless porridge?"

Ike makes a low peeping sound, like a bird. It's the sound he makes when my responses don't work with his operating system. It's basically a 'does not compute' noise.

I put a packet of the rations into a bowl and shove it into a cupboard that rehydrates and heats the food. As I close the door, Ike sits up, his normally blue lights turning to red, something I've never seen before.

"What is it?" I whisper to him, as if there's anyone else on board.

A strange ripple runs over his silvery, scaly body, and at the same time, somewhere there's a crunching sound. A shudder runs through the structure, and a loud hiss has me running out of the rations room. Something has hit us, and I'm terrified that it's the sound of air escaping.

Up until now, the only danger of being in space seemed to

be from dying of boredom. But the real danger was from something damaging the ship, the air escaping, and me suffocating while I scream my last. A thought that I had put right to the back of my mind. With good reason, it turns out, as my legs turn to jelly.

Ike zips alongside me. "Mistress Kat. Docking."

He often speaks in riddles, and I keep running towards the noise, not entirely sure what I'm going to do when I get there, but maybe Ike can help me plug the leak or something. Maybe the awful porridge will prove to be good for spaceship leak plugging.

"Oh, fuck!" I skid to a halt as I reach the end of a corridor and it opens into a wider space. Outside, through a small port hole, I can see something that wasn't there yesterday.

It's another ship. Angular and streaked with black, it's slowly seating itself in line with the one I'm on.

"Mistress Kat," Ike chimes, his little wings whirring like a hummingbird. "Visitors."

Too many thoughts run through my head, but the one that crystalizes is my fear of the lizard aliens. Perhaps they've come back for me?

That's the last thing I want. Even staying alone on this ship for the rest of my life would be preferable to being at their mercy again. I back into the corridor and watch as finally, the other ship clamps onto mine. What I always thought was some sort of cupboard in the wall lights up. White lights running around the rim, getting quicker and quicker until finally, with a low groan, a door slides up into the ceiling, and I see there's a short passageway between the two craft.

The door at the other end is firmly closed. I put my hand to my lips, biting on my thumb as inaction freezes me in place. If they find the place empty, they might just leave. As I struggle to decide what to do, I hear a new sound.

Voices.

Whoever or whatever is on that ship has just opened the door.

And they're coming in.

Strykr

The airlock lights turn green, and I unholster my laser gun. Proto is supposed to be gone, at least from Ustokos, and tech shouldn't be deadly anymore, but for all we know, this space station could be an isolated outpost, and I'm not taking any chances.

"Mylo, with me," I call out. "Jay, take up the rear. Ayar, Vypr, search formation. Please try not to kill anything or destroy any tech we come across. You heard Lyon—discharging a laser weapon in space is not advisable."

I'm pretty sure I hear some grumbling from Ayar, but I ignore it. That vrexer only ever wants to kill something.

I don't blame him. Killing, fighting, destroying, it's the undercurrent that drives me. I should have left it behind me when Ryak rescued me two cycles ago. Instead, it follows me, dark and dangerous, an undercurrent of violence that stains my soul.

It's the thing I have to hide.

Something silver appears in the doorway of Proto's space station and is gone.

"Bot!" Vypr calls out.

"Do not shoot it!" I snarl at him. "If there are any working bots, we might need them."

With Jay at my side, I edge up the airlock passage until we reach the station. A quick glance shows that the entrance is completely empty. Whatever it was we saw, it's no longer there.

"Spread out and search for anything we might use. Look sharp!" I order and watch as Ayar and Vypr take one corridor.

Mylo, the vrexing big bastid warrior that he is, hoists his huge cannon onto his shoulder, takes the other, leaving a third for me and Jay.

Lyon told us that this was a space station as we got closer to it. Apparently, these things are supposed to remain in orbit around a planet and provide a suitable docking point for any spacecraft that can't land on the surface.

All my instincts tell me that this was something to do with Proto, but I'm tasked with finding the evidence and then getting Lyon on board to deal with the tech.

Other than smashing bots since I was a youngling, neither I nor the rest of my team have much experience with tech. It's always been too risky to activate anything, given that it only ever attracted Proto, which meant death or capture.

And capture meant a slow death in the camps.

Something else has set my senses on edge. There's a scent in this place that is familiar and enticing.

"Can you smell that?" I ask Jay as we make our way through the station, checking each room for bots or tech. Most of them are empty.

"Smell what?" Jay replies with a shrug, his long laser gun raised. He's the only one of my team I'd trust shooting in this place. He knows exactly where to put a laser bolt, every single time.

"Nothing," I mumble and attempt to concentrate on

moving through the station. There has to be something useful we can take back to Ustokos.

"Commander!" Jay calls out, just up ahead of me. "You need to see this."

He has his weapon pointed into a small room that can only be a cell. In one corner is a tangle of blankets, in another a bowl of half-eaten nutrislop.

"Vrex! There were organics on board." I run my hand over my face. The scent is stronger in here.

Mentally, I run through some calculations—how long it's been since Proto was defeated and driven off Ustokos and so how long the station has been empty of the sentient AI and its killer bots. Long enough for any organic life to still be living. If it's still here.

"What do we do?" Jay asks.

I press on the comm device that Lyon insisted we all wear in our ears. I thought we were going to have to hold down Ayar until he accepted his, but he begrudgingly inserted it himself after I threatened to tie him up and leave him in the hold.

I might have had to warn them all about not touching tech, but Ayar will never voluntarily touch anything other than a weapon. I saw the chair he was strapped to when we found him in one of Proto's camps, and ultimately, I can't say I blame him for hating tech.

"Unit, there may be an organic on board. Proceed with caution, but please, capture not kill!" I motion to Jay to continue, and as he stalks ahead, I struggle to take my eyes away from the small cell. There's something about it that makes my heart ache and my feathers prick up.

"Commander!" Vypr's voice crackles over the comm. *"We've got a problem."*

"What?" I fire out.

"You're going to have to come to us."

"Come on," I call to Jay, and we retrace our steps through the station as swiftly as we can back to the airlock.

Vypr has Mylo over his shoulder. Blood drips from a vicious wound on his side and is pooling on the floor.

"What the vrex happened?"

"We don't know. We heard him yell and found him like this," Vypr says as a grinding sound comes from somewhere in the station.

"Did you see any other organic life? Any bots?" I look at Mylo's wounds. They have to be from a joykill bot or something similar.

"Nothing, Commander. We've seen nothing," Ayar replies.

"Get him back on board the *Perlin*." I gesture for Vypr to return to our craft. "Jay, you go with them. Ayar with me."

If there's a joykill bot anywhere on this station, Ayar is the warrior I need. "Take me to where you found Mylo."

He races ahead of me, and we work our way through the interminable corridors until we reach a small, open space where there is a pool of blood.

"He was here," Ayar says, his voice dull.

"Did he say anything?"

"He pointed at that." Ayar gestures with his laser cannon to a wall.

I walk up to it, pulling out my dagger. The one surefire way to deal with a joykill. The wall in front of me morphs, and I step to one side as the vrexing bot appears, it's laser whip crackling. Ayar leaps backwards, and before I can stop him, he fires his weapon.

The wall ahead of us explodes, and an intense wind whistles through the entire area, pulling both of us towards the crack. I grab hold of Ayar's wing and with every ounce of strength I have, I fling him back down the corridor.

Grabbing onto the wall, I heave myself around too.

"Let's go, you vrexer!" I bellow at him, and with my fist planted firmly behind his wings, I propel both of us back towards the *Perlin*.

The air is already getting thin as we reach the airlock, panting hard.

"What did I say about discharging a weapon?" I shake my head at Ayar, who's grinning wildly at all of the excitement.

"Don't?"

"Is there ever going to be an occasion when you follow my orders?" I rub at my temples as my comm fires up.

"Commander, Lyon says he can't maintain the airlock with the station. We're going to have to disengage," Jay says.

"That'll be down to Ayar," I reply. "We're at the airlock now. We're coming in."

I indicate to Ayar to get ahead of me and follow him as he troops back towards our craft. He's reached our airlock, and I hit the sequence to close the one on the station, so we can free our ship as quickly as possible.

It's then that I see her. The human female with long dark hair and a face as pale as Ustokos's moons. She stares at me, big blue eyes round with fear, as a tiny silver bot alights on her shoulder.

It's her. The scent on the station that calls to my soul.

"*Eregri!*"

The word is out of my mouth at the same time as I leap through the gap, and the airlock slams closed behind me.

Kat

Oh, dear god, there are huge, hulking aliens *with wings* on the ship. Not only have they sabotaged it by blowing a hole in it, but one of them is still on board.

The massive creature bellows at me like a bull, and I don't hang around. The huge wind whistling through the ship has slowed, and Ike is no longer chirping at me like a fire alarm. I don't know if that's a good thing or not, but I'm certainly not hanging around for the incredibly pissed off looking alien to get to me.

And I need to find something to defend myself. Although what would possibly stop something that enormous, I have no idea. I run, Ike buzzing alongside me. I use my knowledge of the spaceship to dodge down several corridors until the sound of the new alien dies away, and I slow my pace, leaning up against a wall. Bent double, I pant hard.

I'm out of shape!

"That was close," I rasp through my ragged breathing. "What was that thing?"

"Gryn, mistress," Ike replies. Another response that I don't understand.

"What are we going to do?" I ask myself. Not only am I stuck on this ship, which now has a hole in it, thanks to the new aliens, but I've also got a new problem.

Him.

The thing with the claws, sharp teeth, and wings. First contact with a whole new alien species that doesn't resemble a lizard. He just resembles a raptor instead. Only without a beak, which is some small consolation.

I wonder what he eats.

If the alien is in another part of the ship, I should be able to dodge him as I look for a weapon and gather up some food and water so I can hide until he leaves. That would be a plan, admittedly not a long-term plan, but it'll have to do in the circumstances.

With my breathing back under control, I debate my next move. My new alien might look like a raptor, so he might have the hearing of an owl or something, which means I'm going to have to be quiet. I consider whether or not to take Ike, but the risk is he'll make too much noise if I leave him behind, so I put him on my shoulder. He curls his metal tail around my neck, chirping happily.

Having decided I'm going for food first, I pad down the corridor, heading towards one of the dispenser points, hoping I don't bump into anything big, scary, and predatory. There's a strange scent in the air, ozone mixed with a spice that I've never smelt before.

Rounding a corner, I'm faced with an open space I have to cross in order to get to the food dispenser. At around knee height, there's a thick mist which is freaky. It's then I notice the scorch marks on the hull and a large area of cream-colored foam material clinging to the wall, like a wasp's nest.

I've got to get through all of this, and I take a step into the mist. It tingles against my legs. Then it starts to burn. Without thinking, I let out a cry of alarm and race across the open space as the stuff clings to me. Once I'm out of the mist, I rub at my legs, trying to get any of the stuff off me. But it's no use. I need water, and I need it now.

Somewhere in the station, I hear the sound of the alien creature. It's a long, deep cry that encircles my stomach with fear. It must have heard me.

"Shit!" I start to run again, pelting down the corridor and heading for the one area I know there's water that doesn't just come on twice a day.

The one place I never go.

The dissection room.

Steeling myself, I reach the door and take a couple of deep breaths. The skin on my lower legs is turning red and blistering in places, so I know I have zero options but to enter. I punch the glowing entry button, and the door swishes open.

The smell that hits me is incredible. I gag immediately, placing my hand over my nose and mouth. The pool of blood on the floor has turned black. Discarded instruments, pieces of bloody bandage all stinking to high heaven.

Whatever happened to the robots on this ship, they didn't get a chance to clean up, and that's why I vowed to never come in here, not after the first time. Somewhere, buried in my memory, are things I don't ever want to think about. Things involving this room.

I race over to a metal sink that has a hose above it. Lifting one leg into the container, I pick up the hose and, fortunately, it starts gushing water straight away. I sluice off one leg first and then the other. Neither is in great shape, but I feel considerably better. Without even looking at the room, I race back out. As soon as the door behind me closes, I spit out all the breath I've been holding in order to take in a lungful of cleaner air as I lean against the wall.

Ike chirps in my ear in a way he never has before. It's then I hear the rustling.

He's here. The alien. He's standing only ten feet away from me.

Good god, he's enormous. And he's most definitely male. He has to be at least seven feet tall and maybe just as broad. Giant pale, striped wings sprout from his back, and his shoulders are covered with a leathery skin. His chest is entirely bare, heavily muscled with abs that any bodybuilder would die for. As he cocks his head to one side and runs his hand through tousled dark hair, he looks quite human, if all humans looked like Greek gods. High cheekbones, a sharp aquiline nose over full lips. His eyes are entirely dark, no white visible, and they glitter with a strange interest that has a part of me churning in a way that should be impossible.

He moves, only slightly, and it's then I get a really good look at his vicious black claws. He bares his teeth at me, sharp canines on show.

I think I've worked out what he eats.

Human.

Strykr

When I heard her cry out, it was like a dagger to my chest. My beautiful mate is in trouble!

Any thoughts about escaping the space station are chased away immediately. I have to get to her. I have to help her. There is nothing more important.

The station is worse than the lair for interminable corridors, and all I can do is let my instinct guide me to where she is. It's with a sinking heart that I realize I'm heading for the area where Ayar let loose with his laser weapon. I've noticed a distinct drop in the oxygen levels. My lungs are attuned to such a drop, given that the Gryn can fly at altitude.

It makes me concerned for my mate though. If she's human, and I'm pretty sure she is given that I've seen a few before, she won't be able to cope with any reduced oxygen, and the closer we get to the area where the leak occurred, the worse it will be for her.

When I reach the area of damage, I'm not surprised to see that it's sealed itself. Proto may no longer be in control, but given that this station is not a dead floating hulk, there must be systems independent of the sentient AI that keep it running. One of which is the preservation of the hull integrity.

I've made it my job to learn everything I can from Lyon. He had multiple information downloads from his slave masters, ostensibly to allow him to do his job as a hired killer. It means he understands tech in a way we can't. Generations of being at Proto's mercy means we have simply scratched a living without tech on Ustokos. Learning it all again is an uphill struggle, but I'm determined to master it. Lyon is a solitary figure. He prefers to spend his time with his mate, and I know I'm privileged to have the benefit of his time and knowledge. It helps that he's a good teacher, and I'm a willing student.

Shame that can't be said for the rest of my team. But I guess trust in tech for them will come with time.

The smell emanating from the thick fog swirling around near the hull breach is sharp and acidic, dangerous. I can't even open my wings in this enclosed space, so I have no option but to cross the area with a couple of strides and rely on my thick maraha hide pants to keep the corrosive mist at bay.

Up ahead, a door slides open, and she steps out, breathing heavily. Her eyes are closed as she shakes back her long dark hair and wraps her arms around herself, clutching the short shift that she wears to her body and giving me an indication of the lush curves beneath.

My cock rises as I take every inch of her in, searing this image of my beautiful mate into my mind. She is the most perfect creature I've ever seen. My pants tighten to a painful degree as my secondary cock also swells. Something that's never happened before.

My need to take her, to claim her, is overwhelming me. I have to fill her womb with a youngling. I have to feel her, sheath myself in her. Make her mine.

Her eyes fly open as my wings shift with my desire. I meet

her glorious blue gaze, the color of the tiny flowers starting to bloom everywhere on Ustokos. The human females call them 'forget-me-nots.' It's then I see the red skin on her legs. She's walked through the corrosive mist, and she is injured.

"*Eregri.*" Almost subconsciously, I use the term that the Gryn have for their fated mate. "Let me help you."

I take a step forward, reaching out my hand, knowing that this delicate, spellbinding creature is mine. Knowing I will be by her side forever.

She leaps into the air with a strangled cry and garbles something at me that I can't understand. Then she's racing away from me, and there's something silver hovering over her head. It's a bot, but it's following her. Just like I will do.

"*EREGRI!*" I roar out. She is my mate, and her decision to flee has tripped something primal in me.

She is prey.

And she is mine.

"There's nowhere you can go that I can't find you, my sweet mate." I lift my head up and suck down her scent.

I stroll along the corridor. She's as trapped as I am, and that means that when I catch her, it will be all the more delicious. I palm my cocks through my pants, feeling like I should alleviate some of the pressure. Except all I want to do is spill my seed in her.

Her scent is easy to follow as I dart between doors, right up until one slides open beside me, and I peer in. The room is large and empty. On the floor at the entrance is a small, bright disc. I pick it up. It's perfection. A beautiful thing for a beautiful mate.

The room will be perfect for my nest. Once I have built it, I have no doubt that I can tempt my female in. Females cannot resist a nest or a strong male. Subconsciously, I shake out my feathers, lifting my wings to make myself look big.

In my ear, my comm crackles.

'Commander?'

Vrex it! I'd forgotten all about the mission and my team in my desire to hunt down my prey.

"Yes," I fire out down the comm. "Is Mylo okay?"

"He's eating. Does that answer your question?" It's Lyon on the comm. *"What the vrex happened on there?"*

"There was a vrexing joykill. Ayar shot at it, but there's also a female, a human female on board. We both need to get out of here as soon as possible."

'That's going to be a problem, Strykr. The main airlock was damaged when we disengaged. We can't dock again.'

I swear loudly.

Somewhere on the station, in answer to my curses, a slow, distant cackle rises.

Somewhere on this ship is one of the most feared bots Proto ever invented. A joykill. A bot that computes its targets in such a way it sounds like it's laughing. Laughing as it hits its target. Laughing as it takes your life.

If there is a working joykill on board, my mate is in incredible danger.

"See what you can do about that, will you, Lyon? The hull leak sealed itself, but we can't stay on board. It's too dangerous."

"I'll try and find a solution," Lyon replies and terminates the comm.

I pull out my laser weapon and gaze around my chosen nesting room. If I want to protect and pleasure my *eregri*, I'm going to have to put in some vrexing hard work.

And that's before I find and destroy the killer robot.

Kat

I DUCK DOWN A SIDE CORRIDOR AND WAIT TO SEE IF the huge feathery alien is following me. Instead, all I hear is him bellowing in a language I don't understand.

He seems very annoyed about something. Maybe he's used to a bigger dinner? Maybe he prefers it if his food surrenders itself to him?

I still need to figure out exactly why my body reacted to him like it did. Perhaps I've just been on my own too long, but as much as he was monstrous, he was also rather gorgeous in a strange alien-hawk-man way.

I've been on my own too long. How can I possibly find an alien attractive?

Ike buzzes around my head, his little lights blinking furiously.

"What is it?" I hold out my arm for him to land on, but he refuses.

"Item thirty-seven, mistress," Ike replies, his lights changing to bright red.

Anything he itemizes relates to something to do with the technology on the ship. Normally, it's pretty obvious what he's referring to. The food dispensers are item forty-two. The porridge reheaters are item one hundred and seventy-three. But item thirty-seven? That's a new one.

A noise hits my ears, and it's not relating to the feathered god that gave me the oddest reaction in my life. This is a laugh, except it's anything but a laugh. It has to be the most evil thing I've heard, and that includes the voice of the computer telling me to be calm every time they wanted to stick me with probes or needles. The shudder it sends down my spine means I'm caught between the predator that's stalking me and something that even Ike seems to fear.

I do a quick check to see I'm still alone then, with Ike chirping like a budgie on speed, I run as fast as I can to the food dispenser. Grabbing as much as I can carry and circling back around the ship in the hope I don't bump into either the evil laughter or my delicious winged alien.

"Since when did you start thinking of him as delicious, Kat?" I say out loud, scurrying along. "Since I started talking to myself because there's no one else here."

If I thought that I was in any way sane after everything I've been through, that is my answer in a couple of sentences.

Perhaps I should just give myself up. Let myself be eaten by him.

And why does that thought make my core clench in response? I've definitely been alone too long!

As I hurry along, an open door catches my eye, and I halt in front of it. What was once an empty room has been transformed. There is a huge pile of the strange silvery blankets which pass for bedding on this ship. That wouldn't be too weird, but what is decidedly strange is the items that surround it, that are hung from the ceiling on long slim pieces of wiring. There has to be *hundreds* of little discs that spin and sway in the air currents my presence has created.

It is beautiful as much as it is strange and compelling. I

stand in the doorway, taking in what is a mix between a fairy-tale and a junk shop. Why has this alien done this? What does it mean?

Behind me, I hear a sound that chills me to the bone. Ike's lights go wild, then he shuts down, sliding off my shoulder and dropping into my hand, apparently lifeless.

I turn, slowly, carefully, dropping the food I've picked up, to be confronted by possibly the worse thing I've ever seen. And that includes the lizard men.

Three spiked balls revolve slowly, one on top of the other like a nasty snowman. Each one has similar lights to Ike, only these are all red. Two pincers protrude from the middle ball, one holding what looks like a glowing whip. As I stare, it emits a low cackling sound that is pure evil.

"Ike!" I whisper at the limp robot. "Ike!" He's always explained everything to me, and I could really do with knowing what this terror is that's appeared out of nowhere.

The robot moves towards me.

"Human female." The red lights flicker faster as it fires out the words. "You are to be terminated."

I stare at it.

"That would be a negative!" I reply, regaining some control over my bodily functions. Clutching Ike to me, I turn and run as fast as I can down the corridor.

The thing cackles behind me, and I know I'm no match for its speed and strength. It's getting closer. My lungs are beginning to burn. I probably should have spent more time keeping fit than sitting around moping. It's too late for regrets. Something sizzles past my shoulder, and a searing pain cuts at me. I try to increase my pace, but even with the added adrenaline, my muscles are done.

I am going to be terminated.

I trip, sprawling forward and hitting the floor with enough force to expel all the breath from my body. Ike goes flying, and

I slide, uncontrolled, until I slam into a wall. The cackle gets closer, and I close my eyes, the only part of me that's still working. I can only hope it's quick.

Part of me, the part that I buried a long time ago, the part that wants to live, that wants to be alive, rears up, expecting me to follow, to fight.

But I lost the fight when I broke down at work, sobbing at my desk like a child. They took all the fight from me, and I know I'll never get it back. I may as well die, here, a zillion miles from Earth at the hands of a killer robot.

Because I already died, deep down inside, three years ago. Since then, I've been a shell of my own consciousness and a dead life. I deserve to die alone.

Strykr

The joykill screeches as I drag my dagger through its innards, my weapon making easy work of the bot. I'd heard from the other Gryn how easy it was to destroy these bots, but this is my first opportunity.

I spent my childhood and early adulthood at the mercy of Proto. Stuck in its camps, the joykills were there to keep us in. With nothing more than our claws to defend ourselves, we didn't stand a chance against the laser whips and later laser guns that the bots toted.

To take on a joykill meant almost instant death, and the camps were all about survival. At any cost. They may have cost me too much already.

The thing drops to the floor and rattles an electronic death knell to itself, lights flickering and dimming. I pull out my laser gun and fire into it, just to be sure it stays dead.

Curled up next to a wall, only feet away from the cursed bot, is the female, her gorgeous scent tinged with bitter fear. At my feet is the tiny bot that I saw hovering above her earlier. It's like nothing I've ever seen before, long and slim. Its body is made of a smooth silver metal that's warm to the touch. As I hold it, blue lights appear along its side, and it chirps into life, springing out of my hand and whirring into the air.

"Ike?" My female shifts, and the word is a brief moan that goes directly to my cocks.

"Sweet female, are you hurt?" I'm next to her in a wing beat.

She looks at me, looks at the downed joykill, and opens her mouth.

The sound that comes out is anything but sweet. She scoots away from me until she's pressed into a corner, shaking as the little bot lands on her shoulder. Instinctively, she reaches up to touch it, and, by the Goddess Nisis, I wish she was touching me.

"*Commander*" My comm fires into life at the worst possible moment.

"Captain?" I reply. "Any update?"

"*We're still searching for a way of extracting you, but my sensors picked up a laser discharge*," Lyon says. "*Everything okay?*"

"There was a live joykill. It's possible it was triggered by our presence," I reply, although it definitely seemed more interested in the human female who stares at me with blue eyes as big as Ustokos's second moon. "I've dealt with it. Keep trying to find a way of getting us off this piece of junk. I can't imagine the joykill is alone."

"*Will do.*" Lyon terminates the comm.

I turn my attention back to the female who is incredibly still.

"My name is Strykr. I'm trying to find a way off this station, so I can take you back to Ustokos," I say as gently as possible. Her chest heaves with emotion, and I can't help but notice the delicious swell of her breasts.

If it's at all possible, her eyes seem to get bigger.

"Dynnyhew ur yliyn epe wai frm mi!" she squeaks, attempting to push herself farther into the wall.

Vrex! She hasn't been given any form of translator, not like the human females I've met on Ustokos.

"How long have you been on this station?" I ask, realizing my question is pointless. This female is completely terrified, not just of the joykill, but of me. And I can't even reassure her because we don't speak the same language.

"Vrex it!" I fire out in frustration, and she gasps, hand over her chest.

Swearing isn't going to help. I'm going to have to try something else to calm my terrified female. Something I'm not too good at.

Diplomacy.

I point to myself, placing a finger on my chest. "Strykr," I say, simply. Then I point at her and nod.

She takes in a shuddering breath, water running from her eyes as she blinks, and my heart seems to thunder in my chest. I want nothing more than to soothe her distress, but any move on my part is only going to make our communication issues worse. She shifts, looking from side to side as she strokes the small bot on her shoulder. Eventually, she points to herself.

"Kat," she says.

"Kat," I repeat, with a nod that I hope seems friendly.

"Strykr," she says, and the sound of my name on her lips almost sends my cocks bursting out of my pants. I want to hear her shouting it as I'm buried inside her.

Vrex! I have to get my libido under control. Like so many other Gryn, I've had limited opportunity to mate and always thought I had zero chance of ever finding a mate, given Proto removed all the Gryn females from the camps many cycles ago, before I came of age.

No one knows where they have gone or why Proto decided that it had to dispose of only Gryn females, given that the other species on Ustokos, the Mochi and the Kijg, retained theirs.

The only Gryn female I have a dim memory of is my mother, and even then, it's the feel of her hand on my wing or the soft sound of her voice. Other than her, the other female I know is the mate of our governor, Ryak.

Bianca is a powerhouse. And the female I'm faced with today couldn't be more different.

I am completely out of my depth.

"Come." I hold out my hand.

I can make her comfortable. The food packets discarded around the bot suggest that she was eating before the joykill interrupted her. The least I can do is keep her fed, warm, and safe until we can get off this station.

She stares at me, her eyes wandering over my wings and down onto my chest, taking in the dagger at my belt and the laser weapon.

"Come, Kat," I repeat.

Slowly, hesitantly, she reaches out to me, her eyes fixed on mine. Their brilliance is entrancing, perfect, but when she places her hand in mine, the jolt that hits me almost has me dropping it.

Somehow, I have to convince this untamed creature that she is mine. And that I am no longer hunting her.

I have her in my grasp, and I'm never going to let her go.

Kat

My heart beats so hard, I'm sure it's going to burst out of my chest. It rattles away as if I've never met a winged alien, who close up, could be an angel.

A wicked angel from the way his lip curls up, revealing a sharp tooth.

Strykr.

That's what he said his name was, I think. I was ready to flee, to grab one of the weapons he had on his belt and get as far away from him as possible. Even if he did destroy that horrible robot.

I could have been lunch.

Some parts of me are reacting to this chiseled, feathered Adonis as if they want to be eaten.

Dear God, Kat. Doing anything with this alien angel has to be the biggest nope since you had to knee one of Lana's over-enthusiastic male friends in the meat and two veg!

I simply cannot be having dirty thoughts about an alien. He is very easy on the eye, and when he speaks, a low rumbling language that is part purr, part gravel, it definitely does funny things to my lady parts. It's still wrong though.

I've been abducted. I've been marooned. And I've nearly been killed by an evil robot, then an enormous alien angel saves me and offers me his hand? If I couldn't feel the bruises on my knees and elbows, I'd have chalked all of this up to a dream of epic, bonkers proportions.

So what exactly is the etiquette when an alien offers you his clawed hand? I reach out to him, hoping that this is the right thing to do, and hoping I'm not supposed to fist bump him or something awkwardly American, I place my hand in his.

His big, dark eyes flare for an instant, and he huffs a breath. I very nearly let go, thinking that perhaps I've offended him in some way. His clawed hand closes over mine, and it's warm.

It's comforting.

He says my name again, along with another word I don't understand but the meaning is clear. He wants me to go with him. I get to my feet, making sure Ike is okay on my shoulder. I don't know what happened to him earlier, but he seems perfectly fine now.

Strykr points to Ike and makes a low grumbling noise that has to be a laugh.

"Ike," I tell him. "His name is Ike."

Strykr cocks his head to one side, and I very nearly explode with just how gorgeous he looks. "Iky?" he repeats.

"Ike," I say firmly, pointing to the lettering on the little robot's side. "I.K.E. See."

It's only at this point that it occurs to me that, if this alien doesn't speak English, then there is no way that the letters on Ike's body can be the Latin alphabet. They just look familiar, and I've assigned them a meaning which won't be correct. I feel slightly silly as Strykr continues to look at me, dark eyes glittering as Ike's lights are reflected in them.

"Ike." He nods and gestures ahead, past the destroyed robot. I guess he wants me to leave the area.

"Are you hungry after doing all that, um, robot smashing?" I ask him. "I can't offer much in the way of hospitality, only porridge that tastes of cardboard, but you can have some if you like."

I realize I'm babbling. Talking away to an alien that can't understand me. I've been on my own far too long. My legs are still jelly from running away, my heart still hasn't calmed down. I take in a deep breath.

You can do this, Kat.

After everything I've been through, the one thing I do know is that I'm a survivor. This alien is my ticket to getting off this ship. He has to be.

The problem I have is not the huge, winged alien that's following me, his feathers trailing on the ground behind him, a look on his face that I can't quite fathom. It's that I'm only just holding things together as it is. Anything else, and I can already feel the pit of my stomach churning. Just like before everything went to shit at work. When I was escorted out by security, a soggy mess of tears and snot.

When no one contacted me to check how I was. When all I got was a termination email in my inbox.

And then the blackness that followed. It's a shadow that has forever haunted me, and I know the signs of the shadow darkening.

I need something to ground me. That's what my jewelry business did. The intricacies of handling and polishing gems, of making the mounts. Of being creative without anyone looking over my shoulder. It was never about 'playing with pretty stones.'

I can't let Strykr see how badly affected I am, not until I can work out what he wants. Out here in alien space, I have no other option but to rely on myself, and I can't go to pieces.

Reaching up, I put my hand on Ike and feel him vibrate gently against my touch.

Behind me, Strykr moves closer.

"It's this way." I motion to him, leading the way through to the food dispenser.

It's only when I check over my shoulder and come face to face with a very nice, muscled chest that I realize he thinks he can follow me in.

"We won't fit." I laugh up at him, putting my hand against his bare chest without thinking. "You'll have to stay outside."

Strykr looks down at where I touch him.

"Kat," he rumbles. It's almost a growl. I go to snatch my hand away, and in a move I didn't even see, he has my wrist encircled by his enormous clawed fingers.

I try to remove it, but his grip is firm. He rubs a vicious, clawed thumb over my wrist and says something I don't understand. I should be terrified. This close up, he is formidable with his dark eyes and enormous, beautiful wings that are as built as he is. He's a solid wall of muscle and male that smells divine. Warm, slightly musky, slightly spicy. I inhale him as if I'm a woman starved.

Until now, I didn't know I missed being in proximity to another living being.

Right now, I wouldn't want to be anywhere else but in the presence of this enormous alien predator.

Strykr

I'm doing everything I can not to tremble under her scrutiny. Her gorgeous gaze trails over my body, my wings, and down to where my hand holds her wrist. My restraint is stretched to the breaking point when she breathes out, hot, onto my skin, and the aroma of her arousal hits me. Unable to stop myself, a low growl escapes my lungs, and in a flash, her hand and body has gone. She's on the other side of the tiny room where I'd struggle to enter due to my wings.

Almost immediately, she begins chattering in her strange language, all guttural and at the same time like a song. I lean against the doorframe, folding my arms, and watch her as she empties sachets into a couple of bowls, then places them in a small white box.

The box hums to life. I'm reaching for her, wanting to pull her away from the tech that might just kill her, when it makes a short, sharp noise, and she opens the door again.

The strong smell of Proto's nutrislop reaches me. I have to bite back the memories of the camps. It's food I never thought I'd have to stomach again, and yet my mate is handing me a bowl with a smile on her face that is as beautiful as it is hesitant.

I can't refuse.

I take the bowl from her, and she drops in a small spoon. I try to pick it up, but my hands are not meant for such delicate work. My claws don't completely retract anymore, not after what Proto did to me, and, even though I give it my best go, I can't grasp the spoon.

Eventually, I look up at Kat, frustrated, to see that she's watching me carefully, still smiling. Frustration overflows, and I dunk in a finger, swiping up a portion and shoving it into my mouth as she stares. Her lips form a perfect 'o,' and if I could have gotten inside the room, I would have mated her there and then. Yet again, a growl thunders through my chest, and her eyes widen in alarm.

I can't frighten her.

Backing out of the door, I walk across the hall and lean against the opposite wall from her. I droop my wings and attempt to make myself look as small and as unthreatening as possible. I dip my finger into my food again, licking at my claw and hoping I don't wince at the taste too much.

She appears at the door, her bowl in hand, and as soon as she sees where I am, she relaxes, mirroring my pose and leaning against the wall straight ahead of me.

Having taken a couple of mouthfuls, she begins to talk again. Pointing her spoon at the room where she prepared the food, down the corridor, above her head, and finally, she checks behind her where the little silver bot is perched next to where she prepared the slop. The only word I catch is 'Ike,' which seems to be the name she's given the bot.

That has to be a first, a bot with a name. The tiny thing has to have some sort of purpose other than to sit on her shoulder, but it's hard to see what it is. I have to grudgingly admit it's pleasant to look at. Unlike the bots I've been used to on Ustokos until Proto was defeated. Those were all death and destruction, big, nasty, and feared. Not lithe and silver like Ike.

She's been silent for a while, eating her food, her eyes never leaving me. It's as if she knows exactly what I am and that I wasn't searching for her on the station.

I was hunting her.

Yet she is anything but prey. Holding herself defiantly, ready to flee at a moment's notice. Not that I'd let her get far. She should be in my nest and nowhere else.

"Sweet female. I wish we could understand each other. I want to know all about you, how you came to be on this ship, why you are all alone, whether you will agree to be my mate..." I check, and although she continues to half-smile at me, her brow is furrowed. She can't understand me, and a sense of relief that she doesn't know what I just asked her flows through me.

This gorgeous, delicate creature, long dark hair and skin that is tan like the finest maraha hide, she does not belong on this empty station by herself. I have to get her back to Ustokos. I have to make her mine.

"Vrex it!" I run my hand through my hair and touch my ear to activate my comm. "Lyon? Any update?"

There's a low, hissing sound and for a second, I wonder if the vrexing comm is broken.

"Commander, we're still working on it," he replies, and I'm growling again, despite myself.

"Try harder," I spit out and terminate the connection, pulling the comm away from my ear in agitation.

A short, harsh pant brings me back from my instant anger to the female I hunger for. Kat's eyes are wide, her hands wrapped around her empty bowl as if it can protect her from a Gryn warrior.

Unable to stop myself, I stalk towards her. Silently appraising every inch of my mate. It's then I see her blistered legs, and I drop to my knees. The gasping sound she makes goes directly to my cocks, but I cannot indulge them, not with my female injured in this way.

I curse myself that I have not tended her injury. All of this is wrong. Her being on the station, her feeding me, her not being in my nest.

Kat's frozen in place as I gently take her ankle and lift up her leg. She grabs the shoulder of my wing to steady herself, and I just about stifle a groan at her touch. Gryn have always enjoyed mutual preening, and I have been told that having a mate preen you is one of the best experiences a Gryn male can have. I didn't believe it...until now.

Reaching behind me, I dig into the pouch on my belt and pull out the small med-kit our healer has provided. It has a healing salve that should work on her delicate skin.

"Let me help you." I look up at her, holding up the kit. "I can heal you." I point to her leg.

She bites her lip, then nods.

I don't need any more encouragement. I have to show my mate I can provide for her and protect her.

Then I'll take her to my nest.

Kat

I'm genuinely not sure what to do. Strykr has growled, snarled, and is now on his knees in front of me, spreading some translucent gel on my injured calf.

His touch is incredibly gentle, especially for a creature with claws the size of his, that I'm sure could disembowel me in an instant if he decided he wanted to. His feathers are incredibly soft. I'm not sure what I was expecting when I grabbed at his wing to steady myself. Maybe that they would be cold or hard. Instead, they are silky smooth, slippery even, and, as he works on my leg, I can't help but ruffle my fingers through the tiny white and steely colored feathers covering the edge of his wing.

From my position, I can see where they join his impressively muscled back. The feathers extend down towards his waist in a 'v' of gorgeous darkness, rippling as I continue to touch him.

Strykr releases my leg and picks up the other one, causing me to have to shift my balance and fall a little closer to him.

Another growl is repressed. This alien seems more beast

than anything else. A beast who smells like fresh laundry that's just been brought in from the sun. I shouldn't really be touching him like I am, but it's so nice to run my fingers through the soft feathers. I have to delve deep in order to reach his skin, which is almost hot to the touch, my digits disappearing to the knuckle.

"Kat," Strykr rumbles up at me, one clawed hand still cupping my heel. His dark eyes are full of...predatory need.

He dips his head against me and swipes his tongue over the skin of my inner thigh, returning to look up at me with the most naughty expression on his face. The frisson that his touch sends spiking, fizzing over my entire body.

"Strykr!"

I have no underwear. The shapeless shift I have on is the only piece of clothing I own. Strykr's head, his mouth, his tongue are inches away from a part of me that has decided it wants a piece of alien action.

He doesn't move for a beat, and I wonder if I've imagined the touch of his rough tongue, the one that lapped at his finger in such a dirty way earlier, against the sensitive skin of my inner thigh. Instead, we stare at each other for what seems like a long time.

God! His eyes. I could get lost in them.

I could definitely let him do what I think he wants to do. This alien angel I've only just met.

So wrong...

So right.

I'm trying to work out what it all means when he tips me into his arms.

Strykr strides through the ship until he reaches the room I found earlier. The one with all the hanging discs and the piles of blankets. He gently places me on top of them and then stands back, looking confused and hesitant. I shuffle myself into a sitting position.

"Did you do all of this?" I point at the discs.

Slowly, he nods.

My big growly alien is an interior decorator with a penchant for sparkles. Who knew?

Strykr

I have my female in my nest. But now I'm not sure what to do with her.

Kat stares up at me, her head inclined to one side as her little bot buzzes into the room, looking for her. It does a circuit, lights blinking and making a soft, chirping sound, then it settles down beside her. She runs her hand over it, and it curls into a tight ball.

"Ike." I grin at her.

"Ike," she replies, a smile on her lips.

That smile, it fills me with such joy. It's a smile that tells me I haven't done anything wrong. My heart swelling in my chest, I want to roar my claim over her.

Yet there's something still not quite right. It could be my nest. This station is not the right place for a nest. I should be on Ustokos, deep in the eyrie, creating a cozy piece of perfection, just for her.

But would she want to nest with me? Can I escape the pits enough to take a mate? It seemed so much easier only moments ago when she stared up at me as I tended to her wounds. To see her settled in my nest should be filling me with pride. Instead, it's filling me with a sense of dread.

If Kat knew what I was, what hides within me, would she look at me with that smile or with fear in those bright blue eyes?

I know that if it was fear, it would destroy me.

"Strykr?" Kat's teeth are chattering. She says something else and pulls on a blanket, wrapping it around her shoulders.

The temperature in the station is dropping, and rapidly. My breath fogs. This isn't good.

"Wait here," I tell her, holding out my hand flat and hoping she understands what I mean.

Kat doesn't move, and it looks like the gesture is universal.

Heading away from my nest, I stride through the station until I reach the damaged area. The mist has gone, but there is ice forming on the inside of the hull near the fix. I put my comm back in my ear, only to hear Lyon shouting at me.

"What is it, Captain?"

"Strykr! Thank Nisis! We've been calling for the last half hour."

"I've been busy. Have you found me a way off this heap of floating space junk yet?"

"No, and you've got another problem," Lyon replies.

"Is it anything to do with the temperature drop I'm experiencing?"

"The hull breach hasn't completely sealed. It looks like you're venting atmosphere," he says, and I'm curling my hands into fists.

"Any chance you could explain that to the less technical Gryn on board the space station?"

"The air is getting out, and the temperature is only going to get lower. You have to get out of there."

I pinch the bridge of my nose. I should have stopped Ayar

from discharging his weapon, and I'm kicking myself for the failure.

"There's no way you can dock?"

"No, there was only one airlock, and that's gone."

"I need answers, Lyon, or the female and I are going to die in here." I growl in frustration.

"It's possible that the station might have an escape pod, but it's a design I don't recognize," Lyon says, sounding apologetic.

"Would Proto have built in escape pods?" I query, thinking that bots can survive in zero oxygen and in the frigidity of space.

"If it was keeping organics in there, it might have." It's Mylo's voice on the comm. He's always been a fighter, like me, and it doesn't surprise me that despite his injury, he's involved in my rescue. *"Lyon's shown me some schematics of similar stations built by the Drahon. They all have escape pods."*

My stomach warms despite the chill. It's the first piece of good news so far.

"Good to hear you, Mylo. You'll be pleased to know I've disposed of the joykill that you ran into. Any idea what these escape pods look like?"

"Like Lyon said, this station is a different design. It's most likely that the pods will be at the bottom of the hull, so we suggest you start looking there," Mylo replies.

"Will do," I respond, trying not to let my heart sink to my boots.

This was always going to be a dangerous mission. Tech we don't understand that was created by a sentient AI that only wanted to kill, capture, or sell the organic life on the planet it ruled. None of that was going to make for an easy ride.

Somewhere behind me, there is a noise, and I turn, every sense heightened. My female has left my nest. I told her not to.

The reason?

If I don't know where she is, my instinct has no choice. I

have to hunt her down. This is the darkness I hide inside me. This is what keeps me in the fighting pits night after night. Not the pits where the fights are sanctioned, the illegal pits where all species bet on the winner and there are no rules.

I am a hunter. She is my prey.

Kat

The temperature is dropping like a stone, and alone in this strange room, I'm starting to feel nervous. Something is wrong, very wrong, because this hasn't happened before.

My desire to get off this ship and down onto the planet below rises up within me. It might not be Earth, but I hope I'd stand a better chance of survival down there than in this space freezer. I hear Strykr's voice echoing through the corridors. Presumably, he's talking to the others that came aboard with him. I'm not sure why they left him behind, and I hope he's not some sort of psycho killer that they decided to abandon.

Surely something with eyes as gorgeous as his can't be bad?

He's certainly got a wicked tongue. But what if he is bad? What if he's not an angel, but a devil in disguise? Another shiver wracks my body, and this time, it's not the cold that's getting to me.

Ike chirps. His lights are glowing ever so slightly purple. His little head pushes against my hand, and he vibrates. This usually means he wants to show me something useful.

Perhaps it's warm clothing. That would be both useful

and welcome, especially if there are pants that would stop me from allowing an enormous feathered demon from eating me out.

Although maybe I don't want to stop him...

I'm still not sure what part of me was involved in the earlier decision making which meant he picked me up and carried me to this strange room. Actually, I do. It was the part of me that hasn't seen another living being for probably months. That's all it can be. There's no way I'm falling for an alien. I'm damaged, unable to function in normal human society, let alone alien society.

I thought that being on the station was a good thing for a while. I thought being on my own was okay. Of course, I was completely wrong. I am terrible company, what with the nightmares and the cold sweats about stuff that is never going to bother me again, like spreadsheets and clients and financial planning. Or a boss who demanded my presence in the office 24/7.

I need Strykr to get me off this ship. After that, I can be on my own again. Maybe I can find a small corner of the alien planet that turns below me I can call my own.

Whatever my future might hold, I'm going to take charge of it, and that means no more allowing a damned delicious alien to lick me to oblivion!

"Okay, Ike, what is it?" I release him, and he whirrs into the air, lights cycling through red and blue.

I wrap my blanket around me a little tighter and follow him out of the room. He leads me down the corridor and away from where I can hear Strykr.

It's strange, but the farther away I get from him, the less comfortable I feel. In fact, the more I feel like something is watching me. Lurking in wait.

I suppose I had no idea that there were any other robots on board, especially killer robots like the one Strykr destroyed.

I suppose I should consider him useful, if only crappy stuff hadn't been happening to me after he turned up.

I traipse after Ike, hoping that what he wants to show me is worth the effort because the cold is really getting to me.

"Kat." The growl is unmistakable.

I turn to see my hulk of an alien, wings held high, feathers puffed up. His dark eyes glitter with something else, something predatory.

I'd run, but my feet are blocks of ice. I'd hide, but I don't think I can move my limbs enough to go anywhere.

"Don't be like this," I plead. "I've nowhere to go. It's cold and I'm tired. Also, I think Ike's trying to tell me something, and I'm hoping it's something useful."

Strykr inclines his head. His wings drop, and his feathers go sleek as Ike dances in the air around me, and I shake on the spot with the cold.

"*Eregri*," he murmurs. Eyes softened, he moves over to me, and I'm enclosed in a warm wing, pressed next to a hard, muscular body.

"I don't know what that means, but thank you." I snuggle into the feathers, and they smell like a warm cat, biscuity with a hint of something spicy.

"Ike?" Strykr queries.

"We have to follow him." I point down the corridor, and the little robot buzzes away from us.

Strykr nods, and he puts an arm around my waist, making sure that his wing doesn't leave its comforting position as we walk together in silence. Something I notice he does very well, despite his size and considerable amount of feathers. Presumably that's how he keeps managing to sneak up on me.

I suppose I should expect nothing less from a creature that's clawed and fanged. He's a predator through and through. He's a predator I'm fairly sure was hunting me earlier.

"Kat?" His voice rumbles through me with his query, yet again making my core stumble. Up ahead, Ike circles over a hole in the floor, one I've seen before and explored. Down a ladder, there's an area that's full of strange controls that don't do anything when I touch them.

The little robot's lights flash green in an increasingly complex pattern. There's something down there that he wants us to see.

So there's the dilemma. This place is a prison. I have a choice.

I take the winged alien predator into a very enclosed space, or I stay in the main part of the station and freeze to death.

What a choice!

Strykr

Kat hesitates and shivers. The temperature is continuing to drop, and I know that's not a good thing for humans. It doesn't help that she's wearing hardly anything, and she's been injured.

I shouldn't have hunted her earlier. It's meant that she's struggling to trust me. Rage rises from my gut at my stupid, stupid instinct I should have been capable of repressing.

If only...

The scent of the illegal fight pits rises in my nostrils. The stench of blood and other bodily fluids. The only place where I feel whole, where I can rid myself of any feelings because there is only destruction. My claws in flesh.

As it should be. As the Gryn always have been. In the camps, fighting was the only thing that kept me alive. It just didn't keep me living. My soul and heart are black.

So why would this delicious creature want me? All I've done is take advantage of her and hunt her.

She says something and points down a dark hole in the floor, over which her little bot hovers.

"We need to go down there?" I mimic her point, and she nods, looking me up and down. She's wondering if I'll fit.

"I'll fit." I grin at her, but she doesn't smile back.

The bot dives into the hole, and it lights up. Kat exclaims something in her language, her hand flying over her mouth. She's worried about the bot, and I want her to trust me, so I take a couple of strides and jump down after it.

Perhaps not the best idea I've ever had. There's a short, thankfully smooth tube, and I'm dropped into a circular open area that is just taller than I am. Slowly, lights flicker on around me. They look similar to the consoles that Lyon has on his ship. Could this be the escape pod?

"Strykr?" Kat calls down, her voice full of stress.

"Kat, it's fine. I think Ike was showing us the escape pod. You can come down."

I peer back up the tube and see her concerned face, lips tinged with blue. I hold up my arms and try to indicate she should jump down. She stares at me for a beat, then her head disappears, and her feet swing into the hole. With a short swish, she slides down the tube, and I catch her easily.

Her body is light and warm in my arms. Her scent is intoxicating. If I could never smell anything but her again, I'd be happy until the end of my days. She makes everything good.

She makes my heart beat again without the need for any fight or adrenaline.

"Strykr?" Kat stares up at me, her hand on my chest. She says something else, and I, reluctantly, put her on her feet.

She slowly walks around the pod. Ike lands on her shoulder, chirping at her as she trails her fingers over what I think are the controls. She speaks to the bot, and it croons in return.

I'd want her to trust me as much as she trusts that tiny lump of metal.

Ike makes a high-pitched sound, jumps off her shoulder, and

buries its head into one of the consoles. Kat cries out in alarm, pulling at it. In a blur of movement, a compartment slides open behind her. Two pincer like arms reach out, grab her, and she's dragged back into the compartment, her screams filling my mind.

The compartment slides shut, and I can see her. Eyes wide in fear, she drums on the translucent cover of the compartment.

I leap for it, hooking my claws into the metal, tearing at it in the hope I can free her. Her screams are muffled, but I can tell she's shouting my name. I risk a look at her. She's pale, terrified. Pleading.

An arm extends out of the wall behind her, holding a long, slim syringe filled with blue liquid. She squirms away from it, but in the confined space, only just big enough for a human, there's no escape.

I redouble my efforts. Whatever this tech is, it's not connected to Proto. It has to be on some sort of closed circuit. If I knew anything about tech other than the very basics, I might be able to stop it, but all I can do is use brute force to rip at the door and attempt to free my Kat.

As I'm struggling, I can feel a vibration under my feet. The pod is moving. At this stage, I'm not sure if that's a good thing or not. Finally, I feel something give under my claws, and the door springs open.

Kat is slumped in the corner, eyes closed.

The pod shakes, and she falls forward into my arms.

"Vrex!" Not only are we on the move, but the pod has done something to my female.

Next to me, Ike chirps. I reach out for the vrexing bot and miss.

"What the vrex have you done to her!" I shout out loud. "Wake her up!" I add with desperation. She's limp, floppy, and my gut is in knots. I want her to wake up, to talk to me in her funny language. To smile at me.

Anything else means I'm hollow all over again.

"*Commander!*" Lyon's voice fires through my comm. "*There's something emerging from the station. Is it you?*"

"We found an escape pod," I return to him, gently brushing the gorgeous scented dark hair away from my female's face. "The controls are different from the *Perlin*. You're going to have to help me."

"*You should be okay, Commander. It's probably on a pre-designated course to Ustokos. We can track you.*"

"And if we don't go to Ustokos?"

"*Then you're going to need a crash course on flying an escape pod,*" Lyon replies.

Sometimes his dry sense of humor is not really appreciated.

In my arms, Kat moans and stirs.

"Can we avoid doing any crashing? I think I've had enough excitement for one day," she says as her eyes flicker open, and her gaze rests on me.

Kat

There are worse ways to wake up than staring into a pair of concerned dark eyes and a face that wouldn't look out of place on the big screen.

I should know, given that I've already woken up on this spaceship. On the dissection table.

For some reason, Strykr seems to be shaking as I lie in his arms, trying to work out who was talking about crashing.

"Fuck!" I lurch out of his grip. "Are we crashing? What the fuck is going on?"

"We're not crashing. We're in an escape pod. Your little bot led us here, it must have some sort of safety protocol, given that the station was losing atmosphere," Strykr says.

I stare at him.

Then take a step back.

I stare at his lips. Lips that have already been near a part of my body which causes my core to pulse.

"I can understand you!"

"The pod gave you something." Strykr takes a step towards me, and I can't go any farther back, so I freeze.

"Why?"

He lets out a growl of frustration. "This station belonged to Proto. My best guess is that any organics are given translators before they arrive on Ustokos."

My breath stutters in my chest. He may as well be still speaking another language for all his sentence made sense.

"What's Proto? What's Ustokos?"

Strykr opens his mouth to speak, shuts it again as he contemplates his answer. "It's complicated, but the planet, my planet, is called Ustokos."

"We're going to the planet?"

"Looks that way," he replies gruffly.

My alien has suddenly become a male of very few words.

"Can you fly it?"

Strykr looks around at the interior of the pod. The tops of his wings nearly brush the ceiling, and he takes up a huge amount of space, what with all his muscles and feathers. I suddenly feel rather claustrophobic.

"Maybe."

"I'll take that." I shrug. "Anything I can do to help?"

Strykr's feathers lift, pricking up as he turns and looks at me over his shoulder. "It's my job to protect you," he rumbles, his velvety voice full of depth and chocolate.

"Oh." I fiddle with the edge of my dress. I'm not entirely sure what to say. "Thanks?"

I've been on my own for a long time. Not just on the ship or *station* as Strykr has called it. I haven't been present on Earth, in my life, in anything since it all went to shit. Since I ran from the pressure. Since I hid in my house until it was repossessed.

Why would this alien want to protect me?

"I'd still like to help," I say as Strykr looks at the consoles in front of him. He presses a button, and the wall in front of us disappears, showing a much closer view of the planet. It causes me to let out a short 'eep' sound.

"Do not be alarmed, sweet female," Strykr says, hitching up a lip and showing a sharp canine. "It's only a screen." He says it in a manner of an adult explaining things to a child. "These controls are similar to our other ship. I should be able to land without incident."

He's useful as well as looking like a feathered Greek god. I have a new appreciation for Strykr as he takes on the controls. I suppose, being a winged alien, he should be good at flying. Why did I ever doubt that?

And the pod suddenly lurches sideways, flinging me into him.

"Did you do that on purpose?" I ask from my position on his lap. "Because if you're going to keep doing these sorts of things, we need to have a talk about boundaries."

"The controls are new to me, little Kat." The way he pronounces my name is knicker-meltingly glorious, elongating the 'a' with an incredible, rich accent. Shame about the 'little.' "It might take me a while to get used to them."

He places a warm, dense arm over my stomach.

"Don't you need two hands?" I ask, swallowing hard when I see just how enormous his claws are.

"Not always, but I prefer it, when necessary," he rumbles, dark eyes glittering with something that has to be lust.

I don't exactly regret that I let him get...close to me. It's just, now we understand each other, it's suddenly become a bit...awkward.

And I'm all about the awkward.

"Where are we going, your planet? Who were you speaking to just then? Where is your ship? Why did you get left behind?" I garble out the questions to cover my confusion and to attempt to diffuse the situation.

Whoever or whatever Strykr is, he's confident and experienced. Something I stopped being a long time ago. I've had my fair share of men, but no one like him. Strykr oozes sex appeal like a lion on the savannah. He's dangerous and alluring, beautiful and deadly.

"We should be going to Ustokos. The instruments are not clear, but it looks like we're on a trajectory to land. I was speaking to the captain of our spaceship, the *Perlin*. It's just alongside us, look," Strykr says patiently and points at the screen. A bright dot looms closer, and I can see it's an angular looking thing with about as much grace as a cardboard box. "One of my team made an error on the space station, which is why we vacated. I came back when I saw you."

"You—you came back for me?" I stumble over the words. "Why? You don't even know me."

Strykr doesn't look at me. "I don't leave anyone behind," he mutters, and his claws clack over the console. I get the distinct impression he didn't really know the answer to that question.

"So we're not going to crash?"

"We won't crash, little female. I promise. We will land on Ustokos, and you will meet the rest of the Gryn and the other humans."

I gape at him, my heart hammering in my chest, my breath caught up in the moment.

"There are other humans on your planet?"

Strykr

My gorgeous female trembles in my lap. The idea of going to Ustokos clearly terrifies her. As much as I'm overjoyed we can communicate, somehow, finding the words to reassure her alludes me.

"We have five humans. Five females," I say, deciding to keep the exact nature of what they are on Ustokos to myself for the time being. "How long have you been on the space station?"

"I don't know." Kat drops her chin to her chest. "The robots wouldn't tell me anything. I'm guessing a few weeks. But there were other humans with me, at least in the beginning. Then it was just me and Ike."

She looks over at the little bot that's perched happily on the top of a console, his lights glowing a pleasant calming green.

"Do you think the women, I mean females, you have on your planet could be the ones who were with me?" she asks hopefully.

"I'm sorry, these humans have been with us for quite a number of cycles. From what we understand, Proto has been selling Gryn as slaves for some time. It brought in the humans to breed with us."

Vrex! That was definitely the wrong thing to say. Kat can't get away from me fast enough.

"Breed?" she stutters.

"I didn't mean it like that. No one has forced the humans to do anything they don't want to do. Anyway, we've defeated Proto, so there's no longer any risk to you." From the look in her eyes, I'm not helping.

"So you want to breed with me, is that what earlier was all about?" Her voice is the barest of whispers. "The room with the sparkles?"

Vrex it! Yes! I want my seed in her belly and for my youngling to grow inside her. I want to mate her over and over until we fill the new lair with life and laughter.

"No, not at all. I made my nest to pleasure you," I reply as evenly and as quietly as I can.

Kat shuts her mouth with an audible click.

"You liked it, didn't you?" I'm suddenly concerned that this perfect little female thinks I wanted to take advantage of her because that was the last thing on my mind when I lapped at her skin and carried her to my nest.

"Well, yes, but…" She chews on her bottom lip.

Every atom of my being screams at me to tell her she's my mate, that she belongs to me and only me. But Kat looks as if she'd bolt out of the nearest airlock if she could find one.

I concentrate on the console in front of me, not wanting to terrify her any more than I already have. "There is no breeding on Ustokos unless the female is willing, and her mate has made his nest."

Kat is ominously silent, and when I risk a look at her, she sits on the floor behind me, staring straight ahead at the planet that's rapidly getting larger on the screen, her knees drawn up to her chest and her arms wrapped around them.

All the words at my disposal. Words she can finally understand, and I can't tell her how I feel in case I scare her more than she already is. Only the goddess Nisis knows how long she's been on her own; she needs time to adjust.

She needs to be with the other humans. I know that they can help her. After all, they've been through the same thing.

Only, if I don't assert my claim on her before we reach the planet, she might be taken from me. A boiling rage fills my veins at the thought of losing my mate. The delicate creature I know I need, or I'll lose my mind.

"*Commander, have you been able to determine your trajectory?*" Lyon's voice breaks into my thoughts.

"It's on a fixed course. I can't change it. Hopefully, we won't land too far from the eyrie," I reply. "Please continue to monitor our progress."

"What's the eyrie?" Kat asks, her voice dull.

"The Legion of the Gryn is expanding. That's my species. When we defeated Proto, the sentient AI holding you captive on the space station, we released many of our kind from the camps. As a result, a phalanx of warriors we call mercs have moved to a new lair, the eyrie. It is our home."

Although for me, it's as far from a home as the camps were.

Kat looks at me, and I can see in her eyes that she's unconvinced. "It can be your home too, if you wish?" I suggest, trying to keep hope out of my voice.

"Do I have any choice? Can you send me back to Earth if I don't want to be a breeder?" Her voice trembles, and although she's trying to be strong, I can feel that she is struggling.

"My *eregri*, you can do whatever you want to do. If you want to go back to Earth, I will move all of Ustokos to make that happen."

I'd move all of Ustokos to keep you in my arms forever.

She blinks at me, blue eyes enormous in the harsh lighting

of the pod. Her skin is pale from the time she's spent in space, but it has the most amazing quality. Soft, beautiful, and eminently touchable.

"You'd help me get back to Earth?"

"If that's what you want."

Kat is quiet again. "And I don't have to be a breeder?"

I'm unable to help myself, laughing out loud. "Proto is gone. We are all free. No one has to breed if they don't want to."

I don't look at her because if I do, I'll give myself away. The only thing I want to do is take her to my nest and breed with her. The exact opposite of what she wants. My emotions are at war. The part of me that always wants to fight struggles with the part of me that can command a unit of elite warriors.

Some of whom need a lesson in restraint when it comes to their trigger fingers.

She's the one thing I should be fighting for and the one thing I'm going to have to let go.

"*Commander.*" Lyon is on the comm. *"we've worked out your final landing place. It looks like you'll be going down near one of Proto's old bases. We'll meet you down there."*

"Understood," I reply. "Can you contact the ground and let them know what's happening?"

"Already done, Commander."

"What did they say?" Kat asks, not having moved from her position on the floor.

"They've confirmed we're going to land not too far from the new lair."

Her lack of response makes ice settle in my stomach.

Whatever happens on Ustokos, I can't let her go. That's one thing I know for sure.

Kat

My brain fires in all sorts of dark directions. I'm stuck in a tin can with an alien angel who wants to breed with me, after he's introduced me to more aliens who want to do the same.

Maybe that's disingenuous. He didn't specifically insist on the breeding thing, although his behavior so far is a good indication of his interest.

And you liked it, Kat.

I've just met the first living thing I've seen in weeks. Perhaps it was an unusual greeting, that's all.

My inner sarcastic bitch smirks at me as I continue to stare at the empty wall Strykr calls a screen and watch as we hit his planet's atmosphere. The pod shakes briefly before stabilizing, and then we're descending through clouds.

My gaze wanders onto his back, huge wings that only just fit into the pod, slate gray, they have the softest sheen of silk. I frown at him. He seemed nice. It's hard to believe he and his species are just after humans for breeding. Or that there are other species that want humans for slaves. Admittedly, he said they wanted his species for slaves, too.

The more I think about it, the more my head hurts, and the more I want to get away. I've been a lot of things—employee, failure, business owner—but I've not been a breeder, and that is definitely not something I'm going to sample.

As soon as I can, I'm going to find a way back to Earth, back to my quiet life of making jewelry for people who appreciate it. Back to being independent and able to hide away whenever I want.

Ike curls into my hair, chirping softly, and I stroke over his sinuous metal form as I watch Strykr operate the controls. Could I take him back to Earth with me? He's kind of cute, albeit very alien. He's been handy in a difficult situation, and he's definitely easy on the eye.

Color flames in my cheeks at the thought of what I might have liked Strykr to continue doing to me earlier, and my stomach fills with lead as the view screen flicks to the planet below us. It's a huge city, sprawling out for miles. I'm going to be in a place I ran from many years ago, the heart of an urban conurbation that ate me up and spat me out.

"This is Kos," Strykr says over his shoulder. "It was one of the great Gryn cities of Ustokos. Over there is the main lair." He points at an enormous crumbling building sprawling across the side of a cliff. "Our eyrie is over there." He points to a large empty area over which a huge tower block squats in the landscape.

"What happened here?" I ask. "Why is it so ruined?"

"There was a great reckoning between Proto, the Gryn, and other organic species. We lost, and what you see is what happened to our civilization," Strykr says, not looking at me. "Those who were left were rounded up into camps, along with other organics on Ustokos. But Proto reserved its worst treatment for the Gryn."

His hands curl into fists, and I see his claws cutting into his skin.

"We were tortured, experimented on." A shudder he tries to suppress shakes his feathers. "Some of us escaped and set up a resistance, led by our Prime, Jyr." His head falls between his shoulders. "Some of us had to be rescued."

I ache to touch him, to soothe him and make things better for this strange alien raptor who I thought wanted to eat me. How little I knew about exactly which part he wanted to taste!

"But this thing, Proto. It's gone now?" I say, hesitantly.

"Defeated by the Gryn." Strykr straightens. "We have a world to rebuild. My team are a small part of that," he adds. "That's why we were on the space station. We're trying to recover as much tech as we can. Proto made sure we haven't had access to it for generations. Some of us struggle with it."

"But not you." I nod at the controls.

"I'm a quick learner," he says wryly.

"So, when you mean no tech, do you mean no computers, mobile communicators, that sort of thing?"

Strykr's brow furrows. I guess that's exactly what he means if he doesn't know what those things are.

"We survived, but now we know what's out there." He points upwards. "Now we know that Proto was selling Gryn as slaves to the rest of the galaxy. We're in danger, and we need to find a way to protect ourselves."

It's hard to imagine anything as predatory as Strykr could be in danger, but then I've seen first-hand what the 'tech' he refers to can do.

"Strykr," I say, slowly. "If the other humans I heard on the station are not the ones you have on your planet, then where are they?"

He shakes his head. "I don't know. Maybe they were sold by Proto, maybe they're already slaves. I'm sorry, Kat."

"You don't need to be sorry, Strykr. You didn't take us

from Earth, did you?" I say, although my emotions churn under the surface.

I don't know who to trust. Before I was taken from Earth, I could hardly trust myself. Now I'm at the mercy of a race of predatory aliens. Maybe hundreds of them. Crowds beyond crowds. My heart starts to beat faster, and I know if I don't get a grip on myself, I'm going to have a meltdown.

My skin heats as wave after wave of concern and nausea roll through me.

"Kat?" Strykr is by my side, crouching down, trying to make himself look small. It would be funny if I wasn't already struggling to breathe.

"I'm fine. I'll be fine," I gasp at him, hating myself for not being in control. My vision dims, and the last thing I want, after everything we've been through, is to pass out on him.

"Strykr!" A male voice echoes through the tiny pod. My alien angel is suddenly jerked backwards with a snarl, and several enormous aliens appear in his place.

"What the fuck!" I try to say, only my voice has been robbed by the rising panic that rapidly consumes me.

"It's okay." A feminine voice penetrates the noise that surrounds me. "You're safe." A human woman's face peers at me, surrounded by long blonde hair.

"Strykr?" I attempt to call out, dimly aware of loud roaring and a struggle.

"He's gone, sweetheart. You don't need to worry about him."

And the lights go out.

STRYKR

"Vrex you!" I finally shake myself free of Ayar and Vypr, who have dragged me out of the pod. "What the vrex do you think you're doing, *mercs*?" I spit out the last word.

"They were following my orders." Ryak steps from behind them. "We were told that you were returning to Ustokos with another human, and we wanted to be sure that everything was well."

"You think I might hurt a human?" I growl.

My feral nature is not under control. Ryak might be my commander, but I won't hesitate to tear into him if I think he's going to keep me from Kat. Not that it would do any good. The seniors have an ability to heal that is beyond any other Gryn.

"We've no idea what went on up there, Commander. Which is why we have to take all the necessary precautions. I'll debrief you all in an hour. Come to my chambers." He turns, just as his mate, Bianca, helps Kat from the pod.

"But..."

"No, Strykr. You can see the human later." His voice is firm, and his feathers bristle, shielding Kat from me.

He's waiting for my acknowledgement, and I can't undermine him in front of my warriors. Not after he trusted me with this team.

"Yes, Guv," I reply, putting a huge amount of effort into making my voice even.

Ryak follows his mate and the desire to slam him to the ground rises within me.

"Come on, Commander." Mylo puts a hand on my shoulder. "We should go."

He doesn't want me to get into a fight with Ryak. Mylo alone knows what I'm capable of, and it won't be the first time he's held me back. A quick glance at him shows the state of his injury. He holds his arm over a bloody bandage wrapped around his torso. His wings are streaked red.

"You need to see the healer," I say, trying not to growl, although it's proving very difficult, given that my mate has been taken away, and every part of me wants to hunt her down. "And you need some additional training." I stare at Ayar.

The vrexer grins at me. "I helped you catch a human female though, didn't I?"

I'm not sure I've ever wanted to kill him more than at this moment. "Mylo. Healer. The rest of you, store your weapons, get something to eat, and join me in the training pit," I grunt out.

Mylo hurries away, and Jay, Ayar, and Vypr troop back off towards the *Perlin*. I breathe out, long and low, in an attempt to center myself.

The problem is that there was one thing that could stop the darkness rising inside me. But it's all changed. The only thing that is ever going to soothe my soul has been spirited away by Ryak.

I drum my claws on the wall of the training arena. There's no sign of my team, and I am absolutely certain that I'm going to tear them to pieces when they do arrive.

All I can think about is Kat. The look in her eyes before I was dragged away. A mixture of fear and the fight. She didn't want to be afraid.

To me, she's already the bravest little thing I've ever met. She faced down the joykill and me, neither of which should be taken lightly.

But I don't want her to be afraid of me.

I want her to care for me. I want to feel her fingers in my feathers, her warm body at my side. I want to be sheathed in her.

Vrex it! My cocks are stirring again at the mere thought of her lush body. I can't let her go; I can't let Ryak spirit her away from me.

Kat is mine. Every atom of my being knows it, and we should never be separated.

I think of the pits below the surface. The ones that the seniors don't know about. The ones where reputations are made and lost. Where coin is exchanged, along with other things, such as narcotics. The ones where the Mochi and Kijg come to watch and bet on us.

The ones where no self-respecting warrior would enter. The pits where a commander of my standing has no reason to be.

And the one place I can go to deal with my anger. It's an addiction I can't rid myself of. The thing that makes me whole, that fills the void. The fight, the dirtier the better, drags me in, and I don't have to be anything other than the dark Gryn that will kill if you let him.

"Strykr?"

I look up from my brooding to see Mylo. He has a clean bandage wrapped around him and looks more comfortable. "Where are the rest of them?" My voice is low and dangerous.

"Vypr and Jay are just bringing down some food for you. Ayar is cleaning up the weapons," he replies.

"I don't want anything to eat."

Mylo shrugs and winces. "What happened up there, Guv?"

"I'm not your Guv. Ryak is, Mylo. Don't forget that." Even the fighter within me can't bring himself to threaten an injured warrior. "Get the rest of them down here, and we'll train."

I extend my claws. They glint in the strong light that fills the training pit.

"I need to see the human female, Mylo." My words are a rasp of desperation. "I don't care what the Guv says. She's mine."

He narrows his eyes.

"Let me come with you," he says "The last thing I want is for you to take your frustration out on anyone else."

"That's not going to happen. If I have her, I don't need the pits."

Mylo raises his eyebrows. "In that case, you need to see the Guv," he says enthusiastically. "The day you give up the pits is a day I never thought I'd see."

Kat

When I come to, I'm not in the pod anymore, and there's no sign of Strykr.

Instead, I'm on a bed of what looks like furs, in a room that might have been hollowed out of a cave or cast out of concrete. It's difficult to tell exactly what the material is.

My head aches, and my body is stiff with the residual effects of having run all over the spaceship. Beside me, Ike chimes as he slips out from in between some of the furs.

I put out my hand, and he whizzes around my arm, burying himself in my hair.

"Oh, hi. You're awake?" I jump in alarm at the voice I vaguely recognize. It's the woman I saw earlier. She holds a tray.

"Er..." I scramble to sit. "Yes, sorry about earlier. I'm..."

"You don't need to explain. We were all overwhelmed when we first arrived. Especially by the Gryn. I'm sure Strykr wouldn't hurt you. It's just that these males haven't been around many females." She sits on the edge of the furs, which I'm assuming are a type of bed, and has the tray on her lap. "Sometimes they can be a bit full on."

There's a cup of some sort of brown substance which steams, and a pile of what appears to be Danish pastries.

"Strykr wouldn't hurt me. I know that." I peer at the tray. "Are those..."

"We're very lucky that one of our number is a chef, and she's worked magic with alien ingredients. Go on, try one." She offers me the tray. "I'm Bianca, by the way. Bianca Richards."

"Kat Bolton." I take the proffered tray from her and put it on my lap.

"What the fuck!" Bianca leaps up and paces back from me.

"What?" I stare at her. I'm pretty sure I've not been away from Earth so long that taking a tray is some sort of weird thing to do.

"What the fucking hell is that thing on your shoulder?"

It's only then I remember Ike and that Strykr told me that tech was basically bad on this planet.

"This is Ike. He was with me on the spaceship." I tempt the little bot out of my tangle of hair and onto my arm. "He's completely harmless. Without him, I'd have been completely stuck."

Bianca thaws as she sees Ike curled around my hand.

"Jesus, you gave me a fright. I thought you were turning into the Terminator or something!" She laughs and comes closer to inspect Ike who chimes at her and flashes green and purple. "Cute," she decides. "A pet bot, whatever next?"

I take a bite of the pastry, and it's delicious. Not as sweet as on Earth, and the spice element is...unusual...

"Good?" Bianca asks, sitting back down again.

"Different, but it doesn't matter. I've been living on porridge forever."

"That'll explain some things." Bianca looks me up and down. "Like why you're skin and bone. How long were you up there?"

"I don't know." I take a sip of the coffee and find that it's not coffee at all, but a hot, savory drink. "How long have you been here?"

"About three years, give or take. Ustokos's days are longer than on Earth," Bianca replies. "I arrived with four other women. We were brought here by Proto."

"Strykr told me, to breed with the Gryn."

Bianca gives me a very big smile that's nearly all teeth. "No wonder you were in a dead faint when we found you if that's what he was saying. It's enough to put anyone off. Yes, that horrible creature—Proto—did bring us here to breed with the Gryn, but the Gryn rescued us instead. They let us make their home here with them."

"So you're..."

"I'm mated, which is what the Gryn call being in a relationship, to Ryak. He's one of the senior Gryn."

"And Proto?"

"Gone. Along with all its tech, which is why your pet bot surprised me. We haven't seen any bots since Proto was destroyed. The Gryn are doing all they can to get the tech working again, but it's hard when you haven't dealt with it for generations."

"But they have a spaceship?"

"It's a long story, but yes, they have one spaceship. They were hoping to find another which is why they were up there when they found you." Bianca tries to give me a reassuring smile, but none of this is reassuring.

"I suppose I was lucky then."

"That Strykr found you?" She cocks her head to one side. "If you don't mind me asking, are you mated to him?"

"If you mean have I had sex with him, that's none of your damn business!" I bite back the tears, not wanting to be rude and yet annoyed at the intimacy of the question from a woman I've only just met.

"I'm sorry." Bianca holds up her hands. "I could have been more diplomatic. That's why Ryak sent me. We just want to make sure that you were unharmed, after the way we found you with Strykr."

"The way you found me?"

"Him standing over you like that. It looked like he was..."

"He wasn't," I say emphatically. "He wouldn't do anything to hurt me."

"Good. No Gryn would normally ever hurt a female. It's sort of their thing, protecting females," Bianca says, her voice kind. "They lost all their females, you see. But they can go a little crazy around females, sometimes," she adds. For a second, it looks like she's about to ask me something, then she thinks better of it. "Once you've had something to eat, the other seniors want to meet you. No one expected to find anything living on the space station, so you are *of interest*."

I don't reply, instead taking another bite of my food. I don't like being 'of interest,' and I wish the big feathered male they all thought was a threat to me was here, now.

Doing what he said he would do.

Protecting me.

I DUCK DOWN A SIDE CORRIDOR AND LEAN AGAINST A crumbling wall, breathing deeply to recover my composure. Bianca has run me ragged. I have spent the last day doing everything I hate with a passion.

Most of that being meeting other beings.

And to make it worse, there's been no sign of Strykr.

Instead, I've met the incredibly imposing leader of all the Gryn, Jyr. A male they all call 'Prime.' I've met all the senior Gryn, including Strykr's boss, Ryak. I've met all the human women, all of whom were very friendly, but I got the impression they were hiding something. At least one of them looked pregnant.

I've seen more flying aliens than I could shake a stick at. A very big stick.

But no Strykr.

Overwhelmed doesn't even cover how I'm feeling. I'm longing for the solitude of the space station. I'm also wondering what I've done that means he'd do a disappearing act on me, especially after he told me he wanted to protect me.

Maybe that means something else to an alien like him.

The 'lair' that these aliens live in is split into two. There's the big one I saw on our descent. It's just as decrepit as it looked, if what is basically an alien castle can be described as decrepit. Apparently, there has been an influx of new warriors since they defeated the robots, so instead of overcrowding their current accommodations, they've moved out the warriors who were released from the camps into the eyrie, where I'm staying.

It's a tower block that's again more castle than modern aesthetic architecture. It looks like it was once pretty special, although on the inside, it's more of a shell.

A shell of a building filled with exuberant winged aliens, who, if they are not flying around the internal open atrium that rises the full height of the building and where long, looping green plants hang, they're fighting in the courtyard at the bottom. Even now, their shouts echo up to me.

All in all, it's been an exhausting day, and yet all I could do was look for Strykr everywhere I was taken. I can't shake the feeling of his warm feathers around my shoulder, his light touch, and the concern in his eyes as panic overtook me.

What I need is a long bath and time away from both alien and human to process everything. I can't possibly be dependent on Strykr to save me. I've fought my own battles for so long, I don't need an avenging angel to join my fight.

It won't stop me looking out for him though.

A waft of warm damp air reaches me from farther down the corridor, reminding me that I'm supposed to be looking for the hot baths I've been told about. I've been told that I can go anywhere I like by Ryak, the leader of the warriors who inhabit the eyrie. He and Bianca are apparently married, and I can't quite get my head around that.

So I'm going to take him up on his offer and follow my nose down the corridor, around a corner and find that it opens into a large room, in the center of which is a pool set into the floor, the water steaming slightly as it bubbles from somewhere deep below. Around the edges is a soft, dark green moss that absorbs the occasional spill. The walls are hung with the same plants that festoon the central atrium, some of which, I notice, are glowing.

I stoop next to the pool and dip my fingers into the water. It tingles against my touch, the perfect temperature.

How could this strange place answer my prayers? A hot bath at the end of a long day. If I didn't already think I was dreaming, I'd pinch myself.

But first, I'm going to enjoy the first proper wash I've had in forever.

Strykr

"Report," Ryak raps at me from behind his desk.

His office space is as sparse as it was when we were in the old lair. His nest is through the door at the back, and I'm guessing he wants to keep both spaces separate. Not that I blame him. If I hadn't been chasing down my team in order to get to this meeting, nesting would have been the only thing I would have been doing.

If only to keep my mind and body out of the fighting pits, the place that called to my dark soul once my *eregri* was taken from me.

"The station was functioning when we arrived," I reply as behind me, my team shuffle, feathers rustling.

"Yes, I'm aware of that. It's the lack of functioning after you boarded that I want to know about." Ryak rubs his hand over his face. "You are supposed to be my elite, after all."

"It had life support. It also had functioning bots, including a joykill."

"We knew it wasn't going to be affected by the EMP weapon. Lyon told us that." Ryak steeples his fingers as he rests his elbows on his desk. "But functioning bots? Were they hostile?"

I snort and shoot a look over my shoulder at Ayar, who, for once, has the good grace to look at his boots. "One of them was. It won't surprise you to learn that it was the joykill."

"They will have a residual programming, even without Proto's overall control. If we do encounter live joykills, we'll have to destroy them, even if we do want the tech," Ryak says, partly to himself. The Guv has always been secretive, and I guess old habits die hard.

"There was another bot, a small one. It had flight capacity, but it wasn't a hostile. If I had to say it was anything, I'd say it was friendly," I add, desperate to regain some element of respect from my Guv, who clearly thinks I'm the biggest idiot ever to have crossed his path. "It helped me and the human female to escape."

"Yes, I've met the human female you found and her bot. I've not had a chance to interrogate her yet," Ryak says nonchalantly. "My mate has been taking care of her."

I only hear the first part of the sentence, and I'm leaping over the desk, wings beating and claws outstretched as chaos ensues in the room. Wings, claws, feathers, and limbs are everywhere, until I'm pinned on the floor, and Ryak looms over me.

"She was on that station for a long time, Strykr. You might think she's your mate, but you can't assume she thinks the same."

I can't reply. All I can do is snarl and fight against Jay, Ayar holding me on one side, Vypr and Mylo on the other. It's only when I hear Mylo's hiss of pain that I stop struggling.

"But she's asked Bianca about you, so I'm going to give this situation the benefit of the doubt. I want you to find out what she knows and find out more about that bot." He stares down at me, then holds out his arm.

I'm lucky. He's going to give me a chance. There's plenty of warriors who would have been returned to the lair and on laundry duty for looking at the Guv the wrong way. But I know it's borrowed time.

This was my first proper mission in charge of my team, and I've vrexed it up. Not only that, but my inability to control myself here and now has thoroughly vrexed things with Ryak.

I grab hold of his arm as my team releases me, feathers rustling. The Guv pulls me to my feet and then directly into his chest.

Do that again, and you'll be put in the pits permanently.

Ryak doesn't have to speak. His thoughtbond, a way of transferring his thoughts and emotions is the strongest of all the senior Gryn. He can drop what he's feeling directly into my mind, and from the way these thoughts pound at me, he's not happy.

Don't think I don't know what you do in the dark.

Vrex it! My desire for Kat increases exponentially in an instant because she's the only thing that can hold me. Stop me from wanting to kill everything. She's the only thing that can make me whole, make me the commander that Ryak wants me to be.

I'm in no doubt that, today, he is disappointed in me. Plus I've made a fool of myself in front of my team.

And now I have to convince a wary human female that I'm not a threat, not looking for a breeder, as well as find out what to do about Ike.

Ryak walks over to the door of his office and opens it, motioning another Gryn warrior through.

"This is Syn. He's been trained by Kyt in ancient Gryn tech and some of the new stuff we've been looking at. He's joining your unit from today. Once you have the bot, he can take a look."

The big, broad Gryn looks the least likely candidate for a tech expert, but I'm the first to admit, we need someone with an aptitude for tech, especially if he's been trained by Kyt, the senior quartermaster. Syn glowers at us all.

"He has an attitude problem which I'm sure you can all work out," Ryak adds, and I feel his mirth, even though all he does is glare at Syn. The vrexer has given me this big, angry lump on purpose.

I guess I deserve it, but dealing with another damaged Gryn on my team is not what I need.

"Dismissed." Ryak turns his back on us all.

The mission was a complete wipe out. I've just gained a warrior who looks more deranged than Ayar, if that was even possible, and I have to find my mate.

Except she's not my mate. She's probably even forgotten I existed, or tried to forget, given I nearly killed her on the station, twice. I flick my wings as I exit Ryak's office, my unit trailing after me.

How on Ustokos am I going to convince her that she's mine?

Alone in space, when we didn't understand each other, I could show her how I felt. I've always been better with deeds than words. But now...

I'm actually going to have to speak to her. Given that the last time we talked she thought all I wanted to do was enslave her and breed with her. Then she fainted.

I'm not entirely convinced I can pull this off.

Kat

The water in the pool is the exact temperature of my perfect bath. The liquid is silky, almost slippery, and my poor battered body, particularly my legs, are feeling a million times better from being immersed. The redness on my calves is almost totally gone, and the blistered areas are reduced to some small marks.

I let out a long sigh of contentment. Ike perches on a vine high above me. He wasn't very happy when I first went into the pool, his lights flickering red as he shouted my name, but once I was in, he seemed fine, although not inclined to join me. Silly little robot.

Swimming from one side of the pool to the other means I get another flow of hot water, so I occasionally swish my way over. The pool is so deep in the middle I can't stand up. It's deep and dark, which piques my curiosity. I wonder if it goes anywhere.

Taking a deep breath, I dive down, legs kicking as I try to find the bottom of the pool. The water is crystal clear, but the heat means it's hard to keep my eyes open. My lungs start to burn, and without having located the bottom but having seen that the sides slope outwards and downwards like a bell, I burst to the surface, water flying and gasping for air.

Virtually blind, I thrash my way to the side of the pool and hook my arms over the edge as I regain my breath and wipe my eyes.

As my vision returns, I notice something new in front of me. A pair of boots. Very big boots. I follow the boots upwards, taking in the feathers that trail on the floor, the muscular legs encased in what looks like leather, the obligatory naked torso, and the dark, glittering eyes of Strykr.

"Hello," he says, head cocked to one side.

I run a jittery hand over my hair. Of course I wanted to see him again. After all, I haven't been able to get the big warrior out of my head.

But I had hoped that I might be able to play it a bit cool if I met him again. Not to be covered in water and snot.

"Hi," I say in a tone that is far too high-pitched for my liking. "What are you doing here?" I overcompensate with pitching the question far too low.

"I was looking for you," Strykr says. He doesn't move from his position next to the pool, his eyes boring into me. "I've been asked to make sure you are adjusting."

That's...unexpected. Does this mean he doesn't want to be around me?

"Adjusting?" I query, kicking out my legs in the water. Strykr's eyes widen.

"I mean, making sure that you're comfortable, that you have everything you need," he says, his hands curling into fists.

"I don't really know what I need," I say. I'm not admitting that part of my needs was to see him again, especially as it seems he's here under sufferance. "I've never been abducted by aliens and taken to a new planet before."

Strykr swallows, his throat bobbing, and he is no longer

looking at me. I hope I haven't made him feel guilty because being abducted had nothing to do with him.

"Can I show you around the eyrie, perhaps?" Strykr suggests, his eyes fixed on the center of the pool.

That sounds pretty innocent. It also doesn't sound like he's trying to get rid of me.

"That would be nice," I reply, and I'm wondering why he's staring into the pool because it's starting to piss me off.

Until I remember that I only went into the pool in my knickers. Bianca gave me some clothing, a pair of leather-like pants and a top made of a similar material.

What passes for a bra is more like a short corset, and I didn't think it would stand up to a dunking, so I'm topless, but as I'm at the side of the pool, Strykr shouldn't be able to see anything. I hesitantly put my hand around to my bum and discover that it's completely bare.

A quick look over my shoulder, and I see the gray knickers floating in the water like a rubbish jellyfish.

They must have come off when I dived down. Now I know what Strykr is looking at, and despite what we've shared on the space station, I feel mortification stealing through me.

This is not how I thought we'd meet again. Me buck naked with my underwear twirling in a current of water and Strykr looking drop dead gorgeous, all smoldering alien angel, trying to avert his eyes from my pants.

"Okay, well, maybe I'll see you later?" I say, dropping my bare bum down so that he's not getting the full moon.

"Er, yes," he says and hurries away in a flourish of feathers.

I let out a long breath.

"That could have gone better," I call out to Ike. The little robot swoops down from his perch and lands in front of me.

"Wet mistress," he says in his metallic tones.

"Stupid mistress," I tell him as I retrieve my soaked underwear and heave myself out of the water. "Stupid naked mistress."

"Gryn warrior aroused," Ike replies.

I stare at him. His lights blink at me.

"What?"

"Gryn warrior requires a female."

"Oh, good god, Ike." I groan, rolling my eyes. "Don't you start with that breeding shit."

Ike's lights blink at me, a rolling green and blue. "Gryn warrior requires his mate."

"That Gryn warrior," I point in the direction that Strykr took, leaving a residual scent of cinnamon and his own particular musk, "thinks I'm an idiot."

Strykr

I leave the healing pool where I found my Kat awkwardly. My cocks throb at me. I did my best not to look at her, keeping my eyes firmly fixed on the little bot perched on one of the new vines that have started to grow everywhere in the last cycle, since Proto was defeated.

It didn't work. I palm my erections through my maraha hide pants as I stride down the ramps surrounding the atrium. Even under the water, her scent was intoxicating. How I managed to keep my cocks under control when we were in the enclosed environment of the station *and* escape pod, I'm struggling to work out.

It could be because I know I can nest. My feathers itch and my wings flare. I should have asked to join her in the pool. A bath would do me a world of good. Instead, I made some lame comment about showing her around and ran away.

Not for the first time today, I wish I'd been able to stay in space, just me and her. Instead, I had the torture over the past eve of knowing she was somewhere in the eyrie as I tossed and turned on my ledge surrounded by snoring males.

Males who don't give a single toss that their commander is

fighting for his command or is potentially mated to a tiny female who knows nothing of Ustokos and the Gryn.

To add insult to injury, as I expected, none of them took to Syn, and it's clear that before this turn is out, blood will be shed.

I left them to work it out and just vrexed everything up with Kat instead.

"Strykr?" Her soft voice calls out across the atrium. Instantly, I'm in the air, closing the gap between us and landing as softly as I can.

"Oh!" she says, covering her mouth with her hands. "That was," she searches for the word, "impressive." She reaches out and runs a hand down my flight feathers. I can't help the shudder that runs over me at her touch.

"Sorry." She draws her hand back. "I just hadn't seen you fly before."

"Not much flying to be done in space."

"Isn't space just all flying?" She looks up at me, her mouth hitched up at the corner. I hear the tease in her voice.

Maybe I haven't vrexed up that badly.

An almighty clatter rises up in the atrium, and Kat almost jumps into me.

"What the hell was that?" she asks, her voice hoarse.

I peer over the edge of the solid balustrade and see my entire unit on the ground. Jay spots me, points upwards, and they're all in the air, calling my name.

I turn back to Kat to see she's shrinking back, away from me and away from the atrium.

"It's my unit. They're a noisy bunch of vrexers, but their hearts are in the right place. I can introduce you if you want."

Kat's eyes are enormous, an intense blue that I never want to forget. "I don't get on well with crowds, not anymore," she half-whispers.

My heart is unusually heavy at her concern and fear. All I want is for her to feel protected. By me.

"I can't deny that this lot are a crowd, but I know they'd love to meet you. All Gryn love females." I give her a supportive smile.

Kat slides back a little more, eyes widening, if that was even possible.

"It's only because we don't have any females," I add hastily. "The last female most of these warriors saw before the humans arrived was their mothers." I smooth my wings against my back, to appear smaller, to appear non-threatening.

"You mean they miss their mums?" she stutters out, just as Mylo appears, wings beating hard in the still air of the atrium, reaching for the balustrade.

He gives her a grin, and with a growl, I shove him away.

"We'll come down, vrex off!" He drops back, twirling as he dives, and I hear him shout to the others about where I am.

"It's up to you, Kat." I hold out my hand to her. "I'm happy just to give you the tour I said I would, or you can meet my unit. I want you to be happy, whatever we do."

She relaxes. It's a tiny, imperceptible movement but the way my blood sings in my veins at the fact I've persuaded her, she might as well have jumped into my arms, wrapping me in her scent, her warmth, and all that is Kat. My female.

"I guess we could meet them." Kat seems to come to an internal decision. "They are your unit? How many?"

"I'm the commander of five warriors. We are the elite."

"The elite what?"

"As of today, the elite of vrexing up, but I'm hoping we'll get better," I grumble.

Kat makes a choking noise, and a smile that she clearly wants to hide quirks up the corners of her mouth.

Her face lights up.

Her eyes dance.

I have made her happy.

"Okay, Strykr. My day can't get any stranger or more stressful. Take me to meet your *vrexing* unit."

The sound of my name on her lips and the funny way she pronounces 'vrex' produce the oddest reaction in me.

I am happy too.

Kat slides her hand into mine and, with the reverence I used to reserve for the best weaponry, I close my fingers around her warm flesh. It tingles against mine.

"Are we going to fly down?" she says hoarsely, eyeing my wings.

"If you want. If not, we can walk."

She looks me up and down. "I don't mind flying, if you think you can carry me."

The growl that rips from my throat is her reply. She's in my arms, clutched tightly to my chest as I launch into the atrium, beating with lazy wings, lifting us up to the top where the last few pieces of silica-glass hold on, shielding the atrium from the elements and allowing the plants to grow.

My mate thinks I'm not strong enough to lift us both?

Of course I'm going to prove her wrong!

Kat

I increase my death grip on Strykr as the floor disappears and we hang in the air over the atrium. The drop below us is dizzying, and all he does is climb higher, each wing beat taking us up, not down.

His muscles move under his skin as he performs this maneuver effortlessly. They bunch and contract. Strykr is raw power contained in a single handsome warrior.

After everything I've been through in the past twenty-four hours, I'm flying with an alien predator, who, in the right light, like the shaft of weak sunlight that shines into the atrium, looks almost angelic.

Providing angels are clawed and fanged.

Strykr's dark eyes turn on me.

"Still not sure I can carry you?" His voice rumbles through his chest and buries itself in my bones.

"I never doubted you could," I reply, and it's possible that he laughs before folding up his wings and diving down at a terrifying speed towards the ground.

At the last second, he opens his huge wings and lands as gently as if we are the lightest single feather. With a flick, he folds them and slowly lowers me to my feet. My breath has, frankly, left the building. For a long moment, I'm not sure I can hold myself up and remain, leaning against his warm, bare chest, the scent of his skin in my nostrils, all spicy warm.

"Let me get the introductions out of the way, my *eregri*," Strykr says. "Then I can show you the eyrie." I look up into his handsome face. He is calm and serene whilst I'm all sweaty panting.

"Okay." I wobble upright and attempt to smooth out my clothing and hair, pulling my fingers through the still damp, dark strands and hoping I look vaguely presentable.

For some reason, after all the Gryn I've met today, all of whom were supposed to be bigwigs, meeting Strykr's team is suddenly the most important. I risk a glance up at my big warrior and then look over my shoulder.

If I had anywhere to jump other than into a wall of muscle, I would. Five pairs of dark eyes are trained on me. Five huge warriors stare at me with curiosity on their faces.

"Unit!" Strykr says. At the command, the five of them stand more to attention. "This is Kat, the human who was on the space station."

I give them all a little wave, not entirely sure what else to do. To my immense surprise, in turn, each of these enormous warriors raises their hand and copies my movement.

"We have Vypr, my explosives expert." Strykr guides me in front of a pair of warriors.

"Good to meet you at last, mistress," Vypr says with a smile. His wings are much darker on the edges than Strykr's, but he has a boyish look about him.

"Were you the one blowing holes in my spaceship?" I ask.

"That would be me, mistress. I'm sorry, mistress," the warrior next to him pipes up. His dark eyes show no indication of apology, and the grin on his face tells me he'd do it again in a heartbeat. He has a long scar that runs down his face and over his shoulder.

"This is Ayar. Pain in my backside and my weapons expert." Strykr sighs. "He was responsible for the damage to the station that vrexed up our mission." He levels a commander's gaze at Ayar, who shrugs, giving me another, slightly deranged, twinkle.

"I suppose you didn't kill us." I return his shrug, and his grin widens, even as Strykr growls under his breath. "I'll take that."

"This is Jay, my sniper." Strykr ushers me on, introducing me to a quiet warrior who gives me a hesitant smile.

"Hi, Jay," I say, brightly. He looks more terrified than me. I hold out my hand to shake his.

Jay swallows, his eyes flicking behind me to Strykr. It's only then that I realize how my very human gesture must look to the Gryn.

"When humans meet new humans, the standard greeting is to shake hands. It's a gesture of goodwill and faith in the other human." I step to one side and hold my hand out to Strykr. He takes it with a quizzical look on his face. I lift our hands up and down in a pumping movement. "Pleased to meet you," I say in my poshest voice, hoping I sound a bit like the Queen.

I release Strykr and hold my hand out to Jay. He keeps his eyes firmly on the big warrior hovering behind me but takes my hand and allows me to shake it up and down.

"Pleased to meet you," he parrots, even attempting to mimic my voice.

Unable to help myself, I burst out laughing. Jay releases me as if I'm on fire.

"Sorry, Jay. That was really good, thank you."

I look around at Strykr who has an odd set to his jaw. When I look back at Jay, there's a queue of warriors. Each one taking my hand in turn at this new greeting. Each one delighting in doing something 'alien' to them. The final warrior has a large bandage wrapped around his abdomen.

"This is Mylo, our combat master and strategist," Strykr says, his voice strained as Mylo lifts my hand up and down enthusiastically. "He was injured on the space station by the joykill."

"Joykill?" I query.

"The bot that attacked us. We call them joykills," Strykr explains.

"You have them here?"

"We did. After we defeated Proto, we don't have them anymore," he reassures me.

"That we know of." A new warrior steps forward. He's big like the rest of them, but he's much darker in color. "Like the one on the space station, there could still be some autonomous bots anywhere we find tech," he says without a flicker of emotion. "The bot the human has could be equally as dangerous." He reaches out towards Ike who's curled around my shoulders like usual, half hidden in my damp hair.

There's an ear-splitting roar, and his hand is slammed away as a fury of feathers steps between him and me.

"You do not touch her, Syn," Strykr snarls. "Not unless she invites it. And the bot is not dangerous. It helped us find a way off the space station. It's friendly."

The other warrior snorts in annoyance but backs down immediately in the face of Strykr's ire. I tuck Ike a little farther back, taking comfort in his smooth metal surface.

"Does the mistress require food?" Jay pipes up, clearly looking to break the stalemate between Syn and Strykr who, frankly, looks like he's about to explode.

"I require food." Mylo elbows him in his ribs. "You never ask me if I require food."

"You're not a female," Jay replies, pointedly. "And you're a greedy warrior that eats anything. You can find your own food."

"You never offer for us either," Vypr says in a hurt tone, gesturing to Ayar and himself. "All we ever get from you is 'I need another rifle' or 'watch my back'."

"Vrex you!" Jay half snarls, half laughs. "I'm the one watching your vrexing hides all the time!"

Ayar lets out a feral noise, and Jay squares up to him. In a set of moves I don't even have time to take in, there's suddenly a scrum of bodies and feathers on the floor.

"Shit!" I take a step back. "Strykr?" My gorgeous warrior is looking at the tumble of warriors scuffling in the dust and shaking his head. "Is it always like this?"

"Most of the time." He turns his attention to Syn who is sat on a low bench, watching Ayar biting the shoulder of Mylo's wing. "I was only assigned Syn today. He needs to learn some manners."

As if in response to his words, a hand reaches out of the scrum, grabs Syn by the ankle, and he's involved, trading blows with a roar of anger.

Strykr smirks. "Now, how about that tour?"

Strykr

I can't even...

Could my unit have shown me up any more than by indulging themselves in a fight? Not only that, but I'd have happily joined in. My blood is up with the presence of my mate. A good fight would have been as good as mating her... almost. All I want to do is prove to her that I am the fastest, strongest warrior in the eyrie.

Or on Ustokos.

As for Syn, that Gryn is going to need some careful handling. Whereas Ayar is predictably unpredictable, what goes through his thick head is nothing more than basic needs, to fight, to drink, to party, and sometimes to eat. Syn is different. Something else drives him, and there has to be a reason why Ryak has assigned such a damaged warrior to an existing unit.

His unit. His elite.

Mine now.

From the grunting and snarling going on as I lead a giggling Kat away, that group of warriors are anything but an elite. I'll need to deal with them later.

"Are they always like that?" Kat asks me as I take her through the eyrie and out into the main courtyard.

"Like what? A bunch of untrained, irritating vrexers?" I grumble at her.

"Adorable." She smiles.

"Adorable? You're calling a unit of battle-hardened warriors, fresh from the last great war with Proto, adorable?" I try to keep my face straight.

I've heard my unit called many things, but this has to be a first. For some reason, my heart warms in my chest as I take in the smile on her face.

"Adorable." She nods as if her assessment is final.

"Am I adorable?" I'm desperate to take her in my arms again, like I did when we flew. I want to inhale her, to have her in my nest.

"You're..." Kat hesitates. "My protector." She grins. "You can't possibly be adorable." I pout at her, and she bursts into a delicious laugh that has every part of my body aching for her. "Nope, still not adorable."

"Do you want this tour or not?" I say, attempting to be grumpy and failing in the face of her laughter.

"Of course I do." Kat links her arm with mine. "What do you want to show me first?"

Having determined that Kat loves flying with me, given that I've already taken her to the very top of the lair so she can have a view of Kos, swooped low over the waterfall that flows underneath the lair and feeds the eyrie, to her squeals of delight, I leave her on the roof of the atrium while I fetch some food from our food hall.

"It's not quite the same standard as the food we get in the lair. Our chefs are still learning," I say as I unveil the platter I managed, with some difficulty, to procure from a set of very wary warriors up to their elbows in all sorts of ingredients.

"Doesn't matter. I'm hungry after all that flying, so you must be starving!" Kat pats the floor beside her.

I drop down some furs I stole from our barrack room earlier and indicate she should sit on them. With a smile, Kat shuffles over, and I plonk myself down beside her.

"I'm fine, you eat," I exhort. "You've been stuck with that nutrislop on the station. You need proper food."

"I preferred to think of it as porridge," Kat says, staring at the selection I've put in front of her. "Nutrislop makes it sound even less appetizing than it was. Thanks. What is all this?"

"Maraha." I pick up a piece of the spiced meat. "It's meat. And these are..."

"Bread rolls!" Kat's eyes light up. "Oh, god! I never thought I'd want something as simple as bread this much." She grabs one, biting into it and chewing as her eyes close in pleasure.

Just like they did on the space station when I lapped at her. The mere fact that I'm feeding my female and she is happy makes my pants uncomfortably tight. Kat snags a lump of maraha meat, and I watch with interest as she pulls the roll apart and slips the meat into the middle.

Somehow, I've managed not to scare off this delicate creature. She even finds me amusing. Which is in direct contrast to just how awkward I feel around her.

She assembles another pile of bread and meat, handing it to me. Once again, I'm floored by the fact that she wants to make sure I have food, even though it's my job to make sure she is cared for. I stare at the combination in my hand.

"On Earth, we call this a sandwich. Give it a try." She smiles

I take a tentative bite of my food. Almost immediately, I'm

struck by the way the different flavors burst over my tongue and let out a small, low groan. I've generally viewed food as fuel for my body, not paying much attention to what it was. A long diet of nutrislop will do that to a warrior, but this has to be the best thing I've ever eaten.

"Good?" Kat's cheeks bulge, and I nod vigorously.

"Anything you give me is good."

"Even the nutrislop?" She nudges me with her knee.

"Even the nutrislop. It was the best I've ever had."

Her eyes twinkle with amusement. "Great praise from a mighty warrior."

"A warrior that would want to spend more time with you, if you'd let me." I swallow the last of my roll.

Kat's scent, mixed with that of food, increases in perfume and becomes almost edible. Thoughts of lapping higher up her thighs and at her hot little cunt fills my mind, and I push them away.

We're on Ustokos now. I can't expect that she would want me in that way, or at all. After everything she's been through, after all she's faced in simply getting to my planet. Kat needs time to adjust.

The last thing she needs is a Gryn warrior panting after her. I wish to Nisis I could take the last sentence back.

"I'd like that," she says, not looking at me, instead staring out over the courtyard into the cloudy sky.

She shivers slightly, wrapping her arms around herself. I extend my wing tentatively behind her. Kat looks up at me and smiles, so I curl it around her shoulders, and she shuffles just a little closer to me. She runs her hand down my primary feather, and it takes every iota of self-control not to shudder under her touch. Arousal flares through me like the heat of a fire.

"Soft." She smiles. "Not what I was expecting."

"What were you expecting?" I hope my words don't sound

as strangled as they seem. Kat continues to run her fingers over my wing and through the small feathers and down along the edge.

"They look so strong, I thought they might be hard, like steel." I hold back a groan as she delves deeper. "They are incredible, beautiful. Elegant weapons," she says, almost as if she's talking to herself.

"Elegant weapons. That doesn't sound much like me." I don't want to break the spell, but if she touches me anymore, my cocks will burst right through the maraha hide of my pants. Or I'll mess in them, and I'm not entirely sure I won't even if she stops.

Kat looks up at me, her face tilted to mine. She leaves my feathers, and her hand starts to explore the hard skin on my shoulders, her fingers tripping up my neck until they rest on my jaw.

"I don't know much about you, Strykr. But I know you helped me and protected me, something you didn't have to do."

"I did. I will always protect you, my *eregri*."

"You called me that once before. What does it mean?" Kat's eyes are bright as they stare into mine.

I swallow. Do I tell her? The most recent arrival to Ustokos, trapped for Nisis knows how long in space, that she's my fated mate? My boundless flight? The one creature in all the universes who is made for me.

Do I tell her the darkness in my heart too? That she's bound to a being as despicable as me?

"It's a term of endearment that all Gryn use for females they like," I lie.

"It's beautiful too." She lifts herself up and presses her lips on mine.

My *eregri* tastes sweeter than I could ever imagine. The most perfect thing ever. Her tongue probes at my mouth and, when I open it slightly in surprise, she slips it in, sweeping through and sending my desire to new heights.

Her hands cup my face, and I tentatively place one of mine to span her waist.

Whatever she wants, she can take, but only if she wants it.

Kat

Strykr doesn't kiss me back, even though I could tell how aroused he was from the, frankly alarming, bulge at his crotch.

This alien angel is interested in me, and not because I'm the only other living creature on a space station. I can't deny to myself any longer that he does things to my insides that I want him to do over and over.

But he holds back, and I wonder if I've read him wrong. I release him, and he exhales with a short, sharp pant. He's restraining himself so much, the claws on one hand are digging into his thigh, and it has to hurt.

"I'm sorry, Strykr. I shouldn't have kissed you without asking." I try to move away, but his other hand on my waist stops me.

"A *kiss*? Is that what that was?" He breathes out, dark eyes closing languidly.

"You don't kiss?

Strykr opens his eyes, and I nearly drown in their depths. "Gryn don't kiss. I've seen the seniors kiss their mates, but I never knew that's what it was called."

"Oh." He's never kissed, until now. And my mind is whirling with everything that I've seen and heard and experienced.

Strykr gently traces a claw through my hairline, his eyes studying every inch of me. He grounds me. His beautiful eyes have suddenly become the one thing I can rely on.

"I've never mated," he says, without any embarrassment. "Without females, the Gryn have little opportunity to take a female, unless we go with other species. But they don't kiss either. Only humans kiss."

"Don't you like it?"

In response to my question, Strykr runs his hand around the back of my head and pulls me to him, his lips enclosing mine and his tongue emulating what I did to him earlier. It is at once intoxicating and impressive for a male who admitted his inexperience a second ago. I melt into him. His kiss is absolute perfection, sending sparks of desire to my pussy and tingles down my spine.

When he releases me, I'm the one who's panting.

"I wasn't sure if you wanted me. Things have been different since we got to your planet." I gasp at him, my lips swollen with his attentions. "You're different."

"In what way?" he rumbles, and I feel his words through his muscled chest.

"You're more...measured. You don't look at me in the same way."

"And how did I look at you, little Kat?" Strykr gazes at me, and I know I'm in trouble because the look is back. It almost robs me of my breath a second time.

"Like I'm prey," I squeeze out. My heart drums like it's pounding out the last beats. I remember how I felt on the ship.

When he looked like he was about to eat me all up.

I *wanted* him to chase me. Because I was entirely his.

"Do you like being prey, female?" His words are a rasp, a groan, and an order all in one.

My answer is to rip myself out of his grasp. He might be a big, bad predator, but this prey still has some surprises left in her. I run as fast as I can for the entrance to the roof of the eyrie.

Behind me, I hear the rustle of feathers as Strykr rises, and I check over my shoulder. He's hunched, like he's ready to spring.

"You can hide, little prey, but I will find you...and I will devour you." He growls.

Every single nerve ending in my body fires into life. I'm an alien on a planet in the far reaches of the universe, a rare commodity who's been alone for far too long, and Strykr wanting to hunt me makes me feel more alive than I have in *decades*.

It turns out I am prey.

His prey.

A scuffle behind me has me fleeing for my life, down the decrepit steps and into the body of the building. I've not had much of a chance to explore yet, and most of Strykr's tour didn't quite penetrate my daze of being on a new damned planet, so as I run, I have no idea where I'm going.

All I know is I want him to hunt me down and then deal with me as he would any prey.

Like he did on the ship.

I want to be consumed by him.

I'm running blindly around the top floor of the atrium, looking for somewhere to hide from the oncoming storm that is Strykr. I could make this easy for him, but the frisson of deep desire welling within me wants to make it as hard as possible for this predator to catch me.

There's a short, narrow corridor off to the left, and I'm just about to dart down it when a fury of feathers explodes in front of me, a pair of strong arms grabs me, and I'm lifted off my feet as I feel a set of sharp teeth trail down my neck.

"I have you, my little prey. I can claim you as my own." Strykr's words are a mere breath in my ear and laden with lust. Lust that pulses through me, licking over my skin like fire.

I lie, limp in his arms, playing dead just like any prey would. A deep growl emanates from his chest as he stalks down the corridor I was just about to use as a refuge. He's so large, he fills it, feathers sliding down the walls as he reaches the end and through a door that he slams shut with his foot.

"All good prey should be bare when they offer themselves up," he rasps. "Are you good prey?"

I'm shaking so hard, I'm not sure I can get my clothes off. With trembling hands I pluck at my top to a further snarl from Strykr.

"Too slow."

My top is gone, shredded. I'm in the air again, my back landing on a soft fur bed as my boots are plucked off and my trousers follow my top. I'm well aware of my lack of knickers. They were too wet to put back on, so yet again, I'm bare for him.

"What's this?" Strykr cages me in his arms and wings, claws teasing over the half corset that's doing its best to contain the girls.

"It undoes at the..." My voice is ripped from me at the same time the corset disappears, and I am completely naked.

And completely at his mercy.

"Does prey not get to see her predator, at least once, before she's eaten?" I ask, my voice hoarse.

I've already seen plenty of Strykr. His lack of clothing on his torso has given me an indication of the goods, the acres of muscles that ripple down to a 'v' at his waist, but I really want to see what the bulge in his pants is.

Because I'm a dirty piece of prey who, frankly, hasn't seen action in a long time.

And I'm desperate for this alien male to reveal just who he is to me.

Strykr withdraws from my body, cool air hitting me as he kicks off his boots and shoves his trousers down perfectly sculpted legs. But it's not his legs I'm looking at. Not at all.

"You have two!" I'm not even sure how I managed to speak as I take in his magnificence.

Strykr has two cocks. The fact that both are fucking enormous is not lost on me either. They jut out from a base of dark curls, his balls hanging heavy below. The main cock starts thick, a ridge running the full length, studded with nodes that look like I'll feel every one. His second cock fits underneath with ridges like a crocodile's belly wrapping around it. It's slick with a glistening clear substance.

"And you're going to take every inch of me, little prey." He stalks me, cocks bobbing against his abs, and I gasp as he grabs my ankles. "But only when I'm sure you've been fully pleasured." He pulls my legs apart and draws me to him, his claws dragging up my skin and causing my clit to pulse.

He traces his one clawed finger through my folds, dipping in, only slightly, teasing me and causing me to let out a low moan of frustration until he drops his head between my legs, wings held high above us both. His hands hold my thighs as his tongue laps at me, and I'm in ecstasy at his touch. He fastens his lips over my clit and sucks until I'm nearly back in orbit, writhing and panting beneath him. Strykr captures my hands and pins them above my head.

"Prey doesn't get to touch. Not until she's pleasured and thoroughly eaten." He purrs over my pussy, and I'm convulsing against him, pushing myself into his mouth, wanting more, wanting everything. Wanting him.

"Strykr!" I whisper as I flood him with my moisture. "What else have you got for your prey?"

He releases me, and I sit up, reaching for his cocks, knowing that two can play his game. I grab his members, and his hips snap at me.

"Kat!" His voice is strangled. "I will spill my seed if you touch me."

I run my hands down his cocks. "Too bad. I want to touch you."

Just as I'd hope, they're as hard as hell, each ridge and node designed for pleasure. His second cock is slippery with pre-cum weeping from it, coating both. I need both hands to stroke these monsters and having Strykr at my mercy for a change is deliciously empowering. My predator shakes with desire and need, just as he made me tremble.

"I want you, my *eregri*." He moans. "I want to be sheathed in your tight cunt. I want to make you see the whole of the universe, and I want to fill you with my seed."

He grasps at my shoulders, pushing me back onto the furs. He settles himself between my legs, feathers pooling on either side of us. His cocks nudge at my entrance. Or at least one cock does, his main cock. His other probes gently at my anus.

"I've never had a cock in there before." I pant as he pushes just a little bit deeper, and I cling onto his wings.

"I'll be as gentle as I can, sweet mate." Strykr's teeth are gritted. "But I want you so much, I'm not sure I can go slow."

"I don't need slow." I lift my hips, and with a rush, he slips inside me, a burning stretch at both holes before he's buried deep, and it's all I can do to remember to breathe, I'm so full. "I just need you."

He circles his hips, ensuring I feel every node, and smiles at me. "I can't begin to tell you how perfect you feel with my cocks inside you." He lifts himself up and drops his head to stare at where we are joined. "Such a wicked prey, to devour my cocks like this."

He withdraws, and the top ridge hits my g-spot, sending me spiraling into the heavens and groaning out his name.

"I love my name on your lips, little prey. Call for your predator again," he murmurs as he slams himself back inside me. "Call for me to come and take you!"

"Strykr!" I can't help myself, every node and ridge ploughs into me as he goes deeper than before. I wrap my legs around his slim waist, feeling feathers tickle at my ankles, and it tips me over the edge I've been so damn close to since he entered me.

As he pounds at me, every muscle straining with his desperation to be gentle but his body wanting to take me entirely, my orgasm hits.

It's as if I've been transported into the air with him. The more he plunders my channels, the more I come, my juices running slick over his cocks, lubricating them and allowing him to hit the absolute heights of what I can offer.

I pulse over him, my pussy grasping at the huge cock he has stuffed inside me, my dark hole enjoying every burning inch of his slippery second cock. Stars burst above me as I hit complete and utter ecstasy.

Strykr roars, the noise shaking him and me. He comes with a huge rush, hot cum filling me over and over as his thrusts grow irregular and his breathing more and more ragged.

"Little prey," he pants. "You have captured me."

Strykr

If I had any concept of what mating was like, my mind, as well as my cocks have been blown away. The moment she ran from me, like any good prey, I knew she would end up in my nest. I didn't know just how good it would be to bury myself in her, cocks in both her holes, as I mated her until my world came apart.

Given that my only pleasure until now was the pits, I know now that it was nothing compared to the act of mating. If I could spend forever inside her, I would.

Withdrawing my softening cocks from Kat as carefully as I can, she moans under me. Her eyelids fluttering, her hands on my chest. Then in my feathers and where her touch once set me on fire, it's now the most comforting thing I have ever experienced.

I cover us both with my wings as she breathes deeply beside me, eyes closed, soft exhales on my chest. I have made her content, I hope.

"That was something else, Strykr."

"Something good?" My voice is hoarse with the pleasure still coursing through me.

"Very good." She cuddles against me, her scent mixed with mine and that of our mating.

She wants to stay with me, in my nest.

My heart swells with complete joy at having her in my arms. A delicate being that wants me. Kat opens her eyes, looks up at me, and smiles before taking a languid look around.

"Oh," she says. "What is this place?"

"My nest," I reply, holding my breath, waiting for her reaction.

"Your nest?"

"I made it for you."

Kat sits up. "Does that mean that..." Her hand is clutched to her chest. "I can get pregnant by you? I mean, we didn't use any protection, and I'm not on any birth control." It's as if I can hear her heart beating in her chest, thumping with anxiety.

The last thing I want is a repeat of what happened in the escape pod. I fold her into me, wrapping her in my feathers.

"A Gryn can only impregnate a female if his secondary cock swells for his mate and if he uses both cocks in her pussy at the same time. I would not do that unless you asked me to." I hold her trembling form and nuzzle my face into her fragrant dark hair. "I'll only ever do what you ask me to."

Her shaking stops, and she softens in my arms. A pair of beautiful, bright blue eyes stare up at me.

"I won't lay an egg for you. I'm telling you that now." The eyes close, and her breathing deepens.

"Gryn don't lay eggs." I laugh softly at her, but she's gone. My mate is asleep, and I am content.

I should have returned my Kat to her quarters and gone back to my barracks, but in the warmth of my nest with my mate, that was never going to happen. Instead, I'm woken by the metallic chirping of her bot and a reminder that I have a job to do.

One I don't want.

"Morning, Ike." I address the bot, who is hovering above us. It doesn't respond to me, and I wonder, not for the first time, how it ended up under Kat's control.

"Hello." A tangle of dark hair on my chest shifts, and I brush it to one side to reveal the stunning creature sharing my furs.

"Laid any eggs yet?" I ask her, and she snorts a laugh against my skin.

"I'm saving myself," she replies, and the warmth that emanates from her fits into my soul like she's always been there. "Ike!" she calls out. "Shut the fuck up!"

The bot whizzes low over us, chanting her name and zooming away again.

"He's got some sort of timer, I think. He likes to remind me when mealtimes are." She gives me a wry smile.

"Kat." I run a finger through the impossibly silky strands of her hair. "The Guv wants us to examine Ike, to see if he has any clues to how the space station worked. Would that be okay?" I don't want to ask the question, especially after our mating. I don't want her to think that I only mated to get to the bot.

Kat bites her bottom lip, and all that does is make me want to bite it for her.

"He won't harm Ike, will he? I know he's just a robot, but he..." She looks over to where the bot has perched on a shelf opposite my nest. "He's sort of become my friend too." She drops her head, and I capture her chin, lifting her face up to mine.

"No one will do anything to hurt you, and that means they won't damage Ike, I promise."

"I shouldn't get attached to something that isn't living," Kat says, water hovering in her eyes. "I spent a lot of time on my own, before..." She pulls her chin out of my hand and shifts away from me.

"You're not alone now. You have me." I put my hand out, hovering it over her shoulder, unsure whether she wants my touch. Then I give in and drop it to her warm skin, ensuring I comfort my mate. She doesn't move.

Maybe I'm not enough.

"Thank you, Strykr." Her voice is a bare whisper. "That means a lot to me."

"And I guess now I have to do what Ike did?"

"What's that?" Kat turns to me, flicking away tears with the back of her hand.

"I have to make sure you get regular meals too. But I warn you, our dining hall is not for the uninitiated. Gryn warriors have a habit of making a fight out of thin air."

"They haven't had to fight a human who's been living on porridge for a month yet." She squares her shoulders. "And what they don't know is I fight dirty for a good sticky bun."

The smile is back on her face, and my heart is full once more.

Kat

He did warn me.

Even so, I wasn't expecting the noise, the heat, and the number of warriors sat in the dining hall.

Some of them are sitting, anyway. The rest jostle for position at the various food tables set out at one end of the long, low-ceilinged hall that's lit at one end with natural light. The rest is illuminated by artificial lights set into the ceiling, casting a white light over the whole scrum.

Here and there, the occasional fight breaks out that is quickly resolved with brute force and the sickening thud of muscle on bone and wing, the protagonists either being pulled apart by other warriors or giving up with a flourish of posturing. I can't help but stare and stare.

"Everything okay, Kat?" Strykr murmurs in my ear.

"I'm not great with crowds of feathered aliens." *Or crowds in general.* "But I'll be fine." *I'm with you.*

I swallow down the rising panic and slip my hand into Strykr's feathers. Their warmth and the soft spicy scent that is released is calming beyond anything I've tried before. He puts his arm around my waist, drawing me to him as eyes turn towards us.

Strykr steers me between rows of trestle tables towards a group of warriors who I recognize from yesterday as his unit. At his approach, one warrior jumps up and hurries away, while the rest shuffle up to create a space.

"Commander." Mylo inclines his head. I remember him as the warrior with the bandaged torso.

"All of you vrexers are in training today, not that I expect you to have other plans," Strykr rumbles at him. "You included, Syn," he fires at the dark, glowering Gryn sitting just apart from the rest. "You all need to do some proper vrexing work."

The warrior who left as we arrived returns with a large platter piled with, well, mostly with rare meat. I notice a couple of what look like bread buns and a single item that could be a Danish pastry slotted on the side in what is clearly an afterthought. Looking down the table, I see that all the warriors have platters of meat.

"Thank you, Vypr." Strykr sounds far more amenable towards this warrior. He shuffles his feathers in appreciation and sits down opposite us.

"I guess you all like meat?" I ask conversationally, as I pick up the pastry and take a bite.

"It's what warriors eat," Ayar, sitting opposite, replies, spearing a large chunk on one claw and popping it into his mouth.

"You'd better be quick," Jay says, looking at me shyly, "or Mylo will have it all."

"What?" Mylo is sitting just down from Vypr and Ayar, his cheeks bulging and pieces of meat on his chest. "I like my maraha." He shrugs. "What can I say?" Another huge mouthful disappears.

"As you can see, Kat, this is my team. My elite unit," Strykr says sarcastically. "And they wonder why I keep them training day after day." He rolls his eyes and then tucks into the platter of meat with the same gusto as Mylo, and I hide a small giggle.

"We're not that bad," Ayar grumbles.

"You are." Jay elbows him, and Ayar snarls.

"Dear goddess!" Strykr looks up in exasperation. "Can a Gryn not enjoy a meal without a fight interrupting it?"

"Depends," Mylo says slyly. "Any chance of a party tonight?"

"You lot, partying in the eyrie? Not a vrexing chance. Ryak will have a fit when he has to clean up the mess you leave behind."

There's a chorus of rather pathetic groans. It's clear that these Gryn want to wrap Strykr around their little clawed fingers. And equally clear he'd let them if he could.

"Ryak will have a fit if you don't let him have a look at your mate's bot." A voice rings out from the end of the table.

Syn, the dark Gryn warrior from last night who antagonized Strykr, rises. If he's not deliberately goading him, he's doing a very good job of it.

"You mean you want to inspect the bot." Strykr doesn't even look at him.

"I do. It's important."

In a single fluid movement that almost appears in slow motion, Strykr is in the air and has Syn pinned on the floor, sharp claws at his throat.

"Dear god, can't warriors breakfast without a fight?" A familiar female voice has me looking up from the horrifying scene of Strykr just about to rip Syn's throat out.

"Bianca!" Jay's face is one enormous smile as Ayar and Vypr make a hesitant move towards Strykr.

They're not needed. With a loud huff, Strykr pushes away from Syn and is back on his feet.

"Mistress." He executes a short bow that would be comical if his face didn't look like thunder.

"I came to rescue this one from your clutches." Bianca pops her hip, her intelligent pale blue eyes missing nothing. "I thought you might want to get something else to wear other than my cast-offs," she says to me. "There's a Mochi trader here today who always brings nice clothes for us." She gives me a genuinely warm smile, and for once, the thought of spending time with another woman doesn't fill me with dread.

"What about Ike?" I ask her.

"The boys can have a look at your little bot later." Bianca gives them all a baleful stare that I'm going to have to learn to emulate. "Have you had enough to eat?" She eyes the pastry I've been nibbling on. "Doesn't matter. Jesic normally has food available. Come on."

She turns and walks off. I glance at Strykr. He still looks like he's in a filthy mood.

"I'll see you later?" I garble out, and then I'm up from the table and hurrying after Bianca as she winds her way through the tables and the other winged warriors who barely look up at our passage.

It's only when I reach the door that I check over my shoulder and remember what Syn said.

He called me Strykr's 'mate,' but that can't be because we've only just met. Only just had sex. And mating is something these aliens take very seriously.

Can it?

Strykr

I watch Kat walk out of the dining hall. Each time a warrior looks at her, my desire to kill something increases. Next to me, the sound of rustling feathers denotes Syn getting up.

I haven't finished with him, but here is not the place. I can't be here, or I will do someone an injury.

Without a word, I leave my unit and head out into the atrium, heading for the outside. If I can't be with Kat, then I have to be in the air. My stomach is full of gnawing pain. It's a pain I know can only be assuaged by one thing.

In the morning air, I unfurl my wings and fire myself from the ground in several downward strokes. The flash of flying with Kat in my arms, her delighting in the rise and fall, flits across my mind, and I have to push it back.

She's not said she's mine, even though we've mated.

I've been out of the camps long enough for Ryak to trust me. He gave me command of his old unit and told me that I could prove myself with them.

And then I let a vrexer like Syn get under my feathers like some irritating mite. Like I'm some scrapper in the dining hall.

All I've done is show my mate what a gamble I am. I promised to protect her and behaved like a complete vrexing idiot.

If I were her, I wouldn't take the chance.

I slowly become aware of where my wings have taken me. Circling the pit on the outskirts of Kos, every fibre of my being tells me I should stay away. I don't need a fight. I just need *the* fight. The one that will secure Ustokos and keep the Gryn safe.

Keep my mate safe.

But now I've seen movement below. I'm descending, spiraling down to see what's going on. My palms itch, and I'm aware of the sweat on my brow and chest.

I need this. I need to mete out some violence. Just this once. Then I can go back to the eyrie and find my mate. I can protect her, and I never need to come here again.

"Well, well, if it isn't the big, bad Gryn." A scarred Mochi male saunters out of the dark at the sound of my landing.

"Vrex off unless you're fighting today," I growl at him, knowing that the Mochi only ever take on a Gryn if they're in a pair or more.

Today, I could take on more. My claws extend to their fullest length. My blood pounds through my veins. I shouldn't think of Syn challenging me in front of my mate. Of the glances of the other warriors.

Of my own inadequacies.

But I do, and I'm sweating more, hands shaking, mind fixed on the fight. The fight that will make everything feel so much better.

"Are you fighting? If not, get the vrex out of my way and let me at someone who is," I snarl at the Mochi as a couple more appear behind him.

"Wait, wait, wait." A small, scaly Kijg appears from behind the larger furred Mochi, his skin flushed a deep blue. "We have fights, but a warrior like yourself has short odds. I need time to find a suitable opponent." He looks me up and down. "Or opponents."

"Do what you will, Grid. Send me someone to spar with, or I'll spar with you." I growl in his face.

The need, the deep dark need for violence, is bubbling through me. In the lair, in the eyrie, I can keep a lid on it, most of the time, just as long as I know I can come to this place, with its stench of death and chemicals.

Just as long as I can come here and indulge in the blackness that dwells within me. The one that kept me alive in the camps.

The thing that drew Proto to me. That resulted in the torture and experimentation that lengthened my claws and shortened my temper. That increased the horror in my veins until I became nothing but a tool.

"Sure, sure, sure. Follow me, Gryn." The Kijg turns a pale green and rushes ahead. I don't need a guide. I know exactly where I'm going in this terrible place. Here and there are bodies of prone Mochi and Kijg, not injured, just enjoying the merchandise that the Kijg provide. Their relaxants, their narcotics, their way out.

I don't need any of that, as long as I have the fight.

"I will arrange your opponent as soon as you're on the board and there are takers." Grid shows me into the sparring arena.

"There's no one here, you vrexer." I spin around to see, too late, the newly installed door.

Grid smiles nastily, his gimlet eyes glittering as the door swings shut.

"Need this Gryn fresh for the fight. No sparring," he trills.

I spend the next hours raging and pacing until finally the door opens again. An unfamiliar Kijg steps through as I leap for him. From behind his back, he produces a long, silver stick and slams it into my abdomen.

The pain penetrates my anger.

"The Gryn will come to the fight without incident."

Sweat rolls from me as everything inches down to a pinprick. All the fight, all the pain. Everything is concentrated on what lies ahead. I snarl at him, and the stick crackles.

It's not a deterrent.

It's an incentive.

I will win this fight, and everything will be fine again.

Kat

"That top really suits you." Bianca smiles at me as I come out of the makeshift dressing room in yet another outfit. "Brings out your eyes." She sits back on the chaise-lounge with the air of a woman who knows what she's talking about.

"Thanks," I reply, embarrassed, never having been very good at receiving compliments.

"Perfect for attracting a certain Gryn warrior." Bianca's smile widens.

"I don't know what you mean." I look down at the leather-like pants I'm wearing to avoid her gaze.

"She already has a Gryn mate?" Jesic, the cat lady, appears as if out of nowhere.

I couldn't stop staring when Bianca first introduced us. Jesic has golden fur that shines in the light, two cat ears on the top of her head and a whole bunch of whiskers on her cheeks. Bianca told me that she's from a species called Mochi that are also native to Ustokos. I shouldn't really have stared as much as I did, but winged males are one thing. Ladies who look like cats are entirely different.

However, Jesic didn't seem to be bothered. I guess cats like the attention. She was entranced by Ike, and at one point I thought she was going to try to pounce on him after he hovered around us for a bit and landed on a rack of clothing in the small area set aside down a corridor in the eyrie. It's set up like an old-fashioned salon and is strangely familiar.

"I don't have a mate," I mutter, Syn's words still ringing in my ears.

"Strykr," Bianca says to Jesic.

"Interesting." Jesic sorts through some piles of clothes on a low table.

"They met when he rescued Kat from the space station."

"Very interesting." Jesic gives me the full benefit of a cat smile, and I don't know where to look. It's unnerving.

"It's not like that. He helped me, that's all," I say, wishing that Strykr had said something that might make me understand what he is to me. And I am to him.

"Does he know that?" Bianca asks. "Gryn don't have passing fancies. They're not like human men. When they mate, they mate hard, and they mate for life. If he's chosen you, you've got a shadow, forever." Bianca unfolds herself from the couch and walks over to me. "Hey, I know it's a lot to take in, but it will be okay." She puts a hand on my arm, and I stare at it. "Just as long as he doesn't ask you to take his band immediately. These guys can be a bit full on."

"It's just a lot to take in. To me, it doesn't seem that long ago that I was on Earth, just getting on with life," I say, still not looking at her and wondering what the hell a 'band' is, until I notice that she has a metal cuff around her upper right bicep, and confusion wars with curiosity within me.

"Is the mistress ready?"

I look up to see Jay peering into the salon.

"Out! Out! Gryn!" Jesic leaps at him. "Females only!"

The look on Jay's face is priceless as the diminutive cat lady shoos him away.

"What do you want, Jay?" Bianca calls out.

"Ryak wants to see the bot." His voice winds its way back to us.

"Do you want to try anything else on?" Bianca asks me. I shake my head, which is buzzing with everything she's said. "Fine, I'll take all your new stuff up to your quarters, and you can go with Jay."

"I don't have anything to pay with." I look at Bianca. I might be on an alien planet, but I know nothing comes for free.

"These are on the Gryn." Bianca piles up the clothing I've been trying on.

Great, now I feel obligated. Obviously, I don't want to go around naked or wearing my alien shift dress I've been stuck in forever, but I don't want to owe anyone anything.

"If there's anything I can do..."

"You don't need to do anything." Jesic places a furry paw on my arm. "You didn't ask to be brought here."

The panic rises within me. I know she means well, but all of this is too real, too much like I have to perform. Jump through the corporate hoops. I try to swallow down my rising anxiety as I walk out to meet with Jay.

"Is Strykr around?" I ask him carefully as he guides me back to the atrium. "He said he would be here." I try to sound less needy.

"The Commander is...busy." Jay's hesitation is brief but noticeable. "If he said he would be here, I'm sure he'll be along shortly."

But his hesitation speaks for him. Either there's a problem with Strykr, or he doesn't want to be with me.

Not that I would blame him. Who the hell wants to be around someone who has a panic attack every five minutes?

"Where are we going?" I ask him.

"Syn's set up a workshop in one of the lower levels." Jay guides me down a set of steps that initially start off as if they're contracted and then become rough, as if hewn into the rock. It's cooler down here, and I suppress a shiver.

The steps open out into a large, cavernous room. In one corner, there's a jumble of parts spread over a couple of tables. The parts look like bits of the spacecraft I was on. Syn rummages through some parts, and Ryak stands, arms folded, next to one of the benches.

"Hello, Kat," he says, not unkindly. "Thank you for agreeing to this."

"You won't hurt Ike, will you?" I stumble out, doing my best to remain calm. "I mean, I know he's a robot, but I don't want him damaged, if you can help it."

Syn straightens up with something in his hand that looks like a screwdriver, and I take a step back, hitting Jay, who moves out of my way instantly.

"Where's your commander?" Ryak asks him.

"Commander Strykr is otherwise engaged, Guv," Jay replies. There's something about the inflection in his voice that I don't like. It's a strain that shouldn't be there.

"That's a shame. I would have thought he would want to be here." Ryak doesn't meet my eyes.

Damn these aliens! Why do I get the feeling they all know something I don't?

"Well, he's not here, so shall we get on?" I say with more annoyance than I was intending.

I reach into my hair, and Ike wraps himself around my arm as I draw him out and gently put him onto the bench.

Syn sucks in a breath.

"What is it?" Ryak asks him.

"I've seen one of these before. It's an info bot."

"A what?" Ryak asks. "I've spent time with Proto's tech, and I've never come across anything like this."

"You wouldn't," Syn replies. "They are extremely rare. If what keeps you from destruction is information, you're not going to allow these to roam very far."

"So the space station was important?" Ryak unfolds his arms, not even trying to hide his interest.

"More than important. It was a key part of Proto. The presence of this bot confirms it," Syn says, reaching for Ike. The little robot's lights glow blue at his touch.

"I wasn't the only human held there," I offer, not wanting to draw attention to myself but feeling I have to speak up. "There were others. I heard them. Other women. They did... things to us."

An emotion flits over Ryak's face, but it's gone as swiftly as it arrived.

"Can we get the information out of the bot?" he asks Syn.

"Probably." Syn raises the screwdriver over an unconcerned Ike.

"Look, far be it from me to tell you how to do your job." I put out my hand and grab Ike, settling him back on my shoulder. "After all, humans have only recently managed space travel, and our tech is lightyears behind yours." I look between the two males. "But what if we ask Ike for what you want before you go hacking into him?"

Syn and Ryak exchange glances. I swallow hard, only just realizing what I've done.

I've spoken up for myself for the first time in a long time, but my bravado is rapidly deserting me.

If Strykr is going to put in an appearance, right now would be the perfect time.

Strykr

My head and my left thigh ache like a bastid. Various areas of my skin burn and, as I try to open my eyes, the light hitting them is excruciating.

I look around the hovel I'm stuffed into. It's a far cry from the comfortable nest I built.

The one I should be occupying with my mate.

My painful eyes sight the upended flask and the small container next to it. I let out a low groan. I didn't just indulge my addiction for the fight, I celebrated it, too. The roar of the crowd and the slice of claw through flesh. I took on four fully armed Mochi and defeated them all.

And then I drank and...

My hand finds my face as I relive my shame.

It should not be a part of me anymore. I have my mate. I have a command and a mission.

Yet I have to enter the dirty pit. To degrade myself with these unsanctioned fights for coin. Descending into the depths of narcotics and alcohol.

I should be allowed to embrace what I have.

"Vrex!" I'm out of the hole in which I've folded myself to find that, thankfully, I'm not too far from the eyrie.

I run my hand through my hair and attempt to shake out my feathers. They're sticky with my celebrations and with the blood of my opponents.

Opponents I'm not entirely sure I didn't...

"Vrex!" I shake my head hard so that the world spins.

I was supposed to be with Kat. I was supposed to be in training with my unit, and I've lost an entire day.

"There you are!" Wing beats clatter overhead, and the one Gryn warrior I don't want to see lands with a thump in front of me.

Syn looks me up and down, his lip curling as he takes in my disheveled state. The one saving grace is he can't see what else I've been up to, given that it's contained within the hole in which I slept. Although if he has any sense of smell at all, he'll have some idea.

"Here I am." My thigh burns at me, and I have no option but to put the weight on my other leg. I'm in no mood to trade insults with this male, but I'm in no state for a fight either.

"Ryak wants you. We found out something about your mate's bot that you'll want to know."

"She...Kat...I..." I give up. Kat is my mate. Nothing is going to change that. But if she rejects me, I'm the one who's vrexed it all up. "Where's Ryak?"

"In a meeting with the seniors. I'm to take you to him."

I scowl at the big male. I should go to Kat, beg her forgiveness, not follow him halfway across Kos to some goddess forsaken meeting.

But if I want any chance at really being her mate, I need to ensure I keep my position and my dignity. With a significant effort, I launch myself into the air, reveling in the fact I'm still faster than Syn, even in my current state.

Although how I'm going to be able to explain it to Ryak is another matter entirely.

I'VE NO IDEA HOW LONG WE'RE KEPT WAITING outside the szent room, the large room in the main lair with the imposing table and chairs our Prime and the other seniors use for their meetings.

It doesn't help that my hangover is really kicking in or that the pain in my thigh is not getting any better.

"Strykr!" Ryak's bark makes me jump, and I must have nodded off. "Party last night?" he queries without interest.

He's never been one for a party.

"You could say that."

"Thought you'd be busy with the new female, but maybe I read that wrong." He levels a gaze at me that could be looking into my soul.

Which he probably is, given that the senior Gryn have an almost legendary ability to read thoughts. Something I'm supposed to develop with my mate. If she'll ever look at me again.

"I'm here about the female and her bot. Syn told me you had some information."

"Yes." Ryak rubs his chin and looks at the other warrior. "Fly with me," he says and, with several short steps, he's reached the exit to the lair and is in the air.

"Training," I fire at Syn. He doesn't move. "That's an order. You take your orders from me, not the Guv."

He hitches up his feathers and stares at me, but with a flick, he saunters past and is in the air just before I follow Ryak.

The Guv is circling, and as I reach him, he heads towards the launch pad for the *Perlin*.

The craft is silent when we land. No sign of Lyon.

"Remember when this was home?" Ryak pats one of the external panels almost lovingly.

"I preferred it," I say before I remember myself. "I've never been one for crowds," I add hastily before I realize what I've said.

"We've become a force far quicker than I expected. We were only meant to be a reception center for the new Gryn and yet..." Ryak lets out a sigh. "It was good."

For an instant, he's hunched next to the spaceship, then he turns to me, feathers flying.

"The little bot that the new female has, it contains information about a defense system for Ustokos," he says.

"Syn didn't harm it to find that out, did he?" My stomach hits my boots. I was supposed to be protecting Kat, and instead, I left her in the care of other males.

Ryak narrows his eyes. "No. We just asked it."

I feel a laugh rising inside me that I'm going to have to try hard not to let out. I can just imagine my brave little mate telling Ryak and Syn not to touch Ike and that they should ask it questions instead.

"You know from what happened to Lyon that Proto was selling Gryn all across this galaxy as slaves. Jyr and I have been wondering for a long time why they didn't come directly to the source." Ryak rubs his hand over his chin.

"You think that this planetary defense system has been protecting us? Protecting Proto's investment?" Thankfully, my wits are starting to return.

"Yes, I do. But the question is, is it still doing its job now that Proto is gone?"

"Vrex! All of Ustokos could be at risk if it isn't. We're in no position to defend ourselves against the species out there if they choose to invade. Not yet anyway." Ice fills my veins at the enormity of the task ahead of us and the significant risk posed by what Ryak is saying.

"That's not the only problem." Ryak turns to face me. "Whoever controls that defense system controls Ustokos." There's a glint in his eye I know well. "It's not what the Gryn want, but it's our duty."

We've been the defenders of the planet for eons. Throughout Proto's rule, we provided the muscle to the other species to ensure that they could scratch a living as much as we did.

In the main, our assistance was appreciated. Post Proto, we have an easy alliance with the Mochi and an uneasy one with the Kijg, the cold-blooded reptilians who also occupy Ustokos.

"Does this mean we're going to have to go back to the space station?" I query. "I'm not entirely convinced I left it how I found it."

"Oh, I'm sure you didn't. Not with Ayar on your team. I should have known that vrexer would cause havoc in the vacuum of space." Ryak sighs. "Lyon's confirmed it's still in orbit, and we can always use the suits he has if we need to go back. From the information the bot provided, the controller for the defense system is on Ustokos, and I need you and your team to find it."

I shuffle my feathers and stand up a little straighter.

"Guv!"

"I know you think I'm disappointed in you, Strykr. But what happened on the space station could have happened to any of us. All of this is brand new, and we have a learning curve that's more of a vertical line. You and your team are still my elite." He gives me the full force of his gaze.

"I appreciate your faith in me, Guv."

"Find the controller, Strykr. Ustokos will be eternally grateful." Ryak leans back against the *Perlin*. "You leave tomorrow."

I give him a nod and turn to head back to the eyrie.

"There's just one thing." I turn back to Ryak, who has a look on his face I can't fathom. "The bot only responds to the female. You're going to have to take her with you if you want to find this thing."

Kat

I lie on the bed of furs in the large room that I'm told are my 'quarters.' Given the number of bunks, which are more like shelves that jut out of the walls, this place was designed for more. At the far end, I've discovered a smaller version of the warm pool I found yesterday. It's less pretty and more functional. There's also a number of what pass for toilets on this planet.

Ike chimes in my ear.

"Well, you're a revelation, aren't you?" I run my hand over his lithe metal body.

For a short while, I was caught up in the excitement with Ryak and Syn as they asked me to ask Ike questions and the little robot gave up his information. Eventually, Syn declared he would need some other 'tech' to work best with Ike. Tech appears to be the Gryn word for anything to do with a computer.

I wanted Strykr to share in this moment. I thought we had something, but it looks like I read my alien wrong. Yet again, I've fucked everything up by ignoring what was in front of me. Last time, it was the corporate burn-out that had a grip on my heart and nearly killed me. This time, it was an alien who just wanted to get his rocks off with an exotic human.

There's a soft knock on the door to my room. The last thing I want is a visitor, but I guess that I don't get much choice in the matter anymore.

"Come in," I call out and resume my staring at the ceiling.

There's a rustle of feathers, and I turn my head to see Strykr.

He looks like hell as he leans against the wall, arms folded uncomfortably over his chest.

My heart leaps into my throat at the sight of his handsome face. Stupid heart. Doesn't it understand yet that being alive is the way we get hurt?

"It's you," I grind out. "Finally."

"I'm sorry, my *eregri*." Strykr's voice is low, velvety smooth as always, a hint of pain around the edges. "I know I promised to be there with you."

"You did," I spit out. "And you weren't."

My fucking heart is thundering in my chest, the treacherous organ wanting me to look at him, wanting me to accept him.

Strykr takes a couple of steps into the room and falls to his knees next to me as I scramble to sit up, alarmed.

"Forgive me." He places a huge set of clawed hands on the edge of my bed. His dark eyes are almost liquid as he stares at me.

"What's wrong?" I whisper hoarsely, my hand reaching out, unbidden, to cup his cheek.

The softness of his skin, the warmth of his body, seep into me.

I can't stay mad, not when every element of my being is telling me that he doesn't need my ire, he needs my help.

"I…" He stumbles over the words.

"You're hurt!" I'm running my hands over him as his physical pain spears through me. "Where are you hurt? Why?" I reach his waistband, and he hisses in alarm, attempting to wriggle away from me, and instead, he falls backwards, wings flailing.

"No! You don't need to see. It's not for your eyes!"

"Seriously, Strykr? You must be joking! If you're hurt, I need to know!" My hand touches his left thigh, and he grimaces, only just managing not to make a noise.

I pull at his belt. "Show me!" I use my best stern voice, the one I reserved for board meetings.

"I just need to get to a healing pool, that's all." He drops his chin to his chest, not looking at me.

"A what?"

"The pools in the eyrie, they have healing properties for Gryn." He's still not looking at me, and although it goes against everything I would normally do, such as calling an ambulance, I am on another planet. I should take the lead of the native population.

"There's a pool at the end of this room. Come on." I wrap my arm around my waist and help him to his feet.

For nearly seven feet of solid muscle, he's much lighter than I'm expecting. He lets me help him through to the pool area and then stands in front of me, the very definition of contrition. I fold my arms.

"If you don't take them off, I will."

This should not be turning me on. Strykr is injured in some way; he needs help, not sex.

With infinite slowness, Strykr undoes the catch on his belt and kicks off his big boots. He peels away his trousers.

Gryn obviously don't believe in underwear. His cocks seem to be at half mast, swollen, but not fully erect. When I take in breath, it's not because of the hugeness of his members. It's the huge gash in his thigh.

"Shit, what happened?"

He straightens, and without looking at me, he wades into the pool, sinking down with a sigh that could have come from the depths of his soul. He props his wings on the edge and closes his eyes.

I turn to leave. I've obviously done what needed to be done, and he's happy.

"Wait, Kat. Don't go." Strykr's eyes are fever bright. "I need to explain."

I strip off my top and trousers.

"What are you doing?" His voice is a mixture of gravel and surprise.

"I'm coming in with you, or else it's weird," I tell him firmly. Leaving my knickers and strange corset thing on, I slide into the water opposite him. The pool is small, and he is very large, so our knees touch. "What happened?"

He looks down in the water at his leg, gently smoothing over the gash to clear away the crusted blood. I'm not entirely sure if it's my imagination, or if it's the distortion through the water, but it looks slightly better.

"I'm a fighter, Kat," he says to the water.

"I know that. As far as I can tell, that's exactly what your species is." I laugh weakly, my stomach still hollow given that I was expecting something worse.

Something like him not wanting to be with me anymore.

"No, you don't understand. I *have* to fight. If I don't..." The pain that crosses his face is excruciating for me.

I find myself sliding across the pool until I'm next to him, on his right side, and despite my sensible part screaming at me that this can't be a good idea, I run my hand through his soft feathers, my damp skin sticking to them.

"You don't have to do anything you don't want to, Strykr."

His delicious dark eyes close at my touch. "You don't understand, sweet mate," he breathes out. "It's my mission."

"I don't understand." I push my fingers in deeper so that I touch his skin, and he moans involuntarily.

"The Guv, Ryak, he has me fighting in the pits. It's a way of gathering information on what the other species are doing. Unsanctioned fighting is banned for the Gryn. If I'm involved, if I'm a fighter, they trust me."

"But you don't want to." I'm rifling through his wings now because he's pushing against me, and I love that he's responding to my touch. "So why not tell Ryak that you don't want to fight, that it's causing you pain."

Those dark eyes are open, and he stares straight at me.

"You don't understand. I like it." His breath shudders through him, and he starts to rise out of the water. "I'm not sure I can stop."

"Wait, Strykr." I grab his arm and pull him back down. He doesn't resist. "Your leg needs more time," I tell him.

"All the time in the world won't change what I am," he murmurs, still unable to look me in the eye.

"What's that?"

"A dishonorable male. A male who would rather fight than be with his *eregri*. A male who'd rather party than ensure her protection."

I delve my fingers back into his feathers, more for my enjoyment than anything. Underneath the small, hard outer ones, they are downy soft underneath.

"You shouldn't do that. I don't deserve it." He moans, shifting his wing.

"You've done your duty, so you should get your reward."

Strykr

My sweet female runs her clawless fingers through my feathers. Her preen is almost as good as mating. Almost. My mind empties of the fight and the things I did. Instead, it fills with her scent, her touch, and most of all, it fills with her.

"Please." My voice is pathetic. "You shouldn't care for me."

"It's too damn late for that, Strykr, because I do," she says, delving even deeper into my wings.

My cocks are achingly hard for her, a fact I can't hide, not when I'm naked and entirely at her mercy. My breath comes in short bursts. She is everything I need, everything that can change the male that I am, but I let her down.

"You did what you were supposed to do. If that makes you a dishonorable male, then you're my dishonorable male. If you think that you shouldn't like the fight as much as you do, we can work through it. But I'm not walking away from you." Her fingers stop moving, and I look directly into her eyes. "Unless you tell me to," she finishes.

Her fierceness, her desires, her kindness, they all hit me at once. This is a female who was alone for a very long time with only a bot for company, yet she still made me a meal without even being able to speak to me.

She trusted me when she had no reason to.

"Please," I beg her. "Mate with me."

Kat trails a hand down my chest, over my abs, lower until it's under the water and wrapped around my cocks.

"That all depends, doesn't it?" she says, voice husky as she oh-so-gently begins to stroke me.

"On what?" I can hardly get the words out past the pleasure that's coursing through me, my eyes closed as I hold on to the tenuous restraint I have left.

"On whether you can catch me."

The water sucks away from my body along with Kat's touch, and by the time I open my eyes, she's out of the pool and heading to the barrack room, wet footsteps slapping against the floor.

I rise, my leg no longer hurting. The only ache I have is the hardness of my cocks. Cocks that have to be buried in her, no matter what.

Buried in my prey.

But I'm not going to chase her. This time, she's going to be stalked and devoured, like good prey should be.

"I'm coming for you, little prey," I call out, pausing to shake off the water from my body and feathers. "You can hide, but I will scent you."

In response, there is the most delicious aroma of her arousal filling the air. I creep out of the sanitary area and check around the room full of empty ledges, normally filled with warriors. Kat's body warmth glows at me as she hides under a single low ledge at the far end.

"Oh, prey? Where are you?" I grasp my lengths and pump at them while stalking down towards her. "I have something that I think you'll enjoy."

All I can see of my mate is a single pink toe tip as she trembles. I shove my hand under the ledge and grip her ankle, pulling her out and into the light in one single movement as she lets out a short, sharp shriek of shock and desire.

"Perfect prey." I growl over her. "Needs unwrapping." I let go of her leg, and she attempts to squirm away from me, causing my cocks to bump up against my abdomen in response.

I clutch her to me, her breath hot against my chest as I remove the covering from her pretty little pussy in a single snap. The strange garment covering her breasts disappears in a similar manner.

"Now you're ready to be eaten." I pin her on her ledge, straddling it as her eyes widen, taking in my swollen shafts that I will shortly sink inside her.

"Strykr, don't eat me!" She gasps, a smile on her lips. "Don't you dare!" The command in her voice is absolute.

"Beg me for mercy, prey." I grab the globes of her gorgeous bottom and pull her slick cunt up to my waiting lips. "Beg me or I'll make you squeal."

"Strykr!" She lets out a keening cry as I bury my head between her legs, running my tongue through her wet folds and luxuriating in the taste of her ambrosia as it spills into my mouth.

I discover a gorgeous little bundle just guarding the entrance to her perfect pussy and fasten my lips over it. The noises she makes are just like prey might, all mewls and screams, so I suck harder. I'm rewarded by the feeling of her hips bucking into my hands and yet another flood of her moisture.

"Does this prey need anything before I impale her?" I lift myself from the comfortable position between her legs, wiping my mouth with the back of my hand. "Does she have anything to say?"

Kat's beautiful breasts bounce as she heaves a breath.

"I've only got one thing to tell you…" She props herself up on her elbows.

"What might that be?" I grin at her, all teeth and claws.

"You still haven't caught me yet." She makes a dive for the left, managing to slip out of my grip as I reach for her. She attempts to dart away from me, and my prey drive hits its peak.

"Oh, little morsel, you will pay for that." I fire out an arm and snag her as she attempts to run past me, lifting her up as her legs continue to work.

I hold the squirming female by her waist, her eyes flashing at me, the naughtiest smile on her face which she tries to hide.

"Time for you to take me, and I mean all of me." I lower her down over my lap, and she spreads her legs beautifully.

"Take me, Strykr," she rasps, throwing her head back. "I am your prey, and you have caught me."

Kat

Strykr's eyes are almost black as he lowers me down onto his cocks. I can't believe how wet I am for him, not just from the orgasm he ripped from me with his incredible tongue, but also running from him makes my heart pound and my pussy soaking wet.

And it's even better when he catches me.

The broad head of his main cock breaches my entrance, and he groans out loud.

"So tight."

I can feel myself stretching and stretching around him as he tries very hard to inch his way into me. I moan as he palms my breasts, then fastens his lips around a nipple, lapping and suckling in such a way that I flood him again, and he goes even deeper.

"Fuck! You're big!" The stretch is incredible, painful but pleasurable.

I rock over him, and with a final push, he's deep inside me.

"*Eregri*," he rumbles, his chest vibrating with the word. "I have to claim you for my own."

"Then claim me." I don't know what he means, but I'm

lost in the moment, in the erotic pleasure of having run from Strykr, of having him catch me, pleasure me, and fuck me.

In a smooth movement, Strykr is on his feet and my back is against the wall, my legs wrapped around his waist and his hands under my butt as he begins to thrust up into me.

"You are so beautiful, sweet prey." He growls, sending shivers to my very core. "You make me forget my name, I'm buried so deep in you."

Every node, every ridge scrapes over my channel as he sets up a demanding pace, pounding at me, filling me, delighting me until his mouth meets mine, and I explode.

The stars in the sky descend and dance around us as my climax sheets my vision.

"Strykr!" I call out. "My Strykr!" I pulse over him, and he drives even deeper as my slick eases his way.

"Kat!" My name on his lips is both a shout and a desire. My pussy is already stretched to the limit, but now it stretches even farther, something swelling inside me as he roars out his orgasm. His thrusts irregular, he fires everything he has into me, over and over again.

For what seems like a long time, all I hear is my blood rushing in my ears, until it's just the sound of our panting, our ragged breaths as we cling to each other, damp and sated.

"That was better," Strykr murmurs into my shoulder. "Better than the fight. You complete me, my *eregri*." He lifts his head, dark eyes impenetrable. "I promise I will never leave you. Not for any reason. You are my world, you are my Ustokos, and nothing is more important than you."

"And because you are an honorable male." I snuggle against his chest, enjoying the scent of him, of his feathers and his warm skin against mine.

Strykr does want to be with me, and my heart suddenly doesn't seem big enough for the way I feel about him. The alien angel who has somehow crept into my affections in a way I didn't think was possible.

I've been spinning around myself for far too long. He's knocked me from my orbit, and I can see again. I can see just how wonderful it is to care and be cared for. My big fluffy predator.

I wriggle against his cock, and he moans.

"You can let me down now."

"Can't"

I hold onto his shoulders and pull away slightly, but there's pain. He's right. We're stuck. Strykr lets out a shuddering breath onto my skin.

"My secondary cock has swollen, my sweet mate. It will need to subside before I can withdraw."

In yet another swift, fluid movement, he has me on my back in the furs of my bed, caged by his arms and his huge wings. He nuzzles at my neck, and a feeling of complete calm flows through me. Being in his arms is exactly the right place to be.

It doesn't take me long to fall into a deep sleep in my personal feather bed.

WHEN I OPEN MY EYES AGAIN, STRYKR IS CURLED beside me on the small bed. When I say beside, I mean I'm partially on top of him, finally free of his cocks. The bed is too narrow for both of us, and his wings dangle over the edge.

I'm not sure I've ever seen his face so relaxed. A hint of a smile on his lips, his chest rises and falls in a steady rhythm, along with me. I could stay watching the handsome alien as his eyelids flicker in REM sleep forever, but my bladder is making its presence known.

Should I be worried that we did the deed last night with

both cocks, the only way he says that can cause pregnancy? I delve down inside myself for the rising anxiety that's been ever present for a very long time.

It's not there. Instead, there is only contentment. I might not get pregnant by him. I had my period on the space station not that long ago. We'll just need to be careful from now on.

I slide off him and pad through the big, empty room into the sanitary area and use the facilities with a long sigh of relief. Ike buzzes in, his lights blinking, but he's quiet for a change, and I hope he hasn't woken Strykr.

He seemed like a male who needed a chance to sleep.

"Kat." His voice rumbles from the doorway to the sanitary area. He leans against it, naked, feathers pooling behind him, eyes still drooped with sleep.

"Hey." I wrap my arms around him, luxuriating in the warmth of his body and his smooth skin.

"We need to talk," he says.

Strykr

The panic that raced through me when I awakened and my *eregri* was not in my arms was visceral, instant and terrifying. Until I heard her moving around and the whirr of her little bot.

"Ike!" I call out, but it ignores me, zipping down the barrack room towards its mistress.

I'm already on my feet. My thigh is dramatically improved, the deep gash there already knitted and the pain minimal. When I reach the sanitary area, Kat has her delicious bottom pointed towards me as I call her name, my voice hoarse with lack of use.

Or from the roar that preceded my unbelievable climax. Another new experience that will be burned in my memory for a long time. It's all I can do to persuade my cocks to behave. The last thing I want Kat to think is all I want her for is to mate.

Even if mating is probably the only thing on my mind.

Kat wraps her arms around me, her perfect scent twirling into my nostrils and almost robbing me of my resolve.

"We need to talk." I concentrate on the little bot that's

landed on a high shelf. Its lights flow along its sides like the water in the pool. It goes some way to keeping my raging mate fever under control. "About Ike."

"He was great yesterday," Kat gushes. "You should have seen him with Ryak and Syn. It was hilarious." I should be filling with anger at the thought of her with the two other warriors, but her mirth is infectious.

"What happened?" Curiosity rather than jealously burns at me.

"Ryak, that's your Guv, right?" Kat looks up at me for confirmation, "he was really pissed that Ike wouldn't respond to him. He kept firing questions at him, and all Ike did was make that farting sound and flash red lights." She giggles, and I can't help but chuckle at the thought of Ryak trying to be serious in the face of a rude bot.

"Ryak seems to think that Ike contains information about a defense system that will protect our planet." I drop my chin to the top of her head and inhale the sweet scent of her hair. It grounds me. "I've been given a mission to find the control center, and I'm going to need to take Ike."

My breath stops in my chest, waiting for her response.

"In that case, you'll be taking me too," Kat says happily. "Ike won't respond to anyone but me."

"That's not happening. You're going to stay safe, here in the eyrie. We won't be gone for long," I say, firmly. "Ike, come here." I hold out my arm to the bot.

Kat pushes her face into my chest, and I'm pleased she's accepting what I have to say. There's no way I'm putting her in any danger, that's my job.

The bot remains exactly where it is, blue and green lights blinking and its wings firmly folded against its metal body. It doesn't make a sound.

"Ike. Come here!" I call out again.

Kat makes a squeaking sound against my skin, and the vrexing bot still doesn't move.

"Ike!" I bellow, and this time, Kat dissolves into laughter.

"You and Ryak are the same," she howls. "Ike, come on," she says in a half-whisper.

Instantly, the bot responds, zipping up into the air, circling her once, and then landing on her shoulder.

"Mistress," it chirrups. "Gryn is displeased."

"He sure is, Ike. That's because he didn't get his own way for once." She snorts into my chest, and I lift her off her feet.

"You tell him to follow my orders," I mock growl.

"Doesn't work," she says, her voice still muffled. "Looks like you've got no choice but to take me." She uncurls from me, bright eyes shining. "And anyway, you promised."

Vrex! Mating makes a male do stupid things. Although maybe not as stupid as giving in to my addiction to the fight, whether I'm under orders or not.

"I did promise, and I am an honorable male." I grin at her. "Most of the time."

With a flick of my arms, she's in the air and splashing down in the healing pool with a shriek of anger.

"You utter bastard!" she yells when she resurfaces, flicking her hair out of her face and hitting the surface of the water, sending it in my direction.

I leap into the air, beating down with my wings before I join her, water firing everywhere as I pull her into my grasp.

"Your utter bastid," I growl in her ear as she stills, molding her form to mine. "Yours, always."

I WALK INTO MY BARRACK ROOM WITH A LEVEL OF calmness that means I'm almost floating. Thankfully, for a change, my unit seems to be in harmony with me.

Jay sits on his ledge, tweaking the laser rifle he prefers. Vypr is working his way through one of Ayar's wings, and the male has a beatific look on his face that only ever comes from mutual preening. I heard he was incapacitated yesterday with one of his headaches, so it's good to see him up today.

Mylo is running through one of his slow, steady routines that give him the strength and poise a warrior of his size simply shouldn't have.

Syn lies on his bunk and stares at the ceiling, ignoring them all.

"We have a new mission. One I'm hoping we don't vrex up," I announce.

Ayar is on his feet, preening forgotten. "When?" He's bristling for the action.

"Once you vrexers have sorted your kit."

"What's happening, Guv?" Mylo asks as he joins the rest of the team. I give him a baleful glare. "I mean Commander," he adds as he folds his arms and settles himself on his ledge.

"The space station was part of a planetary defense system. It's controlled from Ustokos. The seniors are concerned that it's what's been keeping the rest of the galaxy at bay, given that Proto has been selling Gryn as slaves."

"And our mission?" Jay asks, putting his weapon down gently.

"We have to find the control center. Kat's little bot is the key to locating it." I look at Syn who's studiously avoiding me. "I understand we have a general idea of where it might be. We just have to take the bot close to where we think it is, and Kat will do the rest."

"The female is coming with us?" Syn sits up.

"The bot only responds to her, Syn, as you know. If we want to find the vrexing control center, I don't have an option." I shove my fist into my feathers and curl it into a ball, hoping the others can't see it.

"Bot? What bot?" Ayar snarls, stepping forward. "Where's this bot?"

"It's not a joykill or anything like that." I move towards him, noting with relief that Vypr has stepped behind him. "It's small and completely harmless. It's friendly."

"Bots aren't *friendly*." Ayar spits out the word. "Bots are dangerous and should never be trusted."

"This one belongs to Kat. She controls it." I decide to take the risk and put my hand on Ayar's heavily scarred shoulder. "It's not dangerous, Ayar. If it was, I wouldn't be doing this. But we have to get to the defense system or we're all in danger."

"We can take anything the galaxy has to throw at us!" Ayar shrugs off my hand. "Let them come!" He spins back towards his ledge and grabs the biggest laser gun that we have in our arsenal.

"You sleep with that? Vrex it! Vypr?" I say, exasperated.

Vypr shrugs, a slight, indulgent smile on his lips. "It's fine, Ayar. You know the Guv will protect us from this tiny killer bot."

Ayar fixes him with a stare that could melt metal, a growl rippling in his chest.

"Ayar, if it makes a single unfriendly move, I'll blast it to pieces myself. But I promise you it's safe," I tell him.

He huffs out a hot breath and stomps out of the barrack room.

"Don't worry, Guv." Vypr wing bumps me as he walks past, following Ayar. "I'll do my best to keep him from destroying anything important."

"You've got half an hour. Meet in the courtyard, and be ready to go," I say to the rest of them as I leave, keen to get back to my mate and make sure she understands about Ayar.

And that Syn might also be a problem I'm going to struggle to control if he keeps goading me.

Kat

I'm certainly clean. Strykr's version of bathing made absolutely sure that every inch of me was licked...I mean washed.

It has at least made the revelation that both Ike and I are the key to some sort of defense system for this entire planet a little easier to bear. A system that apparently the Gryn need to control as they are the defenders of the planet.

Which makes me one of them.

While Strykr's made a good job of redeeming himself, concern rises in my chest like it always does.

What if I can't do this? What if I can't help them? What if he decides that I'm not worth bothering with?

Alone in this enormous room, the walls start to close in on me, heat rising, circling, and the ever-present darkness filling my mind.

"Kat?" For a second, I think it's Ike calling me. The tiny robot kept me sane for so long on the station. But this time, I look into a pair of dark eyes. Strykr.

He takes my hand in his, onyx black claws gently curling around me.

"Kat!" He groans. "I can scent you. We don't have time for mating. My unit will be waiting."

"You can...smell me?" All my fears are dashed away with that revelation.

"You smell amazing to me, all of the time, and even more so when you want me," Strykr says, not bothered in the slightest. In fact, he licks his lips, his rough pink tongue giving me naughty thoughts. "But sometimes it's distracting."

"Shit!" I genuinely don't know where to look. "I'm sorry I smell."

Strykr drops to his knees, and he's nudging at my neck. "Don't be. I can't get enough of you. It keeps me from the fight. It keeps me from everything."

His hands run over my body, and this time, the flood of heat I feel has nothing to do with fear. It's the lust that my gorgeous alien predator brings out in me.

"You're not helping if you do that," I murmur into his fragrant feathers.

"I know." He doesn't release me, just stilling for what seems the longest time. A time I wish could go on forever. "My unit will be waiting for us," he says as he releases me.

"Where are we going?"

"We have to make a stop at an underground lair we have in Mochi territory first. They have a mapping computer there that should give us a route and a fix to the control center." The way Strykr pronounces computer is adorable.

"Exactly how long have the Gryn had access to tech?"

Strykr looks down at his hands, moving his fingers. "A few cycles? I'm not sure. I was liberated in the first wave after Proto fell. I've been free for around that time."

"That's not long," I say, wrapping my hand around his.

"It's not, but we can't stay still. Lyon was sold as a slave to a species called the Drahon, so we know that there's plenty out there that can and will try and take our planet, especially as

Proto has gone. We have to get that defense system online, or we risk the entire planet being enslaved."

"I agree. It's bad enough being taken from one planet, let alone two." I give Strykr's hand a squeeze, taking some of his strength to steady me.

I have to do this. I have to be brave for him and in order to protect my adopted planet.

Strykr presses a kiss to my lips. "My team and I will protect you with everything we have. You will not be in any danger."

"And here's me thinking this was just a walk in the park until you said that." I stare at him in mock horror. "You never told me it would be *dangerous*." I gasp.

"My sweet mate," he croons. "No harm will come to you." He extends his vicious claws. "That is my promise." I take in a breath, and he inhales deeply. "Unless I want to plunder your body, little prey."

STRYKR'S UNIT LOOKS LIKE THEY MEAN BUSINESS when we arrive in the courtyard outside the eyrie. I'm not sure that Ayar and Vypr could be carrying more weapons wrapped around their bodies if they tried. Ayar has some sort of cannon mounted on his back.

Jay holds only one weapon, a long slim gun that looks like a rifle. As we approach, Mylo hands Strykr a belt with two laser guns and a dagger attached, which he straps on. Syn kicks a small stone back and forth, a single laser on his belt.

"Where's the bot?" Ayar snarls at me, and I take a step behind Strykr.

"Ayar." Vypr slides an arm around his waist. "We talked about this. The female and her bot are not the enemy."

"All bots are the enemy," Ayar growls, but the look of pain on his face is too much for me.

"Here." I move out from behind Strykr, putting my hand in my hair and getting Ike to wind himself around my wrist. "Look." I take a step towards Ayar, holding out Ike.

The big, scarred warrior takes a step back, horror painted all over him.

"This is Ike," I tell him kindly. "He looked after me when I was on the space station alone. He showed me where there was food and water. Without him, I wouldn't have survived."

"All bots are bad." Ayar grinds his teeth, and I can already recognize the signs.

Because he's reacting as I might to a stressful situation. Vypr whispers something in his ear, but he's not paying any attention. All of his being is concentrated on Ike.

"What can I do to prove to you that Ike isn't dangerous, Ayar?" I say quietly. "Because whatever you need, I'll do that."

He blinks, his eyes rising from Ike to mine. He takes in a shuddering breath. The last thing I want is Ike to be damaged, but I can tell by the way the rest of the warriors hold themselves that if Ayar can't get over this fear, this trip is going to be in ruins before it starts.

Ike is incredibly still. His lights don't even pulse, just hold steady. With infinite slowness, Ayar moves a couple of paces towards me.

It's as if the entire planet is holding its breath.

"It's small," Ayar whispers.

Ike lifts his little head and looks at Ayar.

The warrior's feathers flare, but he doesn't move away.

"Maybe you can touch him, later," I say. "I'd like you not to be afraid of him," I add as quietly as I can.

"Not afraid," Ayar says gruffly under his breath. He raises his eyes to mine. There's trust there, hovering around the edges. "Maybe later."

He steps back and nods at Strykr. "Guv," he grunts.

I tuck Ike back on my shoulder, out of sight of Ayar, who

shifts his impressive set of weapons around his body and most definitely pretends to be okay, while Vypr watches him carefully.

"Thank you, Kat," Strykr says, his voice low as he takes a loop of what looks like leather from Jay and hooks it over his head and one arm. It hangs low, and I notice the bottom part is wider.

"What's that?"

"It's normally used to transport injured mercs—warriors —who can't fly. It will be more comfortable for you on a long flight." Strykr indicates the loop. I put my bottom in the sling, and it's far more comfortable than it looks. Strykr wraps an arm around me. "Hold on to me," he orders, and I grasp at his impressive bicep.

In one bound, we're in the air, and the rest of his unit springs up to follow in a tight formation.

Strykr was right. I do feel protected, and from that, my confidence grows.

Who knows, maybe I can be the key after all?

Strykr

I keep wanting to check the sling that holds my *eregri*. It's almost a nervous tick because I want to make sure she's safe. I know I've got some way to go to prove to her I am a responsible male on whom she can rely.

Maybe then she will come back to my nest and, I swallow hard at the thought, she might take my band? Bind herself to me in a ceremony that will be witnessed by the entire eyrie?

It's too much to hope for, for an inveterate fighter like me.

I'd better concentrate on the mission.

Checking behind me, my unit remains in a good formation, and I guess I should be grateful for small mercies from the goddess. We've a long flight ahead of us to reach the underground lair before dark.

"Why doesn't Ayar like robots?" Kat says into my ear as I set my wings, keeping up a steady pace through the cloudy skies of Ustokos.

"I don't know the full story, but Ryak and Vypr found him on a machine in one of Proto's camps. He was half mad at the time, incoherent, but he formed a bond with Vypr and

Ryak. He'll do anything for them, providing it involves smashing bots and general destruction," I reply.

"The way he reacted to Ike." Kat shakes her head. "We have to do something to make it easier for him, especially as he's going to have to deal with a robot for a while."

I definitely don't deserve a mate with a heart the size of hers. Ayar is difficult, but the thing that we found him trapped in was truly horrific. None of the Gryn like bots. Those stuck in the camps like me had to deal with their casual cruelty day after day. Those on the outside, they battled with them.

"Maybe if you work with Vypr and just get him used to Ike for short periods? Would that work?" As much as I don't really want her spending time with other males, we are going to be living in close proximity, and anything that can keep a lid on the loose cannon that is Ayar would be helpful.

"It might. I'd like to try." She cuddles a bit closer to me, and I have a spreading warmth that I've pleased her.

We fly on, skirting around a chemical storm that blocks our way at one point. The larger of Ustokos's two suns is beginning to set as we reach the edge of Gryn territory and cross the border into Mochi lands. The evening is clear and beginning to cool as we reach the semi-circular canyon holding the lair.

Having done the standard circuit to ensure our landing is clear, I give the signal to descend, and as one, my unit lands in the dust outside of the lair, our wings stirring enough of it up to cause a cloud.

Kat wobbles on legs that haven't been used for a while. I hold her around her waist until she indicates she can stand.

"We discovered this place," I tell her, "a while back. Our quarters are through there." I point to the cave entrance.

"And the other lair?"

"It's nearby. We're late. We can go there in the morning," I tell her.

Ahead of us, a scuffle breaks out. Ayar rushes forward, kneeling and pulling his cannon over his shoulder. He takes aim at nothing, and the laser retort rings out, slamming into the top of the cliff and causing a large chunk to break off, falling with a horrible slowness down until it hits the ground with an almighty crash.

"Vrex it!" Mylo calls out.

I'm on Ayar in seconds, wrestling the cannon from him.

"What the vrex, Ayar?" I have him on his back, pinned. He's not moving or even fighting me.

"Bot," he says simply.

"Vrex!" I climb off him and haul him to his feet, shoving him at Vypr. "When was the last time he ate or hydrated?" I sniff at him. "Or had a proper bath?"

"I'll deal with him, Guv." Vypr grabs at Ayar's wings. "He'll be fine."

"Don't let him near any vrexing weapons until he's calmed down," I fire out. "Mylo, go get some rations organized. Syn, you go with him." I send the two warriors off. "We could all do with some food and a rest."

"And a party!" Mylo calls out over his shoulder as he hurries away.

"It's true, Guv. We've not partied in a long time," Jay says hopefully.

"I'm not your vrexing 'Guv'." I grumble at him. "How many times do I have to tell you? And as for a party, if you think I'm letting Ayar near any var beer after that little display, you've got nutrislop for brains."

A little pink hand grasps my arm. Kat looks up at me, her eyes wide.

If I wanted to prove to her that I can protect her, that my unit can protect her, I've just failed massively.

"If they need some time to decompress, that's hardly a bad

thing, is it? You've not really stopped since we were in space," she says quietly.

As much as I don't want to give them the satisfaction, Kat's not wrong. Could they get me into any more trouble given that they've nearly killed a senior Gryn and partially demolished a lair full of tech?

Kat

I was excited to see more of Ustokos. We flew over area after area that was just a dystopian wasteland. It looked like a European city after the Second World War, but one that has never been rebuilt. Decimation on a scale I don't think I can imagine.

A war to end all wars. No wonder the Gryn want to secure something that will protect their planet from outside interference, providing it exists. If this is all they have, there's no way they're going to be able to repel any other aliens that decide they want Ustokos, and its inhabitants, for their own.

They've already got enough on their hands trying to get back to what they once were.

Some of these flying inhabitants are currently having what can only be described as a whale of a time in the bowels of the cave system that Strykr led me into. It's hard to see how it can be this high-tech lair that he said we were going to as it looks like it's been carved out of rock millennia ago.

It's warm and dry though, which is appreciated. The circular room that he brought me to is large, almost airy, despite being underground. A ledge runs around the wall, and it's dotted with piles of furs that the Gryn are using as bedding. A large stone table is carved into the center, and it's covered with a huge amount of food that Mylo and Syn have brought in. Next to it is a large wooden barrel, set up on a stand and at which all of the warriors are merrily filling tankards of foaming liquid

"Var beer," Mylo says as I inspect it. "It's our drink of choice." He looks over at Strykr who is talking to Syn and Jay. "When we're allowed," he says *sotto voce*.

"Something tells me that Ayar's little stunt nearly meant you didn't get any." I grin at him.

"Ah, Ayar's always doing stuff like that. We're used to it by now. Don't let it get in the way of a good party." Mylo drains his tankard.

"Vypr and Ayar—are they..." I hesitate, not wanting to seem like I'm prying.

"Mates?" Mylo wipes the back of his clawed hand over his mouth. "I think so. Ayar's never been one for talking, and Vypr, well, he keeps things private unless it involves blowing gak up."

"I think it's good they have each other," I reply as Mylo turns the tap on the beer barrel and obtains a refill.

"Like you and the Guv?" He raises his eyebrows.

"Guv? You mean Strykr?"

"He's our Guv now," Mylo says before he takes a deep draught of his beer.

"I can see why Vypr wants to keep things private." I grin at Mylo. "You're a nosy one."

"Guilty," he replies with a wry smile. "I like to know things. Means I can help the Guv."

My heart warms at this comment. Looking around the room, I realize it's gone reasonably quiet as they all get on with various tasks. It's good to see them all settled, and I feel somewhat responsible for the earlier upset with Ayar. I resolve to speak to Strykr about how we can help the tortured warrior over his concerns about Ike.

"Do you want to try?" Mylo hands me a tankard filled to the brim. I take a sip. It's strong, slightly sweet, without the taste of hops that usually accompanies beer.

"What's it made from?" I ask.

"Um, I'm not sure. Ambrosia, I think." He downs his tankard and calls across to Jay, who ambles over, his own empty tankard swinging. "What's var beer made from?"

"Ambrosia, water, herbs," Jay replies, holding out his tankard to Mylo who obligingly refills it.

"You know some gak." Mylo grins at him.

"One of us in this unit has to." Jay shoulders Mylo with his wing. "Like one of us has to eat all the rations."

"I don't eat all the rations. Not all the time," Mylo replies, cheeks bulging with food I didn't even see he had.

"I think you'll find you do. We have to hide them from you," Strykr rumbles as I feel his warm body behind me.

I snort out a laugh into my beer. Jay fills a tankard, handing it reverentially to Strykr, before filling two more tankards, taking them across to Vypr and Ayar.

"Seriously, Jay, don't give him any!" Strykr calls over.

Ayar fixes him with a glare, swiping the vessel from Jay's hand, the beer slopping everywhere, and he downs it with what has to be a single gulp, not taking his eyes from Strykr. Once done, he smacks his lips noisily.

"Has he had that bath yet?" Strykr fires at Vypr.

"Do I normally look this wet?" Vypr shakes out his wings, water dripping onto the floor. "I made sure he took a bath, Guv."

"Don't need a bath to be a good warrior," Ayar grunts.

"You need clean feathers to be functional," Vypr says with a certain softness to his voice as he runs a clawed hand through Ayar's left wing. He shivers, each feather pricking up until he suddenly lifts his wings over his head, twirling them, shaking hard until they all settle back into place.

The look of surprise on his face tips me over the edge. I'm not entirely sure I've ever seen anything as adorable as these predatory aliens being surprised at their own wings. This time, my laugh isn't a snort, it's a full on bark, and I've got six pairs of dark eyes trained on me.

"Is the mistress well?" Jay finally ventures as I can't seem to stop the laughing.

"Kat?" Strykr puts a hand on my shoulder.

"I can't...Ayar..." I wheeze out, flapping my hand at them as I squeeze my streaming eyes closed. "Too cute!"

There's a chorus of huffs.

"M'not cute."

"He really isn't cute. He's a menace."

"You can talk. You ate all the rations last time we were on a mission."

"And you singed my wings with that supposed 'perfect shot'."

I open my eyes just as Jay leaps for Mylo, the pair of them rolling over and over, bumping into Vypr who dives into the fray. Ayar stalks over and helps himself to another tankard of beer before returning to his ledge and furs, a smug look on his face.

"Vrex it!" Strykr runs his hands through his hair, looking at the ball of brawling.

"Cute," I say again.

"That is not the word for this..." Strykr struggles to find the epithet that can possibly describe the tussle going on in front of us. "There are plenty that can be used, but 'cute' is not one of them," he concludes in exasperation.

Ayar shoves his toe into the scrum of warriors, and they part, panting hard. He jerks his head at Strykr.

"Sorry, Guv," they chorus.

"Just being cute," Jay adds with a wink as they troop past to refill their tankards.

The evening passes relatively quietly. Ayar only threatens to kill Mylo and Jay once. Syn stays out of it, brooding in a corner after he's picked at some food.

Eventually, they all settle down, Vypr preening Ayar until the big, scarred male's eyelids begin to droop. Just looking at them makes me feel sleepy, and I nestle against my warm, feathery warrior who still keeps a watchful eye on his team.

My alpha male, my perfect predator. Sleep takes me even while I'm wondering if he knows just how cute he really is.

Strykr

My Kat fell asleep in my arms last night, and I carefully carried her through to the other quarters. She sleeps still, which is why I'm checking in on my unit and not deep inside her.

In a testament to the power of being a mated male, I don't want to rip my unit limb from limb either. Despite their behavior last night, which proved beyond doubt that they exist only to show me up as a commander.

As I look around the room, I see that the only warrior awake is Jay. He sits, slowly cleaning his favorite weapon, a picture of quiet concentration in the mess that the others have left.

"Guv," he says quietly, noticing that I'm awake.

"How many times..." I start to say, then give up. "It doesn't matter. I hope you all realize this is the last party you'll be having for a long time."

"They needed it, Guv. What with moving to the eyrie and all the other work we've been doing." He references the camps we've liberated and the terrible sights we've seen.

I rub at the back of my neck. "I know."

Mylo lets out a loud snore and wakes with a start, eyes wide and ready for action. In one corner, Ayar still sleeps peacefully, draped over Vypr.

"Where's Syn?" I ask. He's the one member of my team who should be here, integrating himself into the unit.

"He disappeared last night sometime. Probably between the drinking competition and the flight competition," Mylo says.

"There was a flight competition?" I groan.

"I won," Jay says without looking up.

"Only because you didn't do the drinking competition," Mylo grumbles before lying back down.

"Dear Goddess! Give me strength." I ball my hands into fists. "All of you, you've got ten minutes to get your gak together and meet me at the entrance to the underground lair. Tell Ayar if he vrexes up again, I'm leaving him behind."

I stomp away, some of the shine rubbing off my mating glow, and head back to where I left my delicious mate slumbering in my furs.

As I exit the barracks, I almost walk into Syn. The warrior bristles at me but doesn't say anything.

"Where have you been?" I ask him, not bothering to keep the aggression from my voice or tone.

"Preparing the systems for the bot. We need the information it contains. That's our mission, and I'm sticking to it," he says, his eyes not leaving mine, challenging me.

As if he wants a fight. Like he has any idea who I am or what I could do to him.

"We'll deal with the bot when I say. You do what I tell you to. I am your commander."

He snorts out an insolent breath and looks away.

Big mistake.

My arm shoots out, almost of its own accord, and he's

slammed against the rough stone wall, my claws gripping his throat.

"I am your commander," I growl low. "You take my orders."

"What? Like the others? That group of vrexers couldn't follow orders if their lives depended on it," he says, choking. His eyes burn with hatred.

"They are my team, and I trust them with my life. I didn't ask to take you on, but I have, which makes you mine." I increase my grip.

His hands scrabble at my claws, but his gaze doesn't leave mine.

"We'll see what Ryak has to say about that," he says hoarsely.

"Ryak gave you to me. He doesn't get a say in what I do with you. I'll let this slide, Syn, just this once because you're new to me, to Ryak, and to the Gryn outside of the camps, but this is not what we are. We work together, for the good of all. If you can't do that, then you're useless to me and to the Legion of the Gryn."

A light of realization dawns in his eyes. I cock my head to one side but don't let him go.

"You're the fighter," he says.

The growl that rises within me is impossible to stop. He knows what I am. Ryak must have told him.

And the last thing I need is the rest of my unit knowing, but this vrexer will tell them. Then everything is broken. What little respect I have will be gone in an instant.

"You don't talk about that. Not to me, not to the others, and never to my mate. In fact, you never look at my mate, ever. Understand?" I squeeze his throat a little harder, and his eyes bulge.

"Strykr?" Kat's soft voice behind me means I instantly let

Syn go. He drops to the floor, coughing and rasping. "What's going on?"

"Syn was just getting a lesson in how to take orders," I say harshly, flicking my wings over him as I walk over to her and put my hands on her shoulders.

She tenses, staring up at me, her blue eyes filled with doubt.

I need her to trust me, to know that I'll protect her at all costs and, hopefully to help her understand that fate is right, we are meant to be together. Fighting with Syn is not going to do that.

"We need to go," I say quietly. "We have to take Ike to the underground lair and find the location for the central control of the defense system."

Kat gives me a curt nod and calls for the bot over her shoulder. It appears as a little silver streak in the air and hovers around her before landing on her arm.

"We're meeting the rest of the unit at the entrance. Make sure you're there," I fire at Syn as I take Kat by the arm and steer her towards the exit to the barracks.

"What was going on back there?" Her voice is quiet. "I thought Syn was part of your team?"

"He's just been assigned to me," I reply. "He knows about tech, which means we need him."

"It means you can't fight with him," Kat says, not looking at me. Something radiates from her, something bitter.

"I'm sorry." I reach out and take her hand as we walk out into Ustokos's crisp morning air. "I don't want to upset you. You mean a great deal to me, my Kat." I turn her towards me, but she still won't look into my face.

"I...care...about you too," she stutters out. "But I can't do conflict, Strykr. All of this is hard enough without watching you tear another being to pieces."

"I wouldn't do that!" I say. And then I remember I've already told her about my addiction.

About my desire to fight until the very last breath is drawn from the body.

I haven't told her how they drag me from my victim. How they pour alcohol down my throat until I surrender. How they ply me with narcotics to dampen my desire to kill.

Somehow, she knows. Fear hovers in her eyes.

"I just need my team to function," I mumble. "If Syn doesn't want to be a part of that, then I need to know."

"Your team loves you," Kat replies firmly. "You don't need to worry about them."

"Even Ayar?" I say, incredulous that she could determine such a thing about a being so damaged.

"Especially Ayar. He'd do anything for you."

I genuinely wish I had her confidence in my unit. At least I know one thing now. If I want my mate, I'm going to have to do the one thing I didn't think was possible.

I'm going to have to stop the fight.

Kat

Seeing Strykr snarling at Syn was not a pleasant experience. I thought I was done with conflict in my life. Although I suppose given that I've been abducted from my planet and presumably was bound for some sort of slavery, I can't expect life to be a bed of silent roses.

I spent so long creating a life that didn't give me stress, that cut me off from anything that caused me pain, even my friends, the thought of more conflict settles in my stomach like a block of ice.

I hold back the pricking of tears when I think about Lana. She meant well, even if she was seemingly always trying to couple me up with one of her husband's boring city friends. I wonder if she misses me? I wonder if she even notices I've gone? Maybe after I blew her off again, she decided not to bother with me. Her comment about my playing with pretty stones is still quite raw.

The last thing I need is a group of alpha males fighting around me. At least with Ayar and the others, it seems to be a familial thing. What Strykr was doing to Syn? There was malice written all over it.

Yet he has a different side to him, the one that hates the fight. The one that made a nest and took me to the heights of pleasure. That's the Strykr I want.

We walk in silence across the canyon floor towards another opening at the base of the cliff face. Strykr's feathers rustle behind me as we enter and start to walk down a sloping ramp towards a large metal door.

When we reach it, Strykr halts. "We need to wait for the rest of my unit."

"Okay." I stare at my ragged nails for a while, trying to stop the emotions churning inside me from sending me into a meltdown.

I want to be with Strykr, more than anything. I understand he has an addiction, but he's explained how he keeps it in check. If he's letting rip with members of his unit, that can't be a good thing, and I don't know if I can stay to watch.

Except where else do I have to go? I feel trapped, and it's making me itch. It's making my breath short and my body want to be elsewhere.

"Kat?" Strykr is surrounding me with all his muscles and feathers. "What's wrong?"

"Where are they?" I cry out. "Where are the others? We need to get out of here." I'm pushing at him now.

I wanted to hold it together, but it's not working. The desire to be able to breathe, to be out in the open, is overwhelming.

And then I'm surrounded by softness, a delicious fragrance that is calming. A pair of strong arms hold me.

A pair of dark eyes stares into mine.

"Stay with me, Kat. I'm sorry I made you feel unsafe." Lips are pressed to my mouth.

I delve my hands into his feathers, grounding myself at the touch of silk and steel. My head clears.

"My mate." He sounds strained. "Whatever you want, tell

me. I'll pluck the stars from the sky if it makes you feel any better. I'll fly to the sun if you ask me to, just please, please talk to me."

"Strykr." My voice is hoarse, my throat dry as I come back from the brink. I'm clutched to him like a doll, and the scent of his feathers is all warm cat and spice.

"Whatever I did wrong, I'll never do it again." He releases me just enough so he can see my face.

"I don't do conflict," I manage to say. "I know it's stupid, but on Earth, I did everything I could to avoid situations where there were fights of any kind." I drop my chin to my chest. I shouldn't be embarrassed that I stopped being able to cope, that I stopped being brave. "I had a breakdown, at work. I couldn't take the pressure anymore. I had to leave. Ever since, I've spent my life alone. Ensuring that it never happened again."

"And then you were taken by Proto."

I laugh. "Yes, and then I was taken by Proto. If I had thought up a scenario that could put me under the most extreme stress, that would be it."

"But you found Ike, and you survived," Strykr says, still holding me tight.

"And then you burst into my life. Literally." I trace a finger over one of his large pectoral muscles as I look up into his handsome face. A face full of concern, one that grounds me in a way I didn't think possible.

"I don't want you to be in any danger, from me, from my unit, from anything." His voice shakes with emotion. "I mean it, whatever you want me to do, I'll do it."

Noise up at the top of the ramp filters down.

"As long as you're here for me, Strykr," I hear myself say.

The noise gets louder as his unit arrives, a tumble of noise, weapons, and feathers.

"Guv?" Jay stands at the bottom of the ramp.

"You vrexers are to behave today," he fires at them. "Please try not to destroy any more parts of this base," he adds in a softer tone as he looks down at me.

"Where's the bot?" Ayar asks grumpily.

"Never mind the bot," Strykr replies and places his hand on a black touch pad next to the metal door.

"*Strykr, commander of the elite legion of the Gryn. Welcome,*" a smooth female voice says as the door slides open.

"Get in there." Strykr motions at the others. "Let's find the console we need and get on with this mission."

Syn is the last to pass us. He gives Strykr a baleful stare. I feel Strykr tense.

"That male is hiding something," he mutters in my ear.

"He's hiding nothing. All he wants is to be part of your unit," I reply as we follow them into a corridor lined with metal rather than the rough-hewn stone of the rest of the place.

"Do you think so?" Strykr sounds surprised.

"I've seen you all together. He wants to be part of it, believe me."

In front of us, another set of doors slides open, and we're in a large cavern that is half metal, half stone. There are a few other warriors dotted around working at various benches.

"It's this way," Syn says.

Strykr growls under his breath until he remembers himself.

We troop past the other winged warriors who give us all quizzical looks until we reach a side room, and Syn gestures inside.

The room is fully lined in metal. A large console similar to those on the spaceship dominates one wall. The unit drops their packs and weapons in one corner.

"Can you bring the bot over here?" Syn asks me, with a glance at Strykr who gives him a small nod.

"In a minute." I put my hand on Strykr's arm. "What about Ayar?" I mouth at him. He looks over at the scarred warrior.

"Ayar, come here," he says, his voice one that cannot be disobeyed.

Ayar walks over to us, his usual swagger diminishing as he gets closer.

"Hey." I look up at him. All these warriors are huge, most of them close to or even over seven foot in height, and Ayar is no exception. "I wanted to introduce you properly to Ike. You've seen he's not a threat. I thought you might want to try touching him."

The expression that crosses his face is the entire opposite of his fearsome appearance. He's clearly terrified.

"Do I have to?" he says in a very quiet voice, all his feathers tight to him. He actually looks small.

"No, Ayar. You don't have to if you don't want to," Strykr says. "We'd just like you to get used to having Ike around. It's probably safer for all of us if you do."

"But only if you want to," I add.

Ayar looks over his shoulder and through his drooping sad wings at Vypr.

"Okay. I'll look at it," he finally says.

I lift Ike off my shoulder where he's hidden in my hair, and he wraps himself around my arm. I hold it out to Ayar. Ike lifts his head and gives a little chirp. His lights flash in a soothing green color. Ayar doesn't move. It's as if he's mesmerized. I rub Ike on his nose, and he makes a funny farting sound that causes Ayar to flare his wings.

"It's not dangerous," he says, seemingly to himself. He reaches out a claw, and I hold my breath, partially because I really want Ayar to get used to being around Ike.

And partially because I don't want to lose my hand.

He boops Ike on his nose. Ike doesn't respond, and his lights go out.

"What did I do?" Ayar cries out. "I didn't do anything!" he says, anguished.

"He's fine, Ayar. Look." I run my hand over the little robot, and his lights flicker blue and purple as he croons at me.

The look of relief that washes over Ayar is almost tangible. "I didn't break it," he says proudly to Strykr.

Strykr puts a hand on Ayar's shoulder and gives him a smile. "I knew you wouldn't. Well done, Ayar."

The heavy-set warrior shakes out his feathers and relaxes. "Thanks, Guv."

I feel my eyes filling with tears. Whatever Strykr might think about himself, his team respects him in a way that I don't think he can even fathom.

"I need to take Ike to Syn now," I say to Ayar. "Is that okay?"

"Yes!" Ayar says, possibly a little too loudly as confidence radiates from him.

It's Strykr I can't take my eyes off. He looks at once hugely proud of his scarred warrior, and as his eyes dart towards me, there's something else there. A look that at once sets me on fire and allows a pit of lust to uncoil inside me. A look that says he wants me in so many ways.

I don't know how to deal with that from him. It's not that I think what we have is intransigent, it's just that I don't know what I can have with an alien, a flying alien with a fight problem.

Instead, I do what I normally do. I run. Trotting over to where Syn is standing.

"Ike?" The bot lights up white at the sound of my voice. "Time to go to work."

Strykr

I'm not sure anyone has ever got through to Ayar in the same way as Kat. Not even Vypr who looks like he's about to explode with joy at how well Ayar dealt with the bot.

She is truly amazing, and yet again, I'm wondering why the goddess would even consider putting her in my path. I'm a warrior with a dirty past and not worthy of something quite so beautiful.

My mind is still on Ayar and how he reacted to her, so I hardly notice when she heads over to Syn and starts talking to him, holding out Ike. I'm next to her in a wingbeat, a snarl on my lips.

"Ike?" Syn says, not even looking at Kat. "Directions to the central defense system."

"What Syn said, directions to the central defense system, please," Kat repeats to Ike.

The sinuous bot slides off Kat's outstretched wrist and onto the console in front of her. Within seconds, it's attached itself to a small port, and its lights begin to flash slowly, rippling along its sides in a flow of blue and green.

"Is he okay?" Kat asks Syn, and I bristle behind them, irrationally angry that my mate is talking to another warrior.

"It's a bot," Syn says dismissively, then he catches sight of me. Something flashes across his face, some sort of recognition, and he takes a small but significant step towards me. "It can't get hurt."

"I know that," Kat fires back. "But we need him undamaged, don't we? That's the point of this mission, to get to the defense system. So he can't get hurt." Her hands are balled into fists. My little female is angry, and it's glorious.

And it's gone directly to my cocks…

"Yes, mistress." Syn stumbles in the face of her ire. "We need the bot intact. He's—I mean—it's downloading its information to the console, and I should be able to extract some further information about the whereabouts of the central control room for the defense system once it's finished," he says over his shoulder at me.

"Good." Kat sits down on a chair next to the console, not taking her eyes off Ike. "How long?"

A look of pure agony crosses Syn's features, and it's also glorious.

"I'm not sure." He stares at her for a beat. "Not long," he adds.

"In which case, there's time for some training." I stare around at my warriors. "Get your kits, and meet me in the training room." I bend over my mate. "You can stay here with Ike if you wish."

Kat turns and runs a hand down my wing, making me shiver with delight. "I might, or maybe I'll come and train with you." She gives me a big grin.

My sweet female is full of surprises.

I fluff out my wings, making myself look big because females like a big male. "You can come and train with us."

An image of her pinned under me floods my mind, and I'm struggling to wrestle my lust under control.

"Is the mistress training with us?" Jay says with delight as he troops past.

"Not with you!" I growl.

"Oh, I don't know. I think I'd like to learn to shoot a laser gun," Kat says.

"I'll teach you."

Kat levels a gaze at me. She's trying to bring the team together, something I should be doing, because she doesn't want conflict. She wants us to be a unit, and she's absolutely right.

She might be my mate, but I need my team.

"Or Jay can," I say. "He is my best sniper."

I'm not sure I've ever seen Jay look happier. The atmosphere in the room has lifted considerably, and it's all because of her.

"Get moving, vrexers!" I growl at them as we follow them out. "Can't have my team thinking I'm going easy on them," I say in a lower voice to Kat.

"Oh, no! Can't possibly let them think that," Kat says, but I get the impression she's not being entirely truthful.

I wind my arm around her waist and pull her to me as the rest of my warriors depart.

"I hope you know what you're getting yourself into, little prey. I like to train my warriors hard."

Kat presses herself against me, up against my hard lengths. "I hope I am. If not, I'll just have to run again, won't I?"

The lair discovered by Ryak and me over a cycle ago is completely different to the one the Gryn have occupied for many cycles. It was built for warriors, with everything that an elite unit could need, including a training area that is far superior to the one we have back at the eyrie.

The large room has a high ceiling and bright artificial lights, which are only possible because the entire place has its own power.

Ayar and Vypr are already attempting to beat each other senseless in the training ring in a way I think they are both enjoying possibly too much. Mylo and Jay are already at the range, making minute adjustments to each weapon they are using before firing at the target. As usual, Jay is eerily accurate for a warrior who had never fired a laser weapon until a cycle ago.

The last thing I want to do is let Kat leave my side, but I spot Syn studiously ignoring the rest of the unit, and my blood begins to boil.

He knows something. That look he gave me earlier, it spoke volumes. He needs to understand what it is to be part of the Elite unit of the Gryn, and I have a lesson to teach him. One that he will learn because there's no way my mate is going to be upset by conflict.

Syn will learn, and he'll learn the hard way.

"Jay, why don't you show Kat how to be as good a sniper as you are." I take my mate's hand, not wanting to let go but hopefully keeping her distracted while I deal with Syn.

"It would be my pleasure, mistress," Jay says with his customary smile, that drops away as soon as he sees my involuntary snarl.

"Thank you, Jay," Kat says with a smile. I can already see Jay trying to calculate how he can show Kat what to do without touching her.

Kat joins Mylo and Jay at the range, and with some reluctance, I turn my attention to the rest of my unit.

"Syn! With me," I call out. His head jerks up as I indicate that we are to get in the ring.

"Guv?" Ayar queries. He is my go-to for a sparring partner. He's the only one who has the stamina to go wing on wing with me, and his vicious, uncompromising way of fighting keeps me on my toes.

"It's time for Syn to show us what he knows, other than tech," I say darkly as I wing bump him.

Ayar's mouth curls up into a toothy smile. He loves anything violent, and he can see the violence rising inside me.

"Get him a weapon," I say as Syn slides down into the ring to join me.

Vypr tosses Syn a large baton. "What about you, Guv?" he asks.

"I don't need anything." I unsheathe my claws the rest of the way.

Proto didn't do much to me other than torture, but the one thing it did was to enhance my natural fighting abilities. My claws don't retract completely anymore because they're double the length of those of a standard warrior.

Syn assesses me with a coolness I wasn't expecting.

"Whenever you're ready, warrior," I say.

He whirls the baton and runs at me, wings open. I easily bat him away, but he's in the air with a litheness I wasn't expecting and back ready to go at me again.

We dance the vicious dance for some time. The harder he tries to hit me, the more I dodge him. I've been doing this for a long time. He's getting tired, and I can see that too. His weapon is swiped from him, and I have him on the floor, wings pinned under my claws.

"What are you going to do to me, Commander?" he asks, breath ragged from his exertions whereas I've hardly broken a sweat.

"What do you think I'm going to do?"

He attempts to move, but the flesh of his wings grinds

against my claws. His eyes widen. I beat my wings, levering myself off him and standing up. I hold out my hand.

"You fought well, warrior. Even Ayar struggles to go that long in the pit with me." I nod over at Ayar and Vypr who nod.

Syn stares at my hand, not entirely sure what to do.

"You're one of us now. You've fought with the Guv," Vypr calls out. "Most warriors don't last more than five minutes," he says with undisguised awe.

I shove my hand at Syn again. This time, he takes it, reluctantly, and I haul him to his feet, pulling him against me.

"I want you to be part of my team, Syn. If we are a whole, we are invincible, and we need to be invincible. Are you prepared for that level of responsibility?" I hiss into his ear. "Whatever Ryak told you, I can guarantee it wasn't everything. If you want to know everything, you'll need to be part of this unit."

"But Ryak, he said..." Syn stares into my eyes, confusion warring over his face.

"Ryak told you I was a dirty fighter he tried to keep out of his way? He's right, only I'm part of something much larger."

Syn holds my gaze.

"Then I want to be part of it...Guv," he says, finally.

Across the room, Kat stands with a laser weapon in her hand and a smile on her face that would light up Ustokos.

She radiates with happiness, and that makes my world complete.

Kat

I can't quite believe what I'm seeing. Strykr and Syn wing bump each other in an almost friendly way as they climb out of the shallow pit where they were fighting. Jay and Mylo did their best to distract me initially, clearly knowing what their commander was going to do, but once the fight started properly, they stopped to watch.

Now I know why Strykr is tasked with the fight by his superiors. He is simply poetry in motion. It didn't matter what Syn did, he couldn't even get near my warrior. At every turn, it was clear that Strykr could have ended the fight whenever he wanted. His huge claws extended, swiping and slashing but never actually making contact with Syn. All he did was keep the big warrior on the move, tiring him out to the point he was hardly able to stand.

It was as hot as hell.

Syn is grinning like a big idiot as he climbs out of the ring, helped by Vypr. Feathers fluffed, he shakes himself out.

Mylo makes a low crooning sound under his breath. "I've never seen Strykr like that before."

"The Guv let him live!" Jay laughs quietly.

"He did." Mylo looks at me thoughtfully, and then the pair of them step to one side as Strykr approaches.

"Go get cleaned up," Strykr says to the three who have been fighting. "Mylo, Jay, your turn."

Jay grumbles under his breath. Mylo takes the laser rifle from me and puts it back in a rack as Jay sets his wings and strides towards the ring.

Strykr spends the next half an hour putting both warriors through their paces, and when he's finished, they are both a sweaty mess, and he has hardly a bead of perspiration on him.

"I hope you are satisfied, my *eregri*," Strykr says as he joins me, all feathers and warmth.

"Satisfied you didn't kill Syn?" I raise an eyebrow at my huge warrior.

"Satisfied that not everything is about the fight."

"Some parts of the fight are not that bad, but I'm pleased that you've been able to accept Syn," I tell him.

Somehow, I can tell he wants to be close to me, and I move into him, putting my hands on his hard chest as I stare up into his face.

"Everyone is better if they're part of a whole, even you."

"I know that." Strykr dips his head, sneaking a kiss from my lips. "At least, I know that now, thanks to you, my sweet mate."

"Am I your mate?" I hold my breath. The word seems imbued with a sort of reverence that goes beyond merely 'boyfriend' or 'husband.'

"If you want to be." Strykr's dark eyes are like liquid pools of want. "I know you are. All Gryn know when they meet their fated mate, their *eregri,* their boundless flight."

"Is that what I am to you?" My breath seems caught in my chest.

I never expected to be anything to anyone, let alone this huge alien who is at once angelic and imbued with devilment.

As if in reply to my wondering, he hitches up a lip, exposing a sharp canine. He's a very bad alien, no matter how soft his feathers are.

"You are my *eregri*." He wraps his arms around me. "I built my nest for you, both on the space station when I hardly knew what I was doing and again in the eyrie. Please say you will be mine."

He's begging me. This beautiful male who could have anyone he ever came into contact with, if the Gryn had any females. My vicious warrior who delights in the chase and the capture. In all the pleasure.

Who would taste every inch of me if he could.

"I'm yours," I whisper. "I'm yours."

"Guv?" Syn's voice interrupts us, and I look across to see a rather soggy warrior. Barefoot, water runs off his feathers as he hastily belts his pants. "The bot, it's finished. We have a destination."

"Good." Strykr puts an arm around me. "Let's see where we're going."

We follow a wet Syn through the base and back to the console room where Ike is now perched on top of the console. He chimes at me, red and purple lights flowing over him, and he takes flight, circling the room, shouting my name until I hold out my arm, and he lands on it, lights finally back to green.

"Did you find what we were looking for?" I ask him as I scratch the top of his head.

"Gryn defenses are operational," he chitters at me. "Gryn defenses need to be primed," he adds.

"That's not all they need," Syn mutters to himself, frowning at Ike.

"What do you mean?" I ask. He says nothing but doesn't meet my eyes.

"Syn?" Strykr asks, his voice low, and his arms folded.

"Answer her."

Syn drops his chin to his chest, feathers drooping behind him. If I thought that Ayar could look pathetic, he has nothing on this soaking warrior who looks like he has the cares of Ustokos on his shoulders.

"Syn?" Strykr sounds concerned. "What is it?"

"It's the Kijg." Syn sighs deeply. "They know about the defenses, and they're looking for them, too."

"How do you know this?" Strykr asks, hands balled into fists.

"Before Ryak found me, I was with the Kijg." Syn won't look at us, staring instead at his bare feet. "I was their captive."

"The Kijg kept you captive?" Ayar fires out as he and the others walk into the console room. "What the vrex happened?"

"Hold on. Who or what are the Kijg? And does it matter that they kept Syn captive? No one should be kept captive, we all know that!" I hold up a hand to try and head off any aggression between the males, although looking at Syn, any fight he might have had in him has long gone with his admission.

Ayar huffs, shaking his wings, but he doesn't say anything else.

"The Kijg are a bunch of cold-blooded bastids that think they should be in charge of Ustokos," Mylo mutters.

"There are two other species on Ustokos, the Mochi, which you have met, and the Kijg. They are a reptilian species." Strykr sighs, rubbing the back of his neck as he looks at Mylo. "They always begrudged paying for the services of the Gryn to protect them before Proto fell."

"Why would they have Syn captive?"

"They want their own army," Syn says, still not looking at the other warriors. "Even if that army is warriors that they had enslaved."

Next to me, Strykr growls under his breath. "Why have

you decided to tell me this now?"

I manage to refrain from thumping him on his arm.

"I was ashamed to tell anyone after I escaped," Syn murmurs. "I told Ryak, when he and Lyon took me in."

"Vrex it!" Strykr thumps his fist on the console with a cracking sound and glares around at his warriors. "Anyone else keeping a secret? Speak now!"

"I'm hungry?" Mylo ventures, opening his wings and fluffing up the feathers.

Strykr runs his palm over his face.

"Mylo, that sort of information will never be a secret. The whole of Ustokos knows you're hungry all the vrexing time." When he looks up, he can't hide the smile on his face.

"Go, eat, all of you." He waves his hand at his warriors, and they obediently troop out of the door, all except Syn. "I mean you too," Strykr says to him. "Get some food. You don't know when you might eat again."

"I'm sorry, Guv. I should have told you earlier," he says.

"You told me eventually. At least I know what we're up against," Strykr replies. "Go with the others."

Syn heads out of the door, and Strykr sinks onto a chair. "Vrexing Ryak, I should have known," he mutters.

"What is it?"

"Ryak knew all along. He just didn't want to tell me." Strykr puts his head in his hands.

"Tell you what?"

"I'm going to have to fight for this defense system."

"That's okay." I run my hand through the soft feathers at the edge of his wing. "You've got your team. You've got me and Ike. We can do this."

Strykr looks up at me. The ache in his eyes fills my soul. "If only that was true, my *eregri*. But the fight will be in the Arium pits. The most formidable fighting pits on Ustokos. And I can only go there alone."

Strykr

The ball of ice churns in my stomach as I allow the scent of my *eregri* to fill my nostrils in the hope that it can calm my emotions.

Because I want this fight, more than anything. Blood thunders in my ears, my veins already full to bursting at the thought of the pits. But this is not the time for indulgences. My duty to my mate is far more important than any addiction.

"Are you sure about this?" Kat says, combing her fingers through my feathers and sending a frisson of desire through me. "I know that this defense system is important, but can't one of your team do it instead? You've done enough fighting that you don't want to do."

The sigh that escapes my lips is part delight that I have a mate who cares for me and part resignation at what is going to come.

"I'm not going to tell you not to fight," she says, burying her head in my wing. "You are what you are, but I don't see why it should be you."

"The only other male capable of holding his own in the

pits is Ayar, and he's too unstable at the best of times. He'd make a mistake that would get him killed."

"What exactly is this place?" Kat's eyes are full of horror.

"It's the best place to get the information we need from the Kijg and to find out what they're planning. It's always been a den of deceit and intrigue." I lean into her as she works her fingers through my feathers. "Which is why Ryak sent me there." A further sigh escapes my lips as she finds a knot and skillfully clears it.

"So, you have to go. Only you. What about your team?"

"I have plans for them." I groan as her clever digits continue to cause pleasure to spike through me in a way I haven't experienced before, even when I've had another male preen me.

"And me? Do you have plans for me?"

"That depends, little prey." My voice is husky, low and full of lust. "Do you intend on running?"

Just like that, her hands are gone, and so is she. All I see is a flash of her dark hair as she disappears out of the door, the sound of her feet on the floor as she runs as if her life depends on it.

My blood is already up, I want to wait, to draw out the delicious chase, to savor it as if it's my last on Ustokos with my mate. Only, as usual, I can't wait. I have to give into my baser instincts. With a roar, I'm on my feet and chasing after her, following her perfect scent through the base and wondering where she might go that I can catch her.

In the distance, I hear the sound of her feet and her laughter. My body goes into overdrive. I'm half flying, half running after her, stopping briefly to scent the air, attempting to taste her. It's only when I reach a part of this lair that I've not been in before that I slow, turning in a circle as I work out which way my prey went, holding my breath so that I can hear hers.

I know exactly where she is. Hiding in a dark alcove, she

shivers, the smell of her arousal nearly driving me out of my mind.

For an instant, I think about letting her run again, but I can't. I can't help myself. Before she can blink, I have her caged, claws around her shoulders, my throbbing cocks pressing up against her beautiful body, wings enclosing us both.

"Did you think you could hide from me, little prey? Did you not think I would find you and devour you?"

"You're going to eat me?" Kat breathes into my chest, one finger tracing over my skin and setting me on fire. "All of me?"

"Only the parts that matter, prey. First, you'll need to remove every single piece of your clothing," I demand.

I could, I should, find a nest for us both because I want to be the male who fills her belly, who adores her body as she grows round with my young.

With trembling hands, Kat begins to strip.

"Wait." I nuzzle at her neck. "This is my job. To adore you, to worship you always."

I pluck at the top she's wearing, and she raises her hands to allow me to pull it over her head. I trail my lips down to the funny covering she wears over her breasts, and she moans at my touch.

The perfect prey, giving herself to me.

She's wriggled out of the covering, and she's bare, allowing me to take one taut nipple in my mouth, and I suck on it, gently at first as she whimpers under me, then drawing the delicious peak into my mouth and suckling with everything I have.

"Strykr!" She arches her back, pushing her gorgeous breasts into my hands, and I revel at the feel of the heavy globes spilling creamy flesh into my palms. "My angel." She moans. "My wicked alien angel."

"Perfect prey, perfect mate. I want to take you, every single inch of you. Will you let me? Can I have your all?" I pull at her pants, and they drop to the floor. She kicks off her boots and is completely naked.

"I want you." Her lips find mine, her tongue sweeping my mouth as her hands pull at the mag catch on my pants, hands that delve in and pull out my cocks, stroking them and causing my hips to jerk towards her. "I want all of you."

"You have me, precious Kat. I am entirely yours." I moan against her. "You are my world, my stars, and everything in between. Nothing will ever take you from me. Nothing." I gasp as she drops to her knees and wraps her lips around my cocks.

I nearly spill my seed there and then as her hot mouth sucks at me. I grasp at her head, the silky strands of her hair under my fingers.

"*Eregri!*" I groan at her. "You are destroying me."

Kat

My enormous warrior is entirely at my mercy as I run my tongue around the tip of his main cock, lapping up his sweet, salty pre-cum. His second cock pulses with the urge to be inside me, but I want to torture my predator just a little bit longer. I separate it out and angle my head so I can take him deep in my throat.

Strykr moans my name, eyes closed in pleasure, his claws scrabbling in my hair, wings flaring.

"I will spill my seed, *eregri*!" he warns. His eyes fly open, and he stares down at me. "I love your lips around my cocks, but my seed is for your hot, tight cunt only."

With a roar, he grabs me by my shoulders and lifts me bodily into the air, slamming me against the wall. He impales me on his cocks in a single movement. I'm soaking for him, and he slides easily inside as I wrap my legs around his waist.

"You are perfect," he murmurs, burying his head in my hair and inhaling deeply. "When I have you like this, you smell perfect, of me and you, entwined. Of our mating. You make me never want to be outside of you." He rolls his hips and drives himself deeper, each node and ridge on his cocks hitting all the right spots, and I feel the first pulse of my oncoming climax.

"Look at you, stretched around my cocks." He stares down at where we are joined and throws his head back with a growl of lust.

"Strykr." I take hold of his head, making sure his eyes are concentrated on mine. "Whatever happens, I want you to know I feel more alive, more protected, and more whole than I ever have in my entire life."

"Kat," he moans as he thrusts into me, pumping and pounding. "My sweet prey, you have captured me, and your body devours me."

My orgasm hits and it hits hard. My pussy milks his cocks with everything I have. My vision fades, even though I don't want it to because I want to look at my handsome alien warrior, his wings flared as he plunders my body, forever.

Sweet eregri!

The words fall into my head, at least I think they do. I'm not sure because I'm shaking, the thunder of my climax overtaking my rational thought as Strykr slows his strokes. They become irregular as he groans, my pussy stretching as his secondary cock swells in me, a brief pain and then ultimate pleasure as it hits my g-spot perfectly. He comes with a roar of triumph, hot streams of his seed firing inside me, painting my channels with everything he has. He clasps me to him, holding me tightly, murmuring my name into my ear.

A name I've forgotten in the roll of my orgasm ripping my body to new heights. He is the master of me, plucking my body as if it's an instrument made only for him.

For a long while, there's just the sound of our breathing as I drape myself over him. It's then I feel it, a calm blue green that floods through my body. It's contentment, but it's not just mine.

It's Strykr's.

"I can..." I pant, unable to work out what's going on. "I can feel you. I can feel your..." I don't know what to call it.

"It is the thoughtbond," Strykr says, breathing ragged. "All true Gryn mates have such a connection."

"Can you feel me, too?" I ask, luxuriating in the delicious warmth of him, both body and mind.

"A little, I think," he says. "The bond can only grow between us the more we mate and the more our youngling grows inside you."

Do I want this huge warrior's children? Is it even possible? I'm not sure, but basking in the afterglow of his contentment, I know that I never want to be without Strykr. He has placed me at the center of his world.

And he is mine.

"Will you nest with me, my Kat?" he asks, his eyes gazing into mine as his swelling subsides and his cocks slip from me, followed by a rush of wetness. "Will you bear my young and take my band? I promise I will always be there for you, to protect you and care for you. A Gryn's promise is his bond, and I want to give you my bond." His dark eyes study my face, desperate for an answer.

"I don't know what half of that means, but I am yours, Strykr. I've never been happier than when I'm with you."

"Let me take you to be cleansed, and we can make preparations," he says.

"I thought you'd already built your nest?"

"Not good enough." He huffs. "Not good enough for my *eregri.*" He helps me gather up my clothing.

"I liked it," I tell him, because I did.

"I want you to love it." He places a clawed finger under my chin and angles my face up to his for a kiss. "I want you to love it as much as I love you."

"What's the plan, Guv?" Ayar wipes his mouth with the back of his hand as he finishes the enormous mouthful of whatever he's been eating.

Along with the rest of Strykr's unit, they're heavily armed again, and more weapons lie tidily near the door to what appears to be a type of canteen.

"I'm going to the pits. You lot are going to check out another Gryn base Syn has identified from the information Ike held," Strykr says, swiping a foil-covered dish from a pile on the table and handing it to me.

"We're not going with you?" Mylo sits up a bit straighter.

"Do you think taking a patrol of Gryn to the Arium pits is a good idea?" Strykr fires at him, moodily picking up another dish and ripping the top off.

"Probably not, Guv," Mylo replies.

"How many times..." Strykr starts to say.

"Don't call me Guv," the rest chorus.

"Too late, Guv." Jay grins at him.

Strykr shakes his head and puts a hand in the small of my back, guiding me to a seat. I pull the top of my dish back and find inside is a selection of food, some of which I recognize as meat. There are some colored items that could be vegetables. I give them a sniff, and the smell isn't bad, but they could do with heating up.

On the wall behind where Mylo and Ayar are sitting is a bank of what looks like microwaves. I get up and walk over. I press a button, and one of the doors pops open, and I slide the dish inside. There are only two other buttons, so I press one in the hope that it's the heater.

The alien microwave begins an oddly familiar hum, and behind me, I hear a loud rustling of feathers and scraping of furniture, along with several ominous clicks. Turning around, I see four enormous warriors pinned up against the far wall, wings outstretched. Mylo and Jay have weapons trained on the wall. Ayar looks like he's about to explode, and Vypr is only just holding him back. Strykr leaps in front of me with a feral growl at the others.

"Wait! No! It's just a machine that heats up food! Don't shoot!" I call out through his feathers.

The alien microwave stops buzzing, and there's a, thankfully, soft chime. I open it and lift out the dish with care. The scent of hot food fills the room.

"What the vrex?" Mylo peels himself away from the wall and stalks over, wings still held high as if he's going to flee at the first opportunity.

He sniff-sniffs at the food then looks at the pile of foil-covered trays. I manage not to laugh as I can see the cogs turning.

"It heats the rations up?" he asks.

"You can try this one if you like." I hold it out to him and hear a growl from Strykr.

Mylo grins at me and takes the dish, shooting a triumphant glance at Strykr. Quick as a flash, I grab his food and shove it into the alien microwave before he has a chance to complain.

"This is vrexing amazing!" Mylo says through a mouthful. "Why the vrex didn't someone tell us about the food heaters?"

Syn shrugs. "I assumed you all liked your rations cold."

Ayar cuffs the back of his head as he walks past and takes his seat again, shaking out his feathers. "No one likes cold food, you vrexer," he snarls.

"Oh, dear god!" I say and start shoving dishes in the various alien microwaves. "I can't believe none of you asked how it all worked? That's the key to understanding tech, you know!" I scold.

Half an hour later, I have seven happy males, all having had some hot food and all looking very fluffy.

"Syn, I need you to get one of those pads, the ones that

glow. One for me and one for the rest of you to download the locations," Strykr orders. "Mylo, I need weapons." He rises, turns to me, and cups my chin in his hand. "Stay here, my mate. I'll be back soon."

He kisses me with a lingering long brush of his lips, and I miss him as soon as he's gone.

"The rest of you, get kitted up and wait for your orders above ground."

Obediently, Vypr, Ayar, and Jay are on their feet. Collecting their packs and belongings, they load up.

"We'll see you later, little mistress," Jay says. "Thank you for the food," he adds, shyly.

"The Guv better take good care of you and Ike," Ayar joins in forcefully.

"I'm sure he will. Do you want to see Ike again?" I ask.

It took Ayar the longest of them all to stop eyeing the alien microwaves with a look that was part terror and part killer. Ayar nods, and I encourage Ike onto my arm until he's wrapped around my wrist. The huge, scarred warrior stands like a little kid, hesitantly reaching for the silver robot as Vypr keeps a careful eye on him.

"Do you know why Strykr wants to go to the pits on his own?" I ask them.

"He has his reasons, I'm sure," Jay says, fascinated by Ayar's reaction to Ike.

"The Guv always has a plan," Vypr agrees, but there's something in his voice that catches my attention.

"You don't agree?"

"It's not our place to challenge what we're told to do," Vypr says, his teeth gritted. "But if you ask my opinion, I don't think it's a good idea, not with what the Guv's had to do in the past."

"What are you vrexers still doing here?" Strykr booms out as he returns.

"Ayar was just seeing Ike again," I explain.

"Didn't break him again, I see." Strykr grunts. "Vrex off. Mylo has my orders," he says gruffly.

"Is this a good idea?" I ask as the three warriors leave us, weapons clanking.

Strykr bristles. "Why? Don't you think I can protect you?"

"I know you can. That's not what worries me. It's just the whole fighting thing, is that a good idea?"

"I have a plan. My unit will be near the pits as soon as they've checked out the other Gryn lair. If we need them, we can send Ike."

"Oh." I hadn't thought about using the little robot that way. He's still curled around my arm, recovering from Ayar's attentions. "I guess we can."

Strykr seems confident that everything is in hand, but I can't escape the uncomfortable feeling in my stomach that he's the last warrior who should be heading into a fighting pit, given his history.

And what's worse, I now know I'm not the only one who feels that way.

Strykr

I pull the sling over my head, and Kat climbs in. There's a rising excitement within me I recognize but know I can't give into.

It's the fight.

I can smell the pits, and blood roars in my ears. I shake my head as we rise into the air. I can't be distracted. This is all about getting the information we need to obtain control of the defense system. That's the mission.

Not the fight.

Kat wraps her arms around my neck, and I enjoy the feel of her mind against mine. The thoughtbond between us isn't strong, but it resonates in a way that it flows through me, calming my hot blood and making me think only of her.

I know I can keep her safe, but we are going into a situation fraught with danger. I need her by my side because she has Ike, and the little bot won't work for me. If we find the control center, we'll need him, or at least that's what Syn tells me. I vrexing hope he's right because if all of this goes to gak, I'm going to need a miracle.

My wings beat on automatically because they know the

way to the pits. I've been there many times and picked up information valuable for Ryak. I've enjoyed my time in the fight, slashing, ripping until I'm dragged away from my opponent, plied with lynk or any other strong alcohol, or anything else that will stop me, at least until I'm turned loose again with a belly full of fire, making me even more deadly.

Until I wake the next day, and the filth of what I've done can't be washed off, not for a long time.

I look at the gorgeous female in my arms. Why am I doing this? It's not because I'm the only one who can. It's because I don't want to subject any of my unit to the horrors of the pits. They're all capable of hand-to-hand fighting. But that feeling of dirt once you've participated? That's almost impossible to get out of your feathers, and no Gryn deserves to be ordered to fight.

Except me.

It's all I've known, until now. Until I have this perfect tasty morsel of ultimate pleasure weighing nothing in my arms, who looks at me like I'm everything to her.

Who tells me I'm her entire world, her protector, her *mate*.

I do not deserve her. Not if I'm taking her to the pits. She's braver than she knows.

Strykr

My name falls into my head, and I look into a pair of bright blue eyes.

It's going to be okay

I want to believe her, very much. But I can't have the thoughtbond upsetting her. I shut it down as I press a kiss to her forehead, an action so natural, I can't believe the Gryn have never done it before.

"We're nearly there," I mouth in her ear. "I'll try to keep you away from the worst of it. The Kijg normally have areas for guests. You can wait there for me."

In my arms, she tenses, and I understand. I don't want be parted from her either.

"We just need to get the information. I probably won't even have to fight."

She doesn't relax because she doesn't believe me. Kat doesn't trust me either, and I don't blame her. We near the crumbling arena that houses the pits. I understand it was once a stadium where the Mochi celebrated their prowess as warriors. Now deep in Kijg territory, it's a place that allows species to rip each other limb from limb instead. The stench rises to greet me, and my heart doubles in speed.

I should do a circuit, check my perimeters, but my desire to be on the ground, to be closer to where I can allow my feral nature to be free, is too much. Instead, I fold up my wings and dive. Kat lets out a short, sharp cry, and her arms tighten around my neck.

I'm too far gone, too close to what I crave. I have put temptation in my way and given in to it.

I make as much noise as I can when I land, wanting to attract the maximum attention. A Gryn warrior is a formidable opponent, and my odds are always good. If I can please the Kijg, I'll get what I want.

Kat wriggles against me, climbing out of the sling and dropping to the floor with a huff of breath.

"You could have warned me you were going to do that," she grumbles, brushing herself down, and then she stops, staring around. "Lizard men," she wheezes, stumbling back into me. "They're here!"

Kat

I don't need some fucking weird psychic link that I don't really believe in to tell me something is wrong with Strykr. His entire body language has changed since we landed in a small courtyard below an enormous derelict stadium.

Sometimes being sensitive is a curse; sometimes it's helpful. Right now, looking at my huge warrior, his feathers lifted to make himself look even bigger, his muscles straining at his skin, his dark eyes seeming dull as he glares around, he is everything he hates about himself. I'd shiver if I had it in me, but I'm not sure I can move. I've let him become my entire world, and it's shrunk down to this one point.

The male I have no choice but to rely on.

"Gryn!" A voice slides out of a dark corner, and it's followed by the one thing I hoped never to see again.

The lizard man isn't green. In fact, he's more of an off mauve, and as I stare at him, it seems his color changes to a slightly darker purple. In all other respects, he's the thing of my nightmares, those that flickered through my brain when I was captive on the spaceship. Ones I haven't suffered from since I met Strykr, and he brought me to his planet.

"Are you here for the pit?" he asks. Strykr gives him a stiff nod. "Excellent, we're down a fighter for tonight's games." The lizard man's forked tongue flickers out, blue and slimy. It makes me feel sick.

He seems to notice my presence, and the tongue slaps out again. "Is this your little pet?" he asks. The emphasis he places on *pet* causes my guts to churn.

I might not know anything about lizard men, other than they are abducting bastards, but he knows far more about me than he's prepared to let on. His gimlet green eyes tell me all I need to know. I shrink into Strykr, but his body is hard and unyielding.

Looks like I'm on my own. Again.

"I will fight, but I want to see Sigid first," Strykr says after staring at the lizard man for a very long time. "Then fight." His voice is no more than a feral growl.

"As the Gryn wishes." The lizard bows and motions us forward, his eyes never leaving me and that blue tongue still tasting the air with a horrible slurping sound.

If Strykr is disturbed by it, he doesn't show any emotion. He strides forward into the darkness of the stadium and down a poorly lit corridor. The only saving grace is that his hand closes around mine as he does, even if it does mean he's towing me along with him. His hand is warm and dry around my clammy one.

"Let me see if Sigid can see you." The obsequious lizard man hurries past us.

"He will see me if you want to add a Gryn to your program this eve." Strykr inclines his head. "A Gryn fighting in the pits. Think of the coin he would lose if I was to just..." He looks back over his shoulder at the outside world. "Fly away."

"Go straight through, honored warrior," the lizard says,

bowing in a show that would put the best Hollywood actor to shame. I glare at him as we pass, and he lifts his head, interested eyes following me again.

Strykr ignores him completely, and I get the impression he would do as he liked in any event, lizard man or no lizard man.

A new metal door looms out of the dark in direct contrast to its disheveled surroundings. Strykr shoulders it with his wing, and it flies open.

In the well-lit space beyond, there's another reptilian male, this one a deep blue color, and he's lounging on a large, overstuffed couch like an enormous monitor lizard.

Providing monitor lizards wear pants and long silky looking tunics. Or have rings on their clawed, three-fingered hands. He is entirely unperturbed by the presence of the massive Gryn warrior who makes the room seem much smaller.

"Strykr!" he calls out. "Commander! It's good to see you again. What can I do for you?"

Strykr lets go of my hand, and I feel very alone. He whirls around and slams the door shut in the face of the other lizard.

"I need information, Sigid."

"Are you going to fight for me, Commander? I have a couple of Mochi who are itching to spar with a Gryn."

"A couple?" Strykr shuffles his feathers and throws back his shoulders. "Where's the fun in that?"

"Did I say couple?" Sigid hisses out a laugh. "I meant four or five."

This time, Strykr shifts uneasily, and I see his hands balled into fists. Sweat beads on his top lip.

He's in the grip of the addiction he confessed to me, and we're in exactly the wrong place for this addict. Facing down a lizard man who knows which buttons to push.

If I hated the lizards for taking me from Earth against my

will, my loathing deepens at the way this one is manipulating my Strykr.

"We still need the information, or he doesn't fight," I say. The last thing I want to do is draw attention to myself, but I'm not going to let any fucking lizards get the better of us.

"You have a mate, I see." Sigid turns his glittering eyes on me, and his skin flushes a deep orange. "A human. I had heard that they were compatible with the Gryn."

As much as I don't want Strykr to do any fighting, I'd happily watch him tear this condescending creature to shreds, and now I'm really mad. Strykr shakes his head as if trying to clear it and takes a step forward.

"I have a mate, and that makes me an even more formidable opponent, as well you know. So, do we get the information we want or not?"

Strykr

The moment we landed, my brain closed down. Everything became as if I were looking down a tunnel, and every single part of me itched to be in the pit. Even Sigid's interest in Kat only just penetrates the fog.

But not enough.

"You know I'm good for anything the Gryn need to know, but after you've fought for me, not before," Sigid says.

My breath is hot as I dip my stuffed head to my chest, holding back the rage that threatens inside of me.

"We'll keep your mate safe for you," Sigid adds as the door opens behind me. "We have guest quarters for her."

"You will keep her safe, or you'll pay with your life," I growl, but in the distance, I can hear the sounds of the fight, and it's calling to me. It's taking me away from Kat, and although I know it shouldn't—I know I made her a promise—its pull is too great.

"Strykr?" Her voice is far away. I turn and see her stood in the doorway, Sigid standing behind her.

"I'll be back. It's just one fight, my *eregri*. Then I'll be with you again." Even as I say the words, I see she doesn't believe me, and the knowledge should destroy me.

But I'm already at the bottom. There's no way out. Sweat rolls off me, and I can't keep my claws sheathed, not any longer. Not until I get to the fight.

I was made this way.

"This way, Gryn." The Kijg laughs at me. "The pit is waiting for you. Give me your weapons."

He knows me. He's led me to the fight on many occasions. He's been the one standing by with the alcohol and the narcotics. He knows nothing of the fight and everything about being a coward. It doesn't matter; he isn't part of this. All that matters now is the fight ahead. I divest myself of my laser and dagger, throwing them at him.

"In here." He opens a door to the sparring ring, and half a dozen heavily armored Kijg stand around the edge, all holding long, slim poles.

"What the vrex is this? Only Kijg? They're not worthy!" I roar out, taking a step inside.

It's enough for the door to close behind me. I open my wings, expecting the rush, the pounding of blood, the absolute perfect agony and ecstasy of the fight to flow through me as I roar out my desire for flesh.

There's nothing.

My body wanted to fight, but my mind does not. Instead, it's filled with the last vision of her.

My mate, my boundless flight. My all.

The being I promised to protect with everything I had.

And the being I left behind.

With several thin cries, the Kijg leap for me, their natural quickness deadened by the armor they wear. The long tubes crackle with white light. I spin and dodge out of self-preservation, but there are too many to avoid completely.

When the light touches, pain explodes across my skin, and

a cackle of laughter rises from the assembled ranks as I snarl at them.

This is not how it should be in the pit. But it's all I deserve. I left my mate, and I am not a worthy warrior.

Despite pounding a number of the Kijg and noting that they have not gotten up, the others have grabbed their fallen comrades' weapons and redoubled their efforts. It's getting harder to push through the white heat of every jab as I swipe out, hoping to get past the long tubes and finally draw blood.

A long, low hiss fills the sparring arena. It's enough to distract me and allow one of the Kijg to thump their stick into the side of my head.

My vision blackens, and I fall to my knees, wings flailing to keep the rest at bay. Once the ringing in my ears stops, there is only silence.

Then I'm being prodded with something metal and sharp.

"Vrex you!" I swipe out, and my claws connect with a pole that I grasp and pull on.

"Finally." A voice purrs in my ear. "It wakes."

"Farok?" I wrench my eyes open to see the striped Mochika standing over me holding a long pincer, which he uses to poke me. "Vrex off!"

"Why are you here, *Commander*? I thought that the Gryn had better things to do these days, such as saving the planet."

"Does Paulur know you're here?" I ask him, staggering to my feet, swaying dangerously.

At the mention of his mate's name, Farok slicks down his fur in annoyance. The Mochi thought himself our equal for a long time. There's an uneasy truce between his pride and the Legion, negotiated by Ryak half a cycle ago at the gathering, where we met his formidable female, Paulur.

He's supposed to be our friend, but if he's here in the pits, it's difficult to tell if that truce still stands.

"I'm here on a delivery. One of the Kijg bastids said that a

Gryn had come looking for a fight, and my curiosity was piqued."

I snarl at him. My head feels clearer than it was before I was rendered nearly unconscious with whatever weapon the Kijg have. Unfortunately, that means I can think about what I've done.

Kat!

"Why are you here, Strykr?" Farok asks. "I thought unsanctioned fighting was forbidden for the Gryn, by order of your Prime." Farok leans back on the wall behind him and folds his arms. "Did Ryak send you? That slippery bastid is worse than the Kijg."

"Can't talk here," I murmur, knowing he can hear me. "My mate," I add pathetically.

"Oh, dear goddess! Not you too?" Farok sighs. "Will the Gryn ever learn?"

He walks over to the door of the sparring ring and pounds on it. "I'm taking the Gryn to prepare for his bout. No more stun sticks!"

There's a scraping sound as a bolt is drawn back on the outside of the door. "They locked us in?" I query.

"They locked you in." Farok laughs. "Even against all those armed Kijg, you were winning."

I take a step forward, and my leg doesn't want to work immediately, causing me to stumble.

"Take care, Gryn." Farok allows me to lean on him. "You want good odds for later. Best not let them see you like this."

"I don't need your help," I growl and push him away. "I need to get this vrexing fight over with. I need…"

The thought of Kat, alone in this terrible place, unprotected, is enough to have me dropping to my knees again.

I thought it was all about the fight.

I was wrong.

Kat

"You're an interesting little thing, aren't you?" Sigid appraises me as Strykr disappears down the corridor, feathers rustling away until I can't hear him anymore.

I can't feel him either and I am empty.

But I'm not going to cry. I'm not.

I'm not going to let the situation beat me. I'm not going to be intimidated by the lizard men.

"You'd know, wouldn't you?" I fire at him.

"Feisty!" His long blue tongue tastes the air over me. "Humans always are."

"I knew it! Where are the others, you fucking bastard?" I run at him, the tears I promised myself I wouldn't shed blinding me. "They're not dead, I know it!"

The sounds of the cries that haunted me on the spaceship fill my ears even as I try to beat on the horrible lizard. He catches my wrists and holds me away from him like I'm some sort of oddity, his glittering eyes roving over my body.

"I don't deal in flesh, female, even if I do run this pit. Those who come here do so willingly. Even your mate."

"There's nothing willing about what he does. It destroys him," I bawl out.

Sigid cocks his head to one side, fixing me with his unblinking stare. He lets go of my wrists and takes a step away, clearly not wanting another onslaught.

"Gryn rarely attend the pits. It is forbidden for them, and they are honorable warriors who obey their Prime." He sits back down on the couch. "I know Strykr doesn't come because he wants to. I always give him what he needs."

He lets out a soft, hissing sigh.

"Not all Kijg are what the Gryn think we are. I have to make a living, just like the Gryn do. I have mouths to feed and this planet..." He sweeps his arm at nothing. "Let's just say that before Proto fell, things were simpler."

"Let's not just say that." I put my hands on my hips. "Why don't you tell me exactly what's going on?" I glare at the lizard.

After all, what have I got to lose? Strykr's been ripped from my life. This foul place and these foul creatures have done that to us both. I need him like I need to breathe. His absence robs me of a warmth and light I've fought to obtain.

And it's pissed me off.

The sooner we can get the information that Strykr needs, the sooner we're out of this awful place. Maybe I can help...if this fucking lizard is as contrite as he seems.

"Proto protected Ustokos from outside influence. For its own purposes." Sigid's tongue waves in the air again. "It made the species that remained outside of its control dependent on each other. The Gryn provided the protection and medicines, the Mochi provided food and furs, we provided other types of trade. The Zio provided silks, ambrosia, and other elements."

"Zio?" I can't help myself.

"They keep themselves to themselves, little human. Almost as rare as you are." He bares his sharp teeth in what is presumably some sort of smile, given that he doesn't have any lips to speak of. "After the Gryn vanquished Proto, Ustokos is ripe for the picking, not just by my fellow Kijg, some of whom are not as honorable as me." He hisses out a laugh. "But by others not of this world."

"There are other humans on this planet. You know about them. I don't mean the ones with the Gryn, I mean the others, like me," I blurt out. "From the space station."

For a creature that can't do much in the way of facial expressions, a look of pain flits over Sigid's currently purple face.

"Your Gryn friends think I'm their enemy," he says. "I'm not. Far from it. The Gryn did Ustokos a great service. There are plenty of my species who see it a different way. And some of those have assisted Proto in the past and the new intruders now."

"New intruders? What do you mean?"

Sigid shakes. He gets up from the couch and strides across the room to a table where a decanter sits along with a couple of glasses. He pours out some green liquid and throws it back, his throat bobbing as he swallows.

"The Gryn and the Mochi, they are the natural inhabitants of Ustokos. It appears that the Kijg were brought here by Proto. We have a corresponding race out in the stars, the Drahon, and they want a piece of this planet before it becomes strong again."

"What about the humans?" I grind out, wishing Strykr could hear this.

"I believe there are other humans, ones that are not under the protection of the Gryn on Ustokos. The Drahon have them," Sigid says, pouring another measure of green liquid.

I feel for Ike in my hair, his warmth grounding me. I know that without Ike, there's no defense system, and that means that neither the Drahon nor the Kijg can get access to it.

"Strykr's going to fight for you. He'll make you a whole load of money." The words are sour in my mouth at the thought of my handsome warrior sullying himself in this awful place. "There's a defense system, controlled from Ustokos. We think it's near here, but we need the exact location. Do you know it?"

"I don't." Sigid swallows the drink. "But I can find out."

"I need to know where the humans are, too."

"I know where they are, but you can't get to them. The Drahon have them now, and they're going to take them off world."

There's a loud bang on the door to Sigid's room. He spins around, clearly not expecting such a noise.

"Hide!" he murmurs. I don't have to be told twice. Not by a lizard. I dive behind the couch that Sigid recently vacated.

I'm just in time. The door bursts open, and three more lizards enter. Two of them are a dark red color, and the third looks different, more crocodile than lizard and far more familiar.

"Sigid," the first one hisses.

"Grid, have you come for the fights this eve?" Sigid says nonchalantly. "Your coin is always welcome."

"You were told to inform us when you had the Gryn in your disgusting pits again, and yet I had to hear about it by way of another party." Grid fingers a short, dull metal spear at his hip, and I watch Sigid eye it with concern.

"He only arrived in the last hour, Grid. I've been busy."

"We want him. You are to give him to us," the larger green lizard man says, his voice sounding oddly strangled.

"If he doesn't fight, I'll make a loss. Who's going to compensate me? You?" Sigid could be sneering, but he manages to look innocent. "The Council won't like to see me out of pocket."

Grid seems less sure of himself.

"Okay, he can fight, but you're to give him this after." He

motions to the second Kijg who steps forward with a vial of clear liquid. "Guaranteed to knock out a fully grown Gryn warrior cold. Then we'll collect him."

"Where are you taking him?" Sigid asks, but he gets a sharp look from Grid.

"Why do you want to know?" His eyes narrow.

Sigid holds up his three-fingered hands and flushes a light green. "You're right. None of my business, and I don't need to know. If the rest of the Gryn Legion come looking for him, I know nothing."

Grid laughs nastily. "I might just put some of my own coin down. Might as well win something this eve."

"If that's everything, Grid, I've fighting pits to run. You're cluttering up the place," Sigid says with a boldness I didn't expect.

"One more thing. The Gryn had a female with him. Human. Have you seen her?" Grid asks.

I hold my breath. This lizard has no reason not to give me up to the others, whatever he's said. I've no idea if Strykr trusts him because my poor warrior has been carried away by the addiction he's unable to escape, given that it dogs him at every turn.

If Sigid gives me up, I can't warn Strykr. I can't even get to him. Whatever these other lizards want with him, it's not going to be good. If I end up in their hands too, we're both fucked.

Despite everything, a tear slides down my cheek.

I wanted so much to find that being abducted, taken away from everything I know, wasn't the worst thing that has ever happened to me. Strykr made me believe that it was, in fact, the best thing.

His sweet nature, his gorgeous exasperation with his unruly team, his deep, dark desire to chase and hunt me. His body against mine, making every atom of me sing. It was all real and it was all so right.

I'm going to lose it all because I've no way of stopping any of this. Ultimately, it's not that I care I might end up in the hands of the lizards.

I care because I'm going to lose my winged warrior. My reason for wanting to make a new life. My Strykr.

And there's nothing I can do.

Strykr

The vrexing Kijg line the corridor with their sticks pointed at me as I stride through, heading to the preparation area for fighters. Farok follows me at, for him, a respectful distance.

"The Gryn requires assistance before the fight," he says to one of the Kijg stood outside the door of one of the cell-like preparation areas.

"I need no such thing. Vrex off, Farok," I snarl, and behind me, there is the distinct sound of crackling stun sticks and the smell of ozone.

"You will have my assistance and like it, Gryn," he says evenly. "All warriors need a little assistance from time to time."

"Vrex you." I stomp into the cell.

Any desire for the fight has been driven away by the image I have of my *eregri*. It's burned into my mind.

"Why are you here?" Farok is behind me, and a pair of furry paws are on my shoulder. Whiskers tickle my ear. "I know the Gryn enjoy a preen. Roll with it and we can talk."

I'm so vrexing tense that I could easily tear him limb from limb, and Farok knows that. The Mochi are not bad warriors, but compared to the Gryn, they are no match. And yet, he's still putting himself in harm's way.

Especially with me.

"I'm here for the fight, Farok. What else?" I growl.

He runs a set of claws through my feathers, and I stiffen further.

"I know you'd prefer your mate do this, but if you want to get back to her, you're going to have to trust me, Commander. You're in great danger here."

"If you touch my feathers again, I will remove your arm." My anger shakes me, my claws fully extended.

"Stay calm, Gryn." Farok's whiskers tickle my neck again. "I don't want to do this any more than you."

"I know I'm in danger. I'm a contender in the dirtiest fighting pits on Ustokos," I grind out. "I need information from Sigid about a Gryn matter. That's all."

Despite my earlier warning, another set of claws rakes over the shoulder of my wing, and I'm gritting my teeth. "Relax, Commander," Farok purrs. "Save yourself for the pits."

"Why do you even care, Farok? Just vrex off and leave me to my mission."

"I care because I've had word from a pride that borders these lands that they've seen a ship land here."

"Vrex!" I try to turn around, but Farok puts an arm around my neck, pinning me to him.

"Don't move, or I will do something you don't like. I miss my mates." He pushes his hips at me.

I spin around, breaking easily out of his grip. In an instant, I have him up against the cell wall.

"You forget, Mochi, the Gryn are very social. *Very* social." I trail my free hand over his chest. "You might just be starting something you can't follow through."

Farok grins at me. "Now this is the Strykr I remember. So much more fun than your boring Commander Ryak."

"Proto had a defense system for Ustokos. We can activate it to stop any more ships from landing, at least until we're capable of defending ourselves from whatever else is out there," I say, my voice low as I press a hand on his fur. "But we need to find the control center first. It's somewhere near this pit. Sigid will know, even if the Kijg can't access it."

"Why do you want to stop more ships from landing? Maybe they can trade with us?" Farok suggests, ever the trader.

"How do you think we got our spaceship, Farok? Do you think some kind passing species from out in the stars gave it to us out of kindness?" My words are growled low and feral at him. "Proto's been selling Gryn for slaves to the rest of the galaxy for goddess knows how long. Maybe it was selling Mochi too. We know this because a Gryn who was a slave escaped and brought the ship here. If we don't activate the defenses, we're all at risk."

"Proto had its uses then?" Farok is trying to make light of what I've just told him, but he has cubs, and I can tell he's worried.

"Proto was the problem. We were a great civilization once. Now we have to start all over." I release him and drop onto the single bench in the sparse room. "I'm going to have to fight. I need you to find my mate and get her out of here. My unit is waiting for me, and she knows how to get to them."

I'm back on my feet, his furry neck in my claws. "You'll do this for me, won't you?"

The door to the cell clicks open.

"It's time, Gryn." A Kijg, even more heavily armored than those in the sparring arena, stands at the door. These vrexers don't miss a trick.

"Farok?"

He doesn't acknowledge my request. My desire, my need to fight has dwindled to nothing. All I want is Kat, to be drowning in her heady scent and the feel of her in my arms.

I thought I knew what it was to have an *eregri*. I didn't know at all.

When fate put her in my path, I should have given everything up for her. It wasn't about giving into my darkness.

It was about putting her in the light.

"Go, fight, Commander," Farok says, his face expressionless. "That's what you're here for, after all."

Why did I ever think that my need to fight was something I couldn't control?

All I ever had to do was think of Kat. She is vrexing perfection, and that was all I needed after all.

I told her she was my boundless flight. I told her that she was the center of my world. I told her that I loved her and would protect her. And yet I still left her.

I am entirely without honor.

Without another glance at Farok, I walk past the Kijg and down the ramp that leads to the pit.

If I win, if I get out of this, I will set my precious *eregri* free. She can choose another and not spend the rest of her life with a warrior who breaks his word as if it means nothing.

Who abandons her to give in to his base desires. I could have let her save me. But I chose another path.

A crowd roars as I enter the pit. The five scarred Mochi shift from foot to foot, ready to spring.

There's no going back now, whatever my heart wants. I've lost the only thing that ever meant anything to me, and all I am is a dirty pit fighter.

And that's how I'm going to stay.

Kat

"Come with me, little human." Sigid pulls me out from my hiding place. "We need to get you out of here."

"I can't leave Strykr." My voice sounds pathetically plaintive in the face of this big lizard.

"He can look after himself."

"He shouldn't be here at all. You know that. I can't leave him." After what I've just overheard, not only do I have to find Strykr, but we need the rest of the unit here as soon as possible.

There's no way I'm revealing Ike to these lizards, but as soon as I can, I'm going to send him to Syn and keep everything crossed that they get here before Strykr goes into the pit.

Sigid opens the door and peers out. "Come on." He beckons me into the dark corridor and sets off at an impressive pace, his tail swinging behind him.

I follow, even if every part of me is screaming to stay put. We only get a short way when he turns on me, grabbing my arm and shoving me through a door.

"Wait," he whispers, closing it on me.

It's not much of a room, but there is a glassless window to the outside. I press my ear to the door and hear voices outside. One way or the other, this is the one chance I have to contact the unit.

"Ike," I call out softly, and the little robot slides down my arm.

"KatKatKat," he chimes.

"Do you remember Syn and the other Gryn warriors?"

"Commander Strykr's unit," Ike replies, his eyes blinking at me.

"Do you know where they are?"

Lights flow along his side. "I have their coordinates," he replies.

"You need to go to Syn and bring them all back here as quickly as you can. You must do whatever Syn asks you to do. But only Syn. Understand?"

"Understand, Kat," Ike replies, but he doesn't move.

"Okay, you can go."

He remains on my hand.

"Kat needs Gryn warrior," he says. "Kat needs Commander Strykr."

My throat closes up. I want to reply, but it's impossible.

"Please, just go," I gasp out hoarsely. Stupid tears pricking at my eyes. "Strykr needs more than me."

Ike rubs his warm, metal body against my fingers in the way he always does to soothe me, only this time it doesn't work. He knows what I need, and he's absolutely right.

His wings spring free from their casings, and he's in the air, zipping out of the window just as the door opens, and I leap behind it.

"Female?" It's Sigid. "Come quickly, before you're seen."

"Where's the fight taking place?" I peer around the door, knowing that Sigid is, for better or for worse, trying to keep me away from the others.

"The pits are no place for a tiny female like you," Sigid says, and my blood boils in my veins.

"So, if I was bigger, you'd not be bothered about me seeing the fight?" I bristle at him.

Sigid opens his mouth and closes it again.

"I need to see Strykr," I say firmly.

"He's already in the pit, little female." A voice purrs in my ear, and I jump out of my skin.

A huge, striped cat man is stood behind me. He has to be over six feet in height, wide and very furry, reminding me of a large, satisfied tabby housecat.

"Farok." Sigid inclines his head in what I assume is some sort of greeting.

"Your supplies have been delivered. I will take the female to her mate," he says.

"It's not safe for her here." Sigid lowers his voice. "Grid is here, with one of *them*."

"I'm well aware of that." Farok looks down on me. "I have spoken with the commander. He needs you, little female. More than you'll ever know."

I hiccup, my breath sticking in my throat. The last thing I want to do after shouting at Sigid is let him see me cry. I don't want either of these males to think I'm weak, not if I'm Strykr's mate. He deserves better than that.

"Take me to him, please?" I probably shouldn't be trusting anyone right now, but innately, I can see the good in the cat man.

Or perhaps I just like cats.

Farok turns, and again, I'm following a tail down the dark corridors. Every now and then, some light filters in from somewhere, letting me see the place is filthy, green and brown stains on dark walls that may or may not have been painted at some long time in the past.

"Strykr is already in the pit, sweet one." Farok turns to face me. "It isn't pleasant. I'm not going to lie to you." Somewhere, there's a roar of a crowd, and my skin turns to goosebumps.

"One of the lizards, the Kijg, intends on drugging him and taking him somewhere after he's fought," I gabble out. "We have to warn him."

"Strykr told me that we were at risk from other species taking slaves from Ustokos." Farok runs his fingers through his whiskers absently.

"I have to help Strykr," I say firmly. "I have to help my mate."

"That's why I'm here, little human." Farok gives me a sharp-toothed grin. "I've dug Commander Strykr out of a hole before." His grin widens like a Cheshire Cat. "He'll be fine, but he needs you."

"His team will be here soon. He needs them," I say, my voice hollow.

"Oh no, little mistress," Farok hisses. "It's definitely you."

He stops at what appears to be a dark hole in the wall and gestures for me to go inside. I can't hesitate now, even if it looks like a doorway into hell.

Because I can feel Strykr. Something resonates within me, like it did before. It's an emotion that's not mine.

His agony is blacker than the darkness that beckons. My heart curls in my chest, beating double time, as if my blood can heal him.

I step through the doorway, and I'm on the very top tier of an enormous pit. Below me are rows and rows of lizard men, dotted with the occasional cat man, not striped like Farok, looking more like lions to his tiger. They yell and scream at what's going on even farther below them.

Deep in the pit, the solid walls streaked with the filth of god knows what, five cat men surround Strykr, the sole Gryn in the entire place. His wings are outstretched, his torso is covered in blood. He wipes a hand that drips with gore over his mouth.

He is monstrous.

And he is mine.

Strykr

The Mochi are poorly trained and over enthusiastic fighters who are likely to get themselves killed.

Not by me. I only desire to finish this fight, get my Kat, and get out of this vrexing place.

If she'll forgive me for leaving her, for preferring to indulge myself than take care of her, I will take her back to the eyrie and build her the best nest Ustokos has ever seen.

I stand back, waiting for the Mochi to make the next move. Wondering if any of them will work out that if they disable my wings, they'll stand a better chance of leaving without a life changing injury. However, so far, they've only gotten a couple of clever blows in and are showing no signs of working together.

Typical Mochi.

As much as I should remain concentrated, my mind wanders to my mate. I can almost scent her, even in the dirt of the pit.

I can scent her! The thoughtbond fires to life, and her concern flows over me like a blanket of swirling fog.

"KAT!" I whirl on the spot, looking for her, terrified that she's in danger. The thoughtbond tells me otherwise. She is, no thanks to me, safe. But she can see me, and her mind is in turmoil.

The dratted Mochi take advantage of my distraction, and one of them launches onto me, sinking his claws into my flesh. I wrench him away, flinging him across the pit where he hits the wall and slides down, remaining unmoving on the filthy floor.

"Kat!" I call out again, beating hard to rise up out of the pit, well aware that if I get too high, I will forfeit.

"Strykr!"

My heart leaps into my mouth as I hear her voice. I want nothing more than to hold her in my arms until everything is all right again.

I look around at the remaining Mochi from my elevated position. None of these young kits need to be here. They're all looking to make names for themselves, and yet they can all make a difference on Ustokos by remaining part of their community and helping rebuild our ruined planet.

I have a lesson they can learn. It's one I should have paid heed to a long time ago.

With a flick of my wings, the first Mochi male is flat on his furry behind. The rest follow in quick succession. The crowd want blood, but I want no part of this.

Not anymore.

With all the Mochi sprawled out, I rise out of the pit, trying to pinpoint the one and only creature who is worth living for.

Who is worth fighting for.

Finally, I spot her, and it's as if everything has contracted around us both. She's tiny in comparison to her surroundings but just by her being here, for me, she fills my world.

I spin around the walls, flicking my wings as I head towards her. Knowing what it's like to have her in my arms is not the same as her being there, so when I land on the tiny platform, I'm not entirely sure what I should do.

I vrexed everything up between us. Although every part of me aches for her, I can't will my feet to reach her.

"*Eregri*, I..." My sentence isn't finished, and she's wrapped around me, her head buried in my wings. My arms are heavy as I take her, hold her, and marvel that she's prepared to take me back.

To give me another chance.

"I'm sorry." I drop my head into her fragrant hair. "I failed you. Can you ever forgive me?"

"Oh, Strykr." She sighs against me, her soft body molding to mine in a perfect symphony. "You had no choice, I understand that. I should have stopped you, somehow."

"I had every choice," I growl. "I could have chosen you and not the pull of the fight. I should have chosen you, and for that, I will always pay. Nothing, *nothing* ever matters to me more than you. You are the light in my darkness, sweet Kat."

Kat pulls away from me, eyes bright with unshed tears. "I need you, Strykr. I..." She hesitates. "I didn't understand what it was before, but I understand now. I understand that I love you."

Her head drops, and I feel her hot tears. I take her chin between my thumb and fingers, lifting it so that I can see her beautiful face.

"I want you by my side, always, my mate. I want us to have younglings together, many younglings. I want us to nest and mate and for everything to be just how you want it, however you want it."

She opens her mouth, and I drop a kiss onto it. She returns it, and I lose myself in her taste and scent, enclosing us with my wings so that the sound of the crowd is muffled, and it's just the two of us.

As much as I don't want to release her, to be apart in any way, I can't drown out the crowd any longer, and we must leave the pits before I'm forced to fight again.

"We have to go, Strykr," she pants. "There's a Kijg here called Grid. He told Sigid that he wants to drug you and take you somewhere. There are other lizard people here, ones that are not from Ustokos, and I think they want to take you off the planet. Also, there are humans, maybe the ones from the space station here too, and we have to find them!" Her breath is short as she rushes out the information.

"You've been busy, my Kat."

"I wasn't sure we'd get to you in time," she says, her hand on my chest as if she still can't quite believe that I'm with her.

"I'm pleased we did."

"We?"

"Your mate is very brave." Farok steps out of the shadows. He stares down into the pit as his fellow Mochi begin to rouse, staggering to their feet. "And you are an honorable warrior. You've no need for this pit."

A sigh fills my chest, rising from somewhere deep inside Ustokos as I look on my gorgeous mate. "I know that now. We came for information, and it appears that Kat has obtained that for me, while I was...otherwise engaged."

"If Grid doesn't get what he wants by way of his plan, he'll take it anyway, you know that. You and your mate need to get out of here. Get back to the lair, tell Jyr and Ryak what he's planning."

"What is he planning?" I narrow my eyes at the Mochi. "What else do you know?"

"There are humans on the ship we've seen," Farok says, staring down at his claws.

"Then we need to get to them," Kat says firmly.

My feathers prick with the boldness in her voice. She is truly an amazing being. After all she's been through, she still wants to ensure that everyone else is safe.

She is vrexing perfection. I can't take my eyes from her.

She is mine.

Kat

Strykr might be sticky and stink of, well I don't want to think about what he smells like, but he knows that I love him, and he's by my side.

And he left the fight for me. The bond between us is a glowing string of emotion, and I can see now how important it is. It's crystal clear, not fogged by his conflicting emotions. Or mine. It's as if we're as one. It's both lovely and very odd.

I still can't quite understand this whole psychic link thing. But then I'm on a fucking alien planet, surrounded by flying aliens, cat aliens, and lizard aliens. And robots.

It's a wonder I'm not running screaming through the night.

Well, it's not a wonder at all. It's all down to Strykr. My huge, damaged, and utterly, utterly devastatingly handsome alien warrior. Part angel, part monster. And all mine. Just having him around made all of this bizarre situation bearable.

He's doing his warrior thing, looming over Farok, but there's something wrong.

Behind us, the noise has increased. I look down into the

pit to see the Mochi cat men climbing on top of each other to get to the lip of the pit.

"Strykr!" I call out to get his attention and point down below.

"Vrexing Mochi!" he fires at Farok. "Never know when to quit." He takes my hand gently in his clawed one. "We need to find Grid before he finds us."

"We need to let the others know where we are," I say as I'm towed back through the dark doorway and into the dingy corridors.

Strykr grabs Farok by the scruff of his neck. "Weapons and my vectorpad."

"Sigid has them."

Strykr lets out a low growl, just as there is a large, loud explosion somewhere.

"Never mind, it looks like the team have found us." He grins at me before turning back to Farok.

"You took care of my mate, and for that, you have my thanks, but this is Gryn business now."

"I've no desire to get in a war with the Kijg or their friends, but whatever happens, Strykr, the Gryn and the Mochi are allies. Don't forget that."

Strykr snorts at him but releases his neck. Farok shakes his fur and gives Strykr a half-smile before he turns and heads back into the dark, tail flicking.

Two more explosions rock the walls, causing trickles of dust to fall on us.

Strykr grabs my hand, his excitement a thread of bright blue in my mind, untempered by the earlier darkness that came from him. There's something fresh within him. It's bloomed as the love between us has opened.

"Stay close to me, sweet *eregri*," he says, sweeping me to him for a kiss that causes my heart to thump hard in my chest.

"Always," I whisper when he lets me go.

We race down the corridors until we end up back in front of the door I recognize from earlier. A sharp kick from Strykr's boot, and it flies open. He walks in as if he owns the place and heads for his weapons that are piled on a small table to one side. There's no sign of Sigid, presumably the slimy lizard has fled.

"Are you sure you don't need something else after your fight, Commander?" I recognize the voice immediately as Grid steps into the doorway. "Some liquid refreshment perhaps?"

"Grid." Strykr lifts the laser and points it at the lizard. All he does is slip out a blue tongue, seemingly unperturbed. "My unit is here." He lifts his head, and as if they know, there's a rattle of short, sharp explosions. "And I believe you have some information I can use."

"The only thing I have for you, *Gryn*," he spits out the word, "is a one-way ticket off Ustokos. I have a contract to fulfill, and you are what they want."

"They?"

"My kin, the Drahon." Grid inspects his claws.

"And I guess they promised you control of Ustokos for your efforts in enslaving the species on your own planet," Strykr says, leaning back as he slides his dagger into his belt.

"Ustokos isn't my planet." Grid laughs nastily. "It's done. There's no coming back from what Proto did, but the Drahon find it fascinating, and they're prepared to pay good coin for Gryn warriors, for whatever reason. As far as I'm concerned, they can have it all, including you."

"Where are the humans?" I blurt out.

"Ah, yes." Grid's eyes glitter unpleasantly. "The Gryn and their found mates. Shame Proto took your females. Good thing it left you with a replacement species."

"You heard Kat—where are the humans? We know they

were on the space station." Strykr takes a step forward towards Grid, but the big lizard doesn't move.

"Same place I was going to take you. I still can. I don't even have to drug you if you'll come willingly." Grid's voice is obsequious, and I want to punch him. "Although you don't mind the narcotics, do you, *Commander*?"

"That's done now, Grid. Finished. As are the pits. I'm going to see to that." Strykr stands proud, and my heart swells for him. "But you *are* going to tell us where the humans are."

"I don't think so." Grid takes a swift step back, but there's a blinding light, and he crashes forward into the room.

"Vrex!" Strykr rushes over to the prone Kijg as Ayar's grinning face appears in the doorway. "I needed the vrexer alive!" he shouts.

"Don't blame me, Guv. That shot was all Jay's doing." Ayar is streaked with filth, probably even worse than Strykr, and I'm not sure I've seen him look happier. "I couldn't have made it with all the luck on Ustokos!"

Grid groans.

"Thank vrex," Strykr mutters and turns him over. A large wound runs with a green substance that I presume is blood. "Where are the humans?" He shakes the Kijg who moans with the pain. "If you want to live, you'll tell me, or I will leave you to Ayar who knows exactly what to do with vrexers like you who think enslaving any other species is a good thing."

Behind him, Ayar lets out a feral grunt, his grin disappearing and his face darkening. Fortunately, Vypr is behind him and puts a hand on his shoulder to distract him.

Grid's eyes dart to Ayar and back to Strykr. He lets out a theatrical groan, and I can't help myself. I give him a sharp kick in the ribs, and he howls.

"Where are the other humans?" I yell at him.

"Or," Strykr says, the corner of his mouth quirked up in amusement, "I could just let my mate deal with you."

He hands me the laser gun.

"You wouldn't," Grid gasps at me. "Humans are soft, pathetic creatures. You don't have it in you."

I slowly track the gun down his body, making sure his eyes are on me until it's pointing at the place I'm assuming he keeps his tiny lizard balls.

"Do you really want to take that chance?" I lower my voice, trying to make it growly like Strykr's, to the sounds of amusement in the doorway. "Punk!" I add with some force.

Grid just looks confused, and this makes me even madder.

"Where are the humans, you piece of shit!" I shake the laser at him, and it goes off in my hand, firing a bolt into the floor directly between Grid's legs.

He screams, high-pitched, as smoke rises. Strykr stamps on his chest to hold him down, grabbing at the gun before I drop it.

"Okay!" Grid squeals. "The humans are in a facility on the border between the Kijg and Mochi lands just to the north of here. That's where the Drahon are and where I was supposed to take you." He whines, twisting under the boot.

"Excellent shot, little mistress!" Jay calls from the doorway. I have an entire audience of warriors, all of whom are grinning their heads off.

I'm shaking as Strykr releases him and pulls me into his arms. "I could have killed him."

"You were trained by Jay, weren't you?" Strykr says, smiling at me. "That was the perfect shot."

"What are we going to do with this streak of gak?" Vypr toes Grid, who seems to be unconscious.

"He was here with two others, one of which looked different from them," I tell Strykr.

"I want to find out what they know, after I get the information I came for," he says, hand rubbing at his chin, feathers rattling as he looks at his team.

He strides across the room and up to a blank wall. For an instant, I think he's going to punch through it. Then he hits a small, raised tile, and a door that was almost invisible slides away.

"Out you come, Sigid. Time to collect my prize."

Strykr

"Don't hurt him, Strykr." My mate is at my side. "He helped me."

There's a whirring sound, and Ike flies into the room, followed by Syn. The little bot chatters Kat's name incessantly and whizzes around her with dizzying speed until it lands on her arm, a rainbow of lights and shining metal.

Sigid stares at the downed Grid. "What have you done? They'll come for him and this place too."

"I'm counting on it. Now, you said you'd help. I need to know what the Kijg are hiding. There's a control center that Proto was using for the planetary defense system. We've tracked it to this area, we know it's nearby, but you know exactly where it is."

Sigid doesn't take his eyes off Grid.

"They've been trying to destroy it, but so far, they've been unable to get in. It seems that you need a key, and Proto didn't leave one," Sigid says. "You'll find it under this building."

"It's under the pits? It's been here all this time?" Strykr grits his teeth and raises a fist. "You never thought to mention this?"

I can feel the heat radiating from him, the white anger rising inside him, raw and visceral.

"Guv?" It's Mylo. He leans on his large laser weapon. "What's going on?"

Strykr lowers his arm, taking in the interested expressions of his unit, his ire dissipating.

"I've been fighting in the pits for the last half a cycle," he says, hanging his head. "It's where I go, why I'm sometimes not around. I know it's forbidden, but I've been here on Ryak's orders. Mostly." Kat hovers in the back of my mind, her presence soothing. She wants me to be honest with my warriors. And with myself. "Some of the time, I was here because I couldn't help myself."

"We know, Guv," Vypr says, Ayar nodding beside him. "We've been keeping an eye on you."

"You have?" I say, taken aback. Next to me, Kat chuckles under her breath.

"You're our guv, Guv," Ayar says. "Of course we have. Someone had to look after you before you found your mate."

"Is this true?" The rest of my unit nod earnestly.

"We wouldn't have let you hurt yourself, Guv," Jay says, shouldering his laser rifle. "You've always been there for us when it mattered, and you've always taken the rap for anything stupid Ayar did."

"Hey!" Ayar fluffs himself up and is held back by Vypr.

"What this bunch of vrexers mean is that you'll always be our guv. We'd follow Ryak anywhere, but you're one of us," Mylo says. "And elite warriors stick together."

Kat lets out a soft sob. "That's the sweetest thing I've ever heard," she whispers.

I'm dumbstruck. All this time, I felt on the sidelines, working a mission I could tell no one about, my one relief coming when I was able to tell my mate, except I only ever felt that I was burdening her. All this time and they knew.

And they were all there for me. Just like Kat is here for me now.

I told you they were adorable. Kat's voice radiates down the thoughtbond. She is so incredibly happy for me, she thinks she's going to burst.

I clear my throat.

"We need to secure the defense system. Mylo and Syn with me," I order before I let sentimentality get the better of me. "Jay, secure that vrexer." I point to Grid. "Try to make sure he doesn't bleed out. Too much."

"Guv?" Ayar says hopefully.

"You and Vypr need to find Grid's *friends*." I look at Sigid. He might have provided me with information, even helped my mate, but he still let me fight and win for him in his terrible pits. "You know what they look like. Go with them," I tell him. "I don't want to make you, but I will."

"What's going to happen to all this, if your defense system is on top of it?" Sigid asks, his voice shaking slightly.

"We're going to burn it all down," Syn says, his voice clear in the room. "Aren't we, Guv?"

I look across the room at him and allow a grin to steal over my face. I always knew he was another Ayar, only he is far angrier and needs far more discipline.

And on this occasion, he also needs the opportunity to let loose with the explosives.

"That's exactly what we're going to do."

Kat sticks close to me as we head down into the depths of the pit. I'm hoping that the explosions generated by Ayar, and as it turns out, Syn too, have been enough to empty the place of its usual patrons and any other fighters.

Those who are foolhardy enough to remain will not enjoy encountering a unit of heavily armed Gryn.

"As soon as we've secured the defense system, we'll get Grid to take us to where the humans are being kept," I tell her, knowing how concerned she is. That much was clear by the way she nearly blew the Kijg's cock off.

I'd give anything to see the fire within her again. To know that she's no longer afraid, and she trusts me.

"I just hope we're in time," she says. "If they wanted you, something tells me the Drahon weren't intending on spending much longer on this planet."

"The system will stop them from leaving, once we get it online," Syn says as we reach the pit level. "Where the vrex is it?"

I walk into the pit, a place where I've wasted too much time indulging myself in something that was never meant to be part of me. Regardless of whether I was ordered to or not.

"Where's Ike?" I ask Kat. She slips her hand onto her shoulder, and the little bot appears on her arm.

"He's the key, isn't he?" she says quietly.

"You are both the key, my *eregri*. The goddess made sure I found both of you on that station."

She made sure I found my fate in you.

I allow the thought to drift down the bond, settle in Kat's mind, and calm her. I promised to protect her, and I will fulfill that with every part of my being.

"Ike." Kat addresses the bot. "Activate the defense system."

Kat

I'm not going to deny that I feel a little silly asking Ike to '*activate the defense system*' because it genuinely sounds like something from a science fiction movie, and, clearly, I'm far beyond science fiction and into science fact.

My silly feeling is compounded by the fact that everyone is watching me and that nothing is happening.

Ike's lights begin to flow over him in a pattern I've never seen before. He lifts off my arm and begins to circle the stinking pit. There's a loud cracking sound, and the floor beneath us shakes violently, throwing me off balance.

"What the vrex?" Strykr catches me and pulls me into his side, his wings flaring to keep himself upright, like the others.

Very slowly and with a loud scraping sound, the floor begins to drop, as if it's on some sort of elevator. The doorway we just walked through appears to rise in the wall.

"I don't think this was ever a stadium," I say out loud.

"Or fighting pits," Syn adds.

"Whatever the vrex this is, we're going down!" Jay says as the momentum seems to increase, and we begin to travel faster.

I'd be more concerned about falling farther down this pit if I wasn't with a group of flying aliens, but as the light above disappears, I can't help but be apprehensive. Strykr's strong presence beside me provides the anchor I need, and I can breathe easy.

The scraping sound increases, and a large opening appears, initially as a long slit, and as we continue to descend, it gets larger.

"What do we do, Guv?" Mylo calls across. Both he and Jay have their lasers at the ready.

"I suggest we make a jump for it. I've no desire to go any farther," Strykr says, gathering me into his arms.

As soon as the opening is wide enough, he leaps for it, huge wings beating and then folding up in a symphony of feathers as he pops through the doorway and lands easily on the other side, lowering me to the ground in one fluid, beautiful movement.

"What now?" I query as the rest of the team fly through.

"Syn?" Strykr calls across.

The big warrior works at his tablet device. "The schematics I have on here downloaded from the bot, they match. It's this way." He hurries ahead, feathers trailing.

"Guv!" There's a shout from out in the pit that sounds like Vypr.

"Go ahead," Strykr says. "We'll catch up." He hurries over to the doorway and pokes his head out. "Down here," he calls out.

In no time at all, both Vypr and Ayar thump down.

"We've got a problem, Guv," Vypr says, looking at me. "We found Grid's vrexing comrades, one of whom is most definitely not Kijg."

"Doesn't bleed the same." Ayar studies his claws, and Vypr sighs.

"The only problem is going to be if he's dead. Jyr will

want to question him, and I'm going to have a hard time explaining why the only other species ever to set foot on Ustokos is not breathing."

"He's still alive," Vypr says hastily as Ayar glowers. "The problem is that he's not alone. He told us that there are others, and they have multiple human captives. Apparently, these not-Kijg took the humans from their planet on behalf of Proto, and now they want them back."

"None of that seems to be a major problem. I presume you've found out where the humans are?" Strykr says.

"The problem is that if this particular not-Kijg doesn't return in the next hour with an unconscious Gryn, they're leaving the planet without him."

"Vrex!" Strykr fires out. "I've no idea how long it's going to take to get this defense system online." He turns to me, agony painted over his face.

"Guv!" Mylo appears. "Syn says he can get it up and running, but it's going to take a while."

"Longer than an hour?" I ask.

"Probably less, but you know tech." Mylo shrugs.

"We have to go and get them." I put my hands on Strykr's chest, looking up into his handsome, strong face. "If they leave this planet, god knows what sort of life they'll face. At least here, I know they can have a life. A good life if they want. I know saving them isn't your mission, but it has to be mine."

Strykr looks around at his warriors and then back at me.

"I want to save the humans," Mylo says.

"And me," Vypr adds. "He'll do anything as long as he gets to blow gak up." He pokes Ayar in the arm.

Ayar grins with a hint of madness behind his eyes.

"Where are they?" Strykr asks.

"About ten minutes' flight directly north of here. There's a canyon where they've been hiding their spacecraft," Ayar replies.

"That's inside Gryn territory!"

"As is this place. Now," Vypr adds. "Sigid agreed."

Jay and Mylo return, and Strykr lifts me off my feet. "I would leave you here with Syn, it's the safest place, but I can't imagine that these humans will be keen to come with us any more than they want to stay with the Drahon," he murmurs in my ear.

I can feel the beat of his heart in time to my own.

"I want to be wherever you are. I trust you." I throw my arms around his neck.

Strykr strides to the entrance, and with an easy beat of his wings, he's in the air. As we climb, Mylo shoots past us, raising his gun. He blasts a hole in the ceiling of the pit and daylight, such as it is on Ustokos, pours in. Strykr surges upwards, head shaking as we dodge the debris, and we're out into the light.

I gulp in a breath of air as he sets his wings.

"Good riddance," I mutter as the decrepit building disappears in the distance and I enjoy the warmth from Strykr's body.

"My *eregri*." Strykr nuzzles at my ear. "You saved me from it all."

"I didn't do anything."

"You stayed, and you fought on your own terms. That was enough. And now you fight for those you don't even know. I cannot wait to get you to my nest again." The picture that fills my mind is utterly dirty and more than enough to have my core clenching around nothing.

"Strykr!" I admonish him.

"I can't help it, my gorgeous mate." The dark fight has left him. All that remains is the white heat of our passion and the goodness of his mission to save my fellow humans and protect his planet. "With you at my side, I have everything I need."

Strykr

The last thing I wanted to do was leave Syn on his own. The team should never split up, but if we don't get to the Drahon and the humans before they blast off, the only other hope is that Syn gets the defenses online, and that will force them back down to the planet's surface.

At least that's what I'm hoping as we fly on towards the area where we've been told we'll find the humans. My blood sings with joy that I have my mate in my arms and I'm heading for a fight with a brand new species.

One that might perhaps provide me with a challenge.

Mylo comes alongside me, and I motion that he and the others are to perform the usual circuit once we reach our destination. I might not have the thoughtbond that the other seniors possess with each other, but my unit understand me. More than I knew.

All the time I was sneaking around, hiding my injuries beneath armor I claimed was for sparring, they were looking out for me.

I look at my mate in my arms. Kat has set her chin, her eyes scanning the ground below us with intent. I feel her emotions down our thoughtbond. She's scared, but there's a strong steel thread of determination that runs through her.

The determination that meant she didn't give up on the space station, and she didn't give up on me.

My love, we will save them.

I push my words down the bond, hoping that she understands. Her blue eyes meet mine, and for an instant, I'm lost, pulled under by how beautiful she is.

My chest catches. I want to see her swell with my youngling. To always have her plump and happy in my nest.

Kat's hand brushes over my cheek.

When this is over, I'm yours, always.

The words tumble in my mind, and I'm delighted that our bond is so strong. But then, why would it not be? She is a strong, brave female, and I am a male with a unit that will always have my wings.

The ground yawns open in front of us as the canyon appears, and I dodge down low so we can remain undetected. Ahead of me, the others also follow the same tactic, and they merge into the dark, dusty landscape, feathers only a blur, before we reach the edge. I drop down and land as softly as I can, placing Kat on her feet.

"What now?" she whispers unnecessarily.

"We need to check out what we're up against."

Kat narrows her eyes and looks around for the others.

"They know what to do once we've recced the area and the Drahon."

She doesn't look entirely convinced, but I head towards the edge of the canyon.

"Wow, a proper spaceship," Kat exclaims.

"What do you mean?" I look down into the canyon. Inside is a long, silver, bulbous craft sitting on three legs with a long ramp that runs down from one side.

"That's what a spaceship is supposed to look like," she

says, as if presenting a fact. "Not the thing that you have. That looks like it's being held together by rust and string."

"When it comes to space craft, we take what we can get," I huff at her. Although, I have to admit, the craft below us is impressive. It would make a great addition to our, admittedly lacking, space fleet. Providing I can capture it.

"Sorry, Strykr." Kat's warm, tiny hand is on my chest. "I was brought up on science fiction movies." I frown at the unfamiliar term that doesn't quite translate. "It means when you're abducted by aliens, you expect ray guns, spaceships, and, well, not a dystopian landscape with little to no tech and ships which look like they wouldn't last more than five minutes."

"And what about Gryn males?" I wrap my arms around her. "Ones who want to claim your body for their own. Who will love you until the end of time?"

She laughs, and the sound is the only reason I will fight today. "A delicious, feathery, fluffy male? One like you, perhaps? You were far more than I bargained for." She pushes her hands into my wings, and I soar to new heights of ecstasy.

Jay thumps down beside us, causing me to growl and the spell between me and Kat to break.

"They don't look like they're getting ready to leave, Guv. We've still got time." He lifts his rifle and checks down the scope that enhances his already eerily accurate sight.

"How many bodies?" I ask him.

"I count five. They look like bigger Kijg, only without the colors," Jay replies after a short pause.

"Lizard men." Kat snorts. "I'm sure it was those bastards that abducted me in the first place."

"I want that ship, Jay. It will be a good prize to take back to the Prime, and the Drahon deserve to be divested of it." I smile at my mate as I raise my eyebrows at Jay.

"If they are the ones who've been taking Gryn or any other

species as slaves, they deserve to be divested of life." Jay growls, and both Kat and I look at him.

The usually mild-mannered sniper actually growled. I'm not sure I've ever heard him do anything of the kind before. His feathers are pricked up, and he looks much larger than normal.

"Okay, then," Kat says, slowly moving her eyes away from the suddenly feral Jay. "What do we do now?"

"I'm going to get the others. We'll head down there to get access to the ship. You stay here with Jay." Kat blinks at me. "He's going to pick off any stragglers, given that's what he wants to do." I shrug at her. "Once it's safe, he'll bring you down."

"I'll look after the little mistress," Jay says, his eyes not leaving the ship.

Of that, I have no doubt at all.

"It's time." I pluck a kiss from Kat's lips. "You know I won't be long," I tell her, cupping her little chin in my hand and making sure I've etched her beautiful face on my mind.

Every atom of my being aches to be in the fight. I take off, circling low around the canyon in order to gather the rest of my unit. At my command, they form up behind me, and we dive over the edge of the canyon, hugging the stone contours as we all power towards the ship.

This will end today. My mate will get her humans, and I will get her into my nest. Whatever these Drahon are, they've never gone up against an elite Gryn unit before.

And it will be their undoing.

Kat

I watch as Strykr gathers the rest of his unit, and they power down into the canyon, looking for all the world like a squadron of fighter jets, their gunmetal gray feathers imposing as they descend towards the ground.

Jay remains incredibly still next to me, as if he's become a stone statue. He watches as the unit reaches the canyon floor before continuing at a heart-stoppingly low level towards the ship. When they are about halfway, he lets rip with a single shot that sizzles over the skin of the vehicle, and the five Drahon spin towards it, pulling at their own weapons.

By the time they realize they've been duped, it's too late. The Gryn are upon them, slamming each one into the ground with a minimum of fuss.

"Mistress?" Jay turns to me, attempting a smile. "We need to go."

"Is everything okay?" I ask him. "You seem on edge."

"There's something." He shakes his head as if trying to clear it. "I'm not sure, mistress." His dark eyes seem even darker than usual, and it's clear he's struggling to process the situation.

Jay is as formidable a warrior as they all are, but in this new dark mode, he's a force to be reckoned with.

He stands and shoulders his weapon. "If you don't mind holding onto me, mistress," he says shyly.

I put my arms around his neck, and once he's sure he has a firm hold on me but not anywhere he obviously deems inappropriate, he lifts off the ground.

Unlike flying with Strykr, I squeeze my eyes closed. It's not that I don't trust Jay, it's just that he's not Strykr, and every part of me wants to be by his side again.

My bones shake as we touch down, and I open my eyes again to a group of males, wings held high, feathers pricked. They look every inch predators. Strykr prowls towards me, and I feel, rather than see, Jay back away.

"You are my prey." He growls low in my ear as he presses himself against me, all hard muscle and cinnamon spice scent. "But you don't get to run here."

He is aroused by the fight, by his blood being high, by seeing me in the arms of another male, and it seeps into me.

"Jay, get rid of these." Strykr points at the bodies surrounding him. "The rest of you, with me."

We walk up the ramp towards the open hole in the side of the ship.

"There's something not right about this," I murmur as we enter.

Inside, it's brightly lit but completely silent.

"I'd have expected more of the Drahon," Mylo says quietly.

"How many did the one at the pits say were here?" Strykr rounds on Vypr who is attempting to coax Ayar inside.

"He didn't, Guv. But I got the impression there were more than five."

"There is something wrong here. This ship is empty!"

Strykr whirls towards the doorway. "Syn!" he calls out. "Vrex it! We have to get back!"

He grabs me and pulls me back outside the ship. "Jay, Mylo, stay here, search the ship, secure it. We're going for Syn."

With that, he grabs me, and we're in the air.

"We've been played!" He growls in my ear. "Sigid. That slimy, cold-blooded bastid!"

"If that's the case, he fooled me too. I was sure he was on our side."

"No Kijg is ever trustworthy, and I was a fool to think he could be," Strykr growls. "And I've just given him the one thing he and his foul kin want. A Gryn warrior."

Our thoughtbond is stretched out, hard and unyielding. I want to comfort him, but he's not prepared to take that comfort. He feels failure as keenly as any other wound.

In the air, he speeds up in a way he never has before. I check behind but Ayar and Vypr are having no trouble keeping up with us. They look as grim as Strykr feels to me, anxious to get to their comrade.

As we head back towards the stadium, another one of the elliptical spaceships hovers over the edge, a long ramp running to the top of the building.

Strykr slows and turns in a tight circle as Ayar and Vypr join him.

"Weapons check?" he calls out.

"I've all the vrexing weapons I vrexing need!" Ayar bellows back. "Let's get these vrexing Kijg!"

Without warning, he flips over and, pumping his wings, he's flying directly at the spaceship, lifting his huge laser and firing.

"Nisis be vrexed!" Vypr cries out. "What's the vrexing plan, Guv?"

I can already tell that any intentions on the part of Strykr for this attack to be coordinated flew away with Ayar.

"Get in, get Syn, drop the explosive charges, and get the vrex out. If you can collect Ayar on your way, I would be most obliged," he says through gritted teeth.

Vypr flies ahead.

"My beautiful mate." Strykr butts his forehead against mine. "I cannot take you into this fight."

"But what if the humans are in there, too? What if Sigid was lying about that? We can't let the Drahon get away with any of this. We have to show them Ustokos doesn't belong to them," I fire out.

Strykr's dark eyes glitter with menace and delight.

"My brave, perfect little prey. I hoped you'd say that."

Strykr

I can't be parted from the fight, no matter what I do. I might not be Ayar, with his messed up head and desire to throw himself into the path of any danger, but I can't resist the heat of the battle.

Especially with my *eregri* at my side. I redouble my efforts to catch up with Ayar before the vrexer does himself an injury he can't recover from this time, and I'm able to give him a thump from behind with my wing, which momentarily stops him from firing his weapon at the spaceship, where it's having zero effect.

"The fight's down there!" I shout at him before diving towards the now ruined roof of the pit.

A couple of laser shots zip past us, but we dodge them easily, and I fold up my wings to dive right in.

"Gryn warriors!" a voice booms around us, artificially enhanced. "You are surrounded. Land and surrender."

"Are we going to do that?" Kat squeaks.

"We're going to land," I reply, making sure that my thoughtbond remains calm. "And they are going to die."

Below us, I've spotted Syn, on his knees, wings pinned out and wrists bound. I know that I will revisit any injury perpetrated on my fellow Gryn twice as hard once I find out exactly who did it.

Surrounding Syn are several large creatures, not quite Kijg, not quite something else. All of them sport a green scaly skin and are heavier set. They hold weapons I don't recognize, but the way they hold them? They have no idea how to use them, not in a way that will deal with a Gryn.

I hit the ground hard, making sure to cushion Kat from the blow, and I'm rewarded by the thumps of Ayar and Vypr behind me. I gently lower Kat to her feet and push her behind my wings as I gaze around at the scene in front of me.

"Where's Sigid?" I snarl. He's going to be first, one hundred percent he is going to pay for his betrayal of our planet.

"You're in no position to make demands, Gryn. We required one for our purposes, but now we have four and another human female to add to our haul." The largest of the Drahon stares me down. "You will drop your weapons and submit to be collared. Or this one dies."

"What makes you think we care if he dies?" I say, feathers itching with the desire to kill something.

The Drahon leader coughs out a laugh. "We've been training Gryn for a very long time. You can be made to do almost anything with the right incentive. One of those incentives is your honor."

One of the smaller Drahon stabs a white pole into Syn's wing, and he howls with pain, his head thrown back. Kat hisses in horror next to me. Her pulse pounds in my ears, the bond between us tinged with bladder-loosening fear.

She's been brave, and I've brought her somewhere that has taken that from her.

She shouldn't be here.

She shouldn't be in danger.

She shouldn't witness any of this.

My heart slows almost to a standstill as I shut down the thoughtbond, knowing what I have to do next.

I promised her I would keep her safe.

"If you don't submit, you all die," the Drahon leader snarls at me.

I should fight. Fighting is what I do. It's all I know.

A hand curls into mine, small and perfect. Its heat flows through me, breaking down the walls.

"No. Nobody dies. You will leave this planet and never come back."

"We have your warrior, *Commander*." The Drahon sneers. "Someone's going to get hurt if you don't comply."

I step forward. "Then collar me. Let them all go. And leave."

"No!" Kat screams out. "Strykr! No!"

I take another step towards the Drahon, noting Syn is still upright and hoping that either Vypr or Ayar has the good sense to take hold of Kat.

The Drahon inclines his head, looking just like a Kijg calculating profit. They may be armed, but they know they're no match for three free Gryn warriors, just like a Kijg would.

"Very well," he says. "No tricks."

"No tricks."

Kat screams as Syn is released and a collar is placed around my neck. I feel it nestling into my skin in an unpleasant slimy movement.

"Do not worry, my *eregri*," I tell her. "I promised you I would protect you, and this is my promise."

She howls, and Ayar holds her to him. "Take care of her." I nod. "I will never be far from her heart."

"This is true, Commander," Ayar responds. "In all the stars, you will shine brightly."

"In all the stars, I will," I repeat.

"Come, Gryn." The Drahon clicks his claws together, and the collar sends a spike of pain down my spine. I freeze and stumble as he hisses a laugh. "You'll get used to it."

Kat

I fight against Vypr who holds me tightly with one arm, the other grasped around Ayar's wing.

"No! We can't let them take him!" I'm screaming and I hate it. I should be strong for my mate, my Strykr, but the old terror is rising within me.

Without him I am...just Kat.

"Hold, mistress," Vypr whispers in my ear. "Hold. The Guv knows what he's doing."

"He's giving himself to their slavery." I wriggle and fight with everything I have, but I'm no match for any Gryn warrior.

Strykr reaches the top of the ramp and stumbles again as he's shoved inside.

I hear a long, keening cry rending the air, and it takes half a second to realize that it's coming from me. The ramp folds, drawing up into the ship.

"I can't..." I finally rip myself from Vypr and run, uselessly, towards the distant ramp as, with a wop-wop sound that I feel rather than hear, the ship lifts farther into the air.

"Mistress." Syn is beside me. His wings are drooping from

where they were pinned. Blood runs from a cut on his forehead, and his whole left side is badly bruised. "Please. This is all part of the plan."

"There's no plan!" I wail, my mind unable to comprehend being cut off from Strykr. "They've taken him. We have to get him back."

"The Guv allowed himself to be taken," Ayar growls. He, too, is freed from Vypr's grasp, and although he doesn't look happy, pacing back and forward, for once, he's not attempting to blow something up. He has a handle on his emotions, only just, but it's there.

Unlike me. I want to rip something apart, anything. I want to burn the whole of Ustokos. Whatever disgusting planet that the Drahon are from, I'd burn the whole galaxy to get to my Strykr.

"He had no choice," I growl out.

Three pairs of eyes are on me. Dark, quizzical eyes.

"You think the Guv would give up so easily?" Vypr asks.

"You think he'd walk away from the fight?" Ayar stills for a second.

"I..." My word stutters out, my comprehension of the situation ebbing. "Then what?"

"Standard Gryn playbook. Make sure those who are in the strongest position remain behind," Syn says, so matter-of-factly it's almost as if he's bored.

"What?"

"The Guv can't fly a spaceship, even if he thinks he's the cleverest vrexer this side of the lair." Vypr laughs. "But Syn can. And he has the defense system. He took a chance that the Drahon are like the Kijg and have a flair for self-preservation."

"Vypr's right. We've got another ship at our disposal now." Syn looks over at Vypr. "I presume?" He raises his eyebrows, and Vypr grins at him.

"And I've got this!" Ayar fingers his enormous laser

cannon lovingly. "And I'm going to use it on those vrexers." He growls, his face darkening.

"Is this...right?" I stare at Syn. The disheveled but unbowed warrior reaches into his pants and pulls out a small tablet, about the size of a mobile phone, very different from the ones I've seen the Gryn with.

"No one searches their prisoners anymore," Syn mock grumbles as he smiles at me. "This is the remote for the defense system. We do need to get close to the atmosphere to use it, and I hear you might have a spaceship for that."

"Surely," I point up at the sky, "they didn't leave thinking you could activate the system?"

"No, they have what they think is the remote. Why else would they just leave us without repercussions?" Syn replies.

"But you have the remote?" I feel stupid and dull. My entire body aches to be with Strykr. Our thoughtbond is cut, and I hadn't realized how much it meant to me to feel him in my head.

"They have my old vector pad," Syn says as he checks over the small device in his hand. "And a recipe for maraha stew."

Ayar barks out a laugh. And then another. All three of us stare at him as he doubles over in mirth.

"Maraha stew!" he says through streaming eyes.

"Okay, then." I look between Syn and Vypr with raised eyebrows. "So, what is the plan?"

I have to trust Strykr believes in his team, he knows what he's doing, and he wouldn't ever do anything that would hurt me.

Even though I am hurting. I thought I'd hurt before. I thought that when my world imploded on Earth it was bad enough, but being ripped away from him like this...

I fight back the tears. I have to be strong for him. I have to share his belief in his team.

"The plan is to get up there and blast them out of the sky!" Ayar snarls, unfurling his wings.

"Dear Nisis!" Syn growls. "Is he always like this?" he fires at Vypr. "Stupid vrexer! What the vrex is wrong with you? The Guv's on that ship!"

Ayar turns on him, lips raised in a vicious snarl, and he leaps for the injured Syn who can't get out of the way. Vypr shoulders the livid warrior, managing to knock his trajectory off so he sails past his intended target.

Instead, he turns on Syn.

"You don't ever call him that. Not ever." Vypr's voice is low, menacing, and his claws are unsheathed. "You don't know anything about us." He steps forward, every element of him bristling at Syn, who is in more danger than he ever was from Ayar.

"Please!" I push my way between the two males, staring up at the rapidly retreating ship. "We don't have time for this. If they get off Ustokos, we've lost Strykr," I plead.

Vypr huffs out a hot breath, his anger almost crackling across his skin. "This vrexer has been getting at Ayar since he arrived," he mutters. "It's time he was taught a lesson."

I look at him, then at Syn who, despite his battered body, looks like he wants to kill Vypr.

This is the last thing I need, the last thing that Strykr needs, but I'm a tiny female stuck between three powerful males who are just about to rip each other to shreds.

A spike of emotion flows through me. Bright red, almost like blood. I grab at my head. It's Strykr, and they are hurting him. As swiftly as I feel it, it's gone, and I am alone.

Incredibly, horribly alone.

Ayar growls, and it brings me to my senses.

"No fighting!" I fire out, aware that my voice is high-pitched but unable to help myself. "Strykr needs us. He needs you. You're no good to him if you're fighting amongst yourselves!" I'm aware that my hands are on my hips as I berate the three enormous males.

Who are now looking very contrite.

"Sorry, mistress," Vypr says, eyes downcast.

I'm aware that Ayar is by my side, his somewhat musky smelling feathers fluttering in the slight breeze down in the pit. He has a look of complete and utter sadness on his face. Vypr puts an arm around his shoulders. Ayar lifts his hand to me, unsure what to do to comfort me.

"We're both sorry," Vypr adds, and Ayar nods, unable to speak. "This is not the time for our petty quarrels."

"You're a unit. His unit. You are his elite, and he's counting on you," I say, trying desperately to keep the tears from my voice. All I want is to get to Strykr.

"He needs you." Ayar's voice is gravelly. He puts a hand against his head, eyes squeezed shut as if he's in pain. "We'll get you to him, mistress. No more fighting, I promise."

When he opens his eyes, I see the purity of the male that Ayar once was. The male Vypr clearly sees.

"Mistress?" Syn approaches me, almost shyly, and holds out something silver.

"Ike!" The little robot bleeps at me and whirls his way around Syn's thick wrist and clawed hand to get to me. "Thank you for keeping him in one piece," I breathe out at the big warrior.

At the corner of his mouth, there is a hint of a smile. "I thought he might bring you comfort, mistress, until we can get you back to your mate. Because that's the plan."

"The only plan," Vypr grinds out.

"What the vrex are we waiting for?" Ayar thunders, shouldering his laser cannon.

"I'm with Ayar," I announce to grins from the other two warriors. "Let's go get Strykr!"

"We'll need to get back to the other ship," Syn says with a wince.

"You're not flying anywhere." Vypr looks him up and down. "You're vrexed."

"I've no vrexing option, have I? I'm the only one who can fly that ship." He stares up at the space vacated by the Drahon. "You're not carrying me."

Vypr folds his arms, cocking his head to one side. "I'm not," he says evenly, watching as Ayar shifts his weapons around. Without any warning, he scoops Syn up. "He is." He grins as Syn snarls out.

Ayar beats his wings, and he's in the air with a wriggling warrior in his arms.

"Mistress." Vypr gives me a short bow. "I know that the Guv won't like my scent on you much, but if you'll do me the honor of flying with me." He holds out his hand like an old-fashioned gentleman.

His gesture makes me want to cry. Tears prick the back of my eyes. I can't show weakness, even if I want to. Strykr needs me. He needs all of his warriors to rally for him.

And we have to save him.

Strykr

The largest Drahon pokes me in my back with the barrel end of his weapon as we enter the ship. "Move, Gryn!" he snarls, unnecessarily.

These males are all cowards and without honor. If they had any ability, they would not rely on their tech including the collar around my neck. They are just larger versions of the Kijg, and just as slippery.

"Vrex off!" I turn on him, and immediately, a shock fires down my spine.

Again, I feign that it hurts more than it does, although it is incredibly painful.

"Shut the zark up, Gryn. You really don't want to make this harder on yourself. You'll have plenty of that later." He laughs nastily.

"What are we going to do with him?" one of the smaller Drahon asks.

"He's been rutting with that human female," the larger one says with a sniff. "Put him in with the other three, see if he'll rut with them. If he impregnates one or both, they'll be worth more with a Gryn hybrid in their womb."

I want to rip his head from his body.

"What about the other one?" the smaller Drahon says, his voice wavering.

"It's contained, isn't it? They won't rip each other to pieces. Gryn aren't like that, about their own kind anyway." The larger Drahon bares his needle sharp teeth at the smaller.

"I am here, you know." I sigh at them. "I do understand you."

My observation is rewarded with another crippling jolt.

"Don't like it, Gryn? Then comply."

I'm booted forward as, for just a second, I catch the thoughtbond. My mate, my sweet Kat, is entirely concentrated on me. Her bravery shines, a beacon in my darkness.

"I'm complying, Drahon," I reply, marching forward with my head and wings held high.

How these creatures ended up so rich in tech is beyond me. They are hopelessly stupid. Now I know that the humans are on this ship and that there is at least one other Gryn who will aid me.

They think treating me like maraha will benefit them.

They are wrong.

I'm shoved and kicked through the ship by a couple of smaller Drahon who wave the collar controller around like it will protect them. As much as I want to end them, I hold onto my temper and put my trust in my unit. They know what needs to be done.

I hope to vrex they do.

One of the Drahon presses his green hand to a pad on the side of a door, and as it slides open, I'm shoved through.

"What about these?" I hold up my bound wrists.

"You don't need free hands to rut, Gryn," one of them sneers. "Just sit one of the females on your lap. She'll either stay on or fall off." He grabs at his crotch in an obscene gesture, and the door slides closed as I snarl at the collar controller being held in his hand.

Behind me, there is a slight squeaking sound. I turn around to see an entirely empty room, save for two doorways and three makeshift beds on the floor. In the far corner, there are two human females clutching each other. Eyes wide, they tremble at the sight of me. Both wear tiny shifts that look like they were once white. One of them has long hair, like my *eregri,* only it's a yellow color. The other has short hair that's in a strange shade of burning orange.

"I'm Commander Strykr, of the Elite Legion of the Gryn." I stride towards them both. "I'm here to rescue you."

The female with the long hair buries her head in the shoulder of the other with a muffled cry of fear.

"I won't hurt you." I stretch out a hand. The short-haired female stares at it as if I'm holding maraha gak, a look of defiance on her face.

"We heard what the croc-guy said about rutting," she spits out. "We're not doing anything of the kind with you!"

From one of the darkened doorways, there is a low, feral growl. The orange-haired female shoots a glance at it. "You don't want to piss him off," she says.

"I am here to rescue you," I say, trying to remain as unthreatening as possible, given the long-haired female seems terrified. "I have a mate, a human mate. I don't want to mate... rut...you. I won't."

The growl is even louder.

"Is that another Gryn warrior, like me?" I query, shaking out my feathers.

"He's another one of you." The female with the short hair barks out a laugh. "But I wouldn't go in there if I were you. The only one he responds to is Jen. Even the croc-guys don't go in."

I sidestep towards the doorway. It's very dark inside, and

the growling doesn't stop. My eyes adjust quickly, and I see there's a crouched figure, Gryn sized, in one corner.

Something hits me on the back of my head, and I stumble away. The blow comes again and, as I go down onto my knees, I see a third female, her black hair flying as she leaps back from me, a large water container in one hand.

"Wait" I reach out, but darkness is descending. "I'm not your enemy."

"You aliens are all our enemy," the female with the orange hair hisses as my consciousness deserts me.

A DEEP, CHUCKLING GROWL VIBRATES THROUGH ME. The scent of blood and unwashed feathers invades my nostrils. Given that I was just dreaming of holding my *eregri* in my arms, it's an unwelcome awakening.

I'm in the dark room, sprawled on the floor. Out in the light, I hear low voices.

"How long have you been here, brother?" I ask, sitting up and holding my head. "Did the humans strike you as well?"

I'm not prepared for the snarling wall of feathers and claws that hits me, chains jingling as he rips at my skin.

"It's not the humans you need to worry about." His words are hoarse. His eyes glitter with a madness I've never seen before, even during my time in the camps. Even in Ayar, despite how we found him and the headaches he suffers from.

This male has been in torture for so long, his mind is lost.

But he's also chained and weakened from his confinement. A ball of anger sits in my stomach, but I hold it back. Shoving at him, making sure not to injure him, I wrestle loose and move towards the door as he lets loose with a shower of obscenities punctuated by a feral roar.

"No!" a feminine voice cries out. "Don't hurt him. He can't help it!"

I whirl around, on my feet with my back to the wall, in case these females want to hit me again. "He's fine. I didn't touch him!" I hold up my hands.

Four pairs of eyes stare at me with undisguised disapproval.

"Don't hurt the monster in the cupboard," the female with the short hair says. "Or we'll set Jen on you."

I slide down the wall, hitting the floor with my ass and huffing out a long breath.

"Honestly, I'm not here to hurt you or rut with you. I really am supposed to be rescuing you."

The female with the long black hair looks around at the others. "He hasn't hurt us, and he's in much better shape than Huntr," she says slowly. "If he wanted to do anything, he would have as soon as he got in here."

"It was your idea to hit him!" the short-haired female chokes out. "Now you want to trust him?"

All three females look strained.

"I promise, I'm here to rescue you, and my unit is coming. My mate is with them. She can explain everything to you." A loud cackle comes from behind me in the dark room. "What other choice do you have?" I add.

The females look at each other.

"I'm Diana," the female with the short hair says. "That's Jen." She points out the female with the black hair who hit me. "And that's Robin." She jerks her thumb at the frightened female with the yellow hair

"I'm pleased to meet you," I say, the phrase my *eregri* taught us what seems like a lifetime ago coming back to me. I hold out my hand to Diana.

She stares at it for an instant, then takes it, slowly shaking it up and down.

"I think he really has had contact with humans!" she says over her shoulder, the first hint of a smile appearing. "British ones, given how polite he is."

"My mate has me well-trained." I risk a wry smile. "Now, if we're going to make the best of this rescue, I'm going to need your help." A low rolling growl comes from the other room. "Yours too, Huntr. If you want to help the females."

Kat

I'm not sure I've ever flown so fast, even with Strykr. The urgency instilled in Ayar and Vypr sees them pushing themselves to the very limit.

I have to admit that, even with the seriousness of the situation, the look on Syn's face as Ayar picked him up was priceless. One of the many occasions in the last whirlwind of days where I wish I'd had a camera.

Ike curls around my neck, clinging on tightly, and I concentrate on his metallic warmth in order not to think too much about that spike of pain I felt from Strykr. Fortunately, it's not long before the other ship comes into view, and we descend rapidly.

Jay and Mylo rise from their seated positions on the ramp. Mylo grins widely when he sees Syn in Ayar's arms, although that smile drops a little when he sees the warrior's injuries.

"Wondered when you vrexers would get here," Jay says. "What's with the other ship taking off and where's the Guv?"

"He's on the ship, and we need to get after him," I say as Vypr puts me on my feet, and I stride past them up the ramp.

On board, Syn hurries ahead of me, seeming to know

where he's going. Behind me, the rest of the unit follow, feathers slicked back. They are all on high alert.

The spaceship is similar in many ways to the space station I was stuck on. All white and silver corridors that twist and turn until finally a door opens in front of Syn, and he steps through.

Into something straight out of a science fiction movie.

Consoles everywhere light up with flickering, colored lights. A huge screen fills one wall, showing a view of the canyon wall.

"Are you sure you can fly this thing?" Mylo says to Syn as he demonstrates that he knows *exactly* what he's doing.

"We have to get to the other ship before it reaches the higher atmosphere. I've already activated the defense system, but I don't know if it's fully functional yet as the Drahon didn't give me time," Syn replies as he works hard, and outside, I see we've risen out of the canyon.

"What are we going to do when we catch it?" I ask.

"We're going to board with extreme prejudice." Ayar snarls, his laser cannon rattling. "The vrexing Drahon are going to pay for taking the Guv."

"What Ayar said." Jay rattles his feathers next to the huge warrior.

Ahead, in the viewer, the other Drahon ship looms larger. I look around the warriors. All of their attention is concentrated on the screen. They are a group of predators who have one aim, and it's not prey. It's getting their boss back.

A bright light appears ahead.

"Brace!" Syn calls out, and the entire ship lurches to the left, but it's not far enough, and the entire structure shudders as the light fills the screen.

"Vrex!" Vypr calls out. "We need to return fire!"

"Too late. That one knocked out the weapons on this flying heap of gak," Syn says through gritted teeth.

"How do we get out?" Ayar paces, wings raised. "I need to get out." He looks at Vypr.

"We need to get out." Vypr grins at the others. "We have all the weapons we need."

"Head back to where we got on, and I'll create a platform for you," Syn says. "Try not to shoot it down. The Guv is on board, after all."

Ayar and Vypr scramble to leave, quickly followed by Mylo and Jay.

"What are we going to do?" I ask Syn as silence descends.

I wish I could feel Strykr again. The thoughtbond seemed freaky to start with, but now, without it, there's a part of me missing. A big, burly predator part that has somehow gotten under my skin, past my defenses, and has made me braver than I ever thought possible.

"We're going to need to get as close to the other ship as possible, stop it from getting any higher," Syn says. "We'll have to leave the rest to the trigger-happy," he says with a laugh. "Ayar has his uses. As does the Guv."

"Oh!" My hand flies to my head. The thoughtbond has fired to life, and this time, there's no pain. Only pure, unadulterated joy. "He's free!" I call out with delight that I can't hold back. "And he's coming for me."

"Let's hope he's going to take the Drahon ship first," Syn says grimly. "Incoming."

Another bright flash fills the screen. I grab hold of a console, but the hit I was expecting doesn't come. Instead, there's an explosion that we zip through.

"Ayar?" I look at Syn who is working frantically on the console in front of him.

"Ayar," Syn says. "Vrex!"

I see it just as he swears, the laser bolt that hits the other ship, forcing it to drop.

"No!" I cry out. "Strykr."

I turn, running as fast as I can back through the ship. I have to stop the others from shooting if Strykr is to have any chance at all.

Because I've had a taste of what it's like to have my heart so full, I might just burst with the love you hold for another. And I know all too well how awful it is to have a heart empty of anything other than my own sorrow.

I'm never going back to being that person. I want Strykr in my life, I want my heart full, and I want to be the best I can be.

Strykr

Getting the vrexing collar off was not something I ever want to repeat. Either fortunately or unfortunately, Huntr had no qualms about hurting me once I'd released him, and he ripped it away as it attempted to shock us both senseless.

Without the control they thought they had over us, the Drahon put up little fight as we make our way through the ship. Behind me, the human females huddle together, with Huntr taking up the rear, laughing maniacally as he lets loose the laser weapon I reluctantly gave him after we overpowered our Drahon guards.

"We have to get to the control center of this ship. Someone tell Huntr to stop trying to blast holes in it," I shout over my shoulder, downing a couple of Drahon.

"Why do we need to get there?" Diana asks me. She's the boldest of the three humans. "Are you taking us back to Earth?"

"I have to get a message to my unit. They should have the other ship by now," I say, ignoring her question about her planet. There will be time for that later.

A Drahon sticks his head out of a doorway, and I grab him, sinking my claws into his scaly skin as he screams in pain. "Where is the control center of this ship?" I hiss in his ear.

"Up ahead." He whimpers.

"Show me," I snarl, shoving him forward.

I can feel the anger rising. Every moment I delay is a moment I'm not spending with Kat in my arms, or in my nest, or under me as I fill her with my young.

I want to hunt her through the eyrie until I catch her and devour her, and these vrexing Drahon are keeping me from her.

The ship lurches sideways, and the lights flicker.

"Fuck! What was that?" one of the females cries out in alarm.

I know it can only be one thing.

My unit and my mate are here, and I have to execute the rest of the plan.

"Keep up," I call over my shoulder and dig my claws farther into the shoulder of the Drahon. He squeals and runs towards a doorway. "Open it."

He presses his hand on the panel, and the door slides open. I fire three shots in before flinging the Drahon inside. There is chaos as Huntr appears by my side. His eyes are wild, red almost. He roars out something that is far more than just anger. It comes from the bottom of his soul as he fires on the remaining Drahon, taking several hits before there is no more fire.

"Thanks for that," I say as smoke fills the control center. "We really needed one of them alive to fly this thing."

"I can fly a vrexing Drahon ship," he grumbles at me.

"You probably could have told me that sooner."

He shrugs, pushing past me to check on the human females, one human female in particular. The way he cups Jen's chin makes my heart pound.

My blood sings in my veins. I have to get to my mate.

"We don't have time for this, Huntr. Get this ship on the ground," I fire at him. "We need my team to deal with any remaining Drahon."

"Yes, *Commander*," Huntr replies, his voice dripping with sarcasm.

Just what I need, another vrexing warrior who thinks he knows best for himself.

There's another judder that reverberates through the ship.

"Any chance you could tell them to stop firing?" Huntr asks me.

"Just get this thing on the ground, that's the plan," I reply.

"There actually was a plan?" He works at the console, and the ship dips forward suddenly.

"I thought you said you knew how to fly this thing?" I flare my wings to keep me on my feet.

"Vrex you!" Huntr says through gritted teeth. "It's been a while."

"You could have told me that, too." I give him the benefit of my best commander smile. I'm pretty sure the look he gives me could have set my wings on fire. "I'm going to clear our way to the exit. As soon as you're on the ground, bring the females."

My mate is close, and I will get to her. I exit the control center, and a barrage of laser bolts fire at me.

Looks like the Drahon are not quite done yet.

Kat

"It's going down! The Guv must have taken control," Ayar says, undisguised glee in his voice.

They are all perched happily on a platform that extends from the ship, wind rushing through their feathers as I cling to the doorframe.

"But the collar?" I frown. "He was in handcuffs."

Vypr takes a moment from firing at the other ship to shoot me a quizzical look.

"That's the plan," he says, before going back to his work.

"This is not a plan!" Unbelievably, I stamp my foot. "This is you blasting the hell out of a ship with Strykr on it and probably the humans too."

"Did he not promise you he would return?" Vypr replies evenly.

I'm so fucking angry, I could pluck out his wing feathers at his tone. God only knows how Strykr kept his temper.

"Yes, he did," I get out through gritted teeth.

"Then he will. The ship is descending." Vypr looks over at Ayar who gives the impression of a dog hanging out of a car window. "Don't shoot it again."

"It's down," Jay says.

"Come on." Ayar hoists me unceremoniously into his arms, and we're in the air long before our ship hits the ground.

Flanked by Vypr, Mylo, and Jay, we spin dizzily around the ship until we reach the airlock.

"Vrexing Drahon!" Ayar says. Slipping his laser cannon from his shoulder, he holds it at his hip and fires.

"Ayar!" I yell in his ear to get his attention. "Stop firing. Strykr could be down there!"

Vypr is beside us. "We have to go in closer."

Ayar growls, but the weapon is back on his shoulder as we dive down to the spaceship.

It sits, the ground underneath it crumpled, dust and steam rising around it. Somehow, I don't think it had a soft landing. The external airlock is open, but there's no sign of any Drahon.

Or Strykr.

"Mylo, Jay, with me," Vypr says. "Ayar, you stay here with the little mistress. The Guv will have our wings if anything happens to her." He runs his hand briefly through Ayar's feathers before taking off for the airlock that looks like the open maw of a dragon, smoke billowing out.

The huge warrior huffs a breath but stays where he is, alert and ready for danger as he follows Vypr's progress.

I wrap my arms around myself. Unsure of what to do. I want to be here, for Strykr, but I feel useless.

"Mistress?" Syn lands beside us both with a thump, causing Ayar to growl. "I need your little bot to check the defense system is activated."

I uncurl Ike from around my neck and hand him over. Ayar ignores him completely, and Syn takes him from me, holding him next to the small, clear device he has.

"Vrex," he says. "It's what I thought—it's not fully activated. There is a gap."

"Doesn't matter," Ayar grumbles at him. "We've got these vrexers now."

There's a rattle at the airlock, and both Syn and Ayar have their weapons pointed at the door, with Syn pushing me behind him.

My eregri

I hear the words in my head as surely as if they are spoken aloud.

"Strykr!" I run out from behind Syn, and I'm half-flying across the rough terrain.

My alien angel appears through the mist and fog of the downed ship. It clings to him, and for an instant, he's almost ethereal. Except he's smeared in blood. Wings held high, he holds his side.

I hit him with all too much force, but only because I need to be with him. To know he's real.

"Why the fuck did you do that?" I shout, wrapping my arms around him. "Why did you pretend to leave me? If you do that again, I will kill you!"

I plunge my hands into his feathers and feel his arms wrapping around my body. His face buried in my hair.

"My *eregri*," he murmurs. "You are the only thing that could bring me back from the brink. I'd give my wings for you. You know that, don't you? There are no bonds, no collars, no species that could keep me from you. I would move the galaxies to be by your side, my brave mate."

"I should think so." I snuggle against him, breathing in the scent that is uniquely and only Strykr. "Because I can't save you all the time, you know." I lift my head to look into his liquid dark eyes. "You are my everything, and wherever you are, I know it's the place I want to be."

He closes his eyes, and my mind whirls with his delight and pleasure, tinged slightly with the pain from the wound on his side.

"I need to get the other humans," he says. "Where is my unit?"

"Did you not see Mylo, Vypr, and Jay?" Ayar is next to us. "They went in to look for you."

"Vrex! I've had to fight my way out. That ship is full of Drahon who think spraying enough laser bolts around is a form of fighting," Strykr replies.

"Good thing I like to do the same," a deep voice rumbles out of the thick smoke.

A warrior steps through, and this one looks like he's from the bowels of hell. He's enormous, filthy, with mad eyes. Holding his hand is a blonde woman who stares at me as if she's never seen a human before.

"There are other humans!" she calls back into the smoke.

Two more women step out into the light, blinking. They all wear the same thing, the tiny shift dresses that I had to wear when I was on the space station.

Next to us, the ship shudders, the airlock grinding as it attempts to close.

"Vypr!" Ayar springs forward.

Strykr catches him just in time. "Wait, I'm not losing anyone else in there," he says as Ayar battles him.

The airlock closes with a groan.

"But I don't want to lose this ship either. Huntr?" he fires at the mad looking warrior.

"Oh, they're not going anywhere, Commander. Not without this." He reaches into his tattered trousers and pulls out a small, clear cube. "Their guidance system."

Ayar attempts to punch Strykr in his wound, and he's slammed to the floor. Strykr has him on his back and pinned beneath him.

"Don't," he says. "I understand, Ayar. I really do. But this won't solve anything."

"Vypr!" Ayar cries out.

I'm on my knees next to them both. Wanting to make everything okay. I put one hand on Ayar's forehead and another on Strykr's arm.

"You know we are strong, as long as we are together. You brought me back my mate, Ayar. We won't lose Vypr. I promise and your guv promises."

My eyes are full of tears as Strykr lets Ayar go and wraps me up in his arms, holding me as if he can't ever let me go.

The airlock whines, groans, and suddenly punches outwards. Two Gryn warriors appear in silhouette.

"Vrexing run for it! They've set it to self-destruct!"

I'm whipped up into Strykr's arms as both Vypr and Mylo come barreling towards us. Each of them snags a human as they leap into the air.

"Where's Jay?" I ask, but my words are carried away as we're in the air and flying hard.

As if in response, there's a loud clicking sound behind us, and a smaller craft emerges out of the shell of a larger one.

"Vrex!" Syn calls out. "That's an escape craft. It's small enough to get through the gap in the planetary defenses."

"Just go!" Mylo yells, accelerating forward with his human cargo.

We head for a low hill that was once covered in buildings and is now only a wreck. A low, dull 'whump,' and the ship behind us detonates. The blast catches up with the sound in half a second, and as one, we tumble over and over in the air until we're slammed into the ground.

Strykr

"Lyon reckons he can repair the second ship, with Syn's assistance," Ryak tells me as the Drahon ship touches down on the launch pad, next to the one that he brought back from Proto.

The silver ship is scorched in places, but the blast from the supposed self-destruct didn't do any real damage. We were able to tow it back to the eyrie using the relatively undamaged craft. An initial search confirmed that Jay was not on board and that there was a missing escape pod.

"We have to go after Jay," I say, staring at the ship. "The Drahon wanted a Gryn male, and they didn't care which one. I know my unit, Ryak. We won't rest until he returns to us, alive."

Ryak makes a small snorting sound which is what passes for laughter from him.

"Some of the other Gryn believe your unit is unkillable," he says.

"About time we had a reputation for anything other than being a bunch of vrexers." I look over to where Vypr and Ayar are in a deep discussion together. Mylo and Syn are side by side looking at a vector pad. Anything to keep themselves busy. To not think about the loss of Jay.

A warm hand winds itself around my waist, and I look down at a mate who is more dust than human at the moment. I trace a hand over her cheek and tuck her into my side.

"Are the humans settled?"

"I'm not sure I'd call it settled. Robin has a broken arm, and the others are understandably worried about her, since, as Diana put it, 'it's a fucking dystopian nightmare'." She sighs. "I've tried to explain, but I'm not sure I've done a good enough job. Diana is adamant she wants to use one of the remaining ships to try to find her sister, who was with her when she was abducted."

"If you're right about Jay, then we're going to have to go after the Drahon." Ryak shuffles his wing feathers, the only outward sign that he understands the strain the loss of Jay has put on my unit.

"The Drahon will be dealt with, but first, we need more functioning spacecraft and a defense system that isn't full of holes," I grind out.

Kat snuggles closer to me, her mind filling mine with the thought of hot water, splashing and...

Naked, pink skin.

I know we have to find Jay, but mating with her, taking her to my nest, claiming her has to be my priority.

Because it's what I promised her. My love, my desires, my protection, and all of me.

And I keep my promises. We are bound as mates as the goddess decrees, but there is more at stake. I want her in my furs and her belly full of my youngling.

I've never wanted anything more.

"All of that will take time, Ryak." I turn to him. "I never leave a warrior behind, you know that because you taught me.

But I'm not taking the fight to the Drahon until we have the weapons and the craft to do so."

My mate gently runs a hand through my wing feathers, and it's all I can do not to groan out loud.

"And I'm not fighting in the pits anymore. The fight is in the stars or out in the open with the Kijg," I tell him. "We know who the enemy is, and we must behave like the honorable warriors we are. There's a reason why the Drahon want us."

Ryak folds his arms, the senior Gryn testing out my thoughtbond even as I shut him down with my newfound ability that has only come from being a mated male.

"And why's that, Strykr?" he asks.

"Because of our honor. We are predators who can be manipulated to their ends. The Drahon are what the Kijg want to be, in control of Ustokos, and because of that, they are even more dangerous than Proto."

Ryak inclines his head as he contemplates the intelligence I have given him. The wily senior Gryn won't ever let me into that dark place he calls his mind, but if I can convince him to look outwards from Ustokos, and not inwards, it will be a safer place for my mate. The Kijg, we can deal with. It's the Drahon who are the threat.

"Let's get these ships in working order, then we can talk," he says.

I wait.

He looks at me and Kat.

We wait.

"And no more fighting in the pits, for you or any other Gryn. You're right. We are honorable warriors. I should never have made you go on fighting so long."

Ryak puts his hand on my shoulder, and this time, I let him in.

You are a worthy senior, my brother

His words fill me with a glow that is good. It surrounds my heart, and I look at my mate.

Her smile is all I need. It sends me into orbit, she is so beautiful.

"If you will excuse us, Guv, we have mating to attend to." I wrap my arm around my mate

"You do, indeed, Commander." Ryak hitches his lips up in a smile that could crack glass. I feel Kat shrink into me.

"After I've spoken with my unit."

This time, the smile is warmer. "I'll speak with them. They'll want to go after Jay. And it's authorized, just as soon as the second ship is repaired."

Kat's arm is warm around my waist, and she snuggles into my side.

My perfect prey.

"Jay will be okay. After all, he's one of yours, isn't he?" She soothes my rough edges as we watch Ryak walk over to the others. They gather around him, and after a short while, Ayar punches the air.

"Bunch of vrexers," I grumble.

"Our bunch of vrexers." Kat traces her fingers over my stomach. "Now, someone promised me a nest?"

I flip her into my arms, opening my wings. "And who could have possibly done that?"

"I think—" Her breath catches as I lift off the ground, heading to the very top of the eyrie. "It might just have been a certain Commander Strykr."

Below us, there is the sound of ribald cheering.

My mate and my unit.

We are one.

Kat

I bob in the big pool as Ike zips above me, flitting from vine to vine. He chirps occasionally, his lights flashing on and off blue and yellow. The hot water invades my bones, silky against my skin.

It's glorious to be bathing here. Quiet and serene, I luxuriate in the silence as I prop myself up on the small ledge, my chin touching the water.

In the center, bubbles rise, and they are followed by an eruption of Gryn proportions. Strykr surfaces, water sluicing off his body and wings as he rises out, splashing great waves absolutely everywhere.

His eyes fix on me, and he's still for a second before slowly swimming towards me, his predatory gaze never wavering.

"I couldn't find the bottom. It goes down a long way. The eyrie is built around a natural rock formation. Presumably, this was part of it," he says as he reaches me, scooting me a little higher as he wraps his arms around my naked body, nuzzling at my neck.

I've lost track of how long we've spent in our nest or in

this pool. It could be days, it could be weeks. And the longer I spend with him, the stronger our bond gets.

I am whole.

"Maybe I should go down and take a look?" I wriggle against him, my body slippery against his hard abdomen.

"You're not going anywhere, little prey," Strykr growls into my neck, spinning us around until I'm pinned against him, and his wings are spread out over the edge of the pool to dry. "You can stay right here. I have to feed you, then I've got some work to do on our nest."

"Again?" I twist up until I can look into his face, gently cupping his cheek in my hand. "I've told you I love it. You don't need to do any more work to it."

Strykr frowns at me. "It's not right, not yet. I think it needs..."

"You know exactly what it needs. You and me. That's all." I laugh at him.

Our nest has become his newest obsession, and I'd be Ustokos's biggest liar if I didn't find his desire for interior decoration the most adorable thing ever.

If I thought what he made on the space station was impressive, what he's done on the planet goes above and beyond.

The last time he 'upgraded,' it was to install something that resembled a chandelier. Part of me has to admit, I'd like to see exactly what he has in mind to top that. The rest of me knows that I love our nest just the way it is.

"You do?" Strykr trails a claw down my neck, responding to my thoughts as usual.

"I love you, Strykr. I love anything you do, but you don't have anything to prove to me."

"Sweet mate, I will always have to prove myself to you."

I feel something pull down the thoughtbond. Strykr has concerns.

"What is it?" I spin around to face him, straddling his lap and putting my hands on his shoulders, longing to run my fingers through his feathers in the way I now know he loves.

"We've been through so much, little Kat." He swallows hard. "You've been through so much, it's been hard to get this time for us."

"I know, but we've got plenty of time."

"It's just..." Strykr shifts under me and not because we're so close. His discomfort is unnerving me.

I fix him with a stare.

"Whatever it is, my love, we can get through it together. You put me together. You showed me that I could be part of something so much bigger again. A family of sorts, two halves of a whole. I didn't even know that was what was missing until you showed me."

"I'm just a dirty pit fighter. Why would a beautiful creature like you want me?" Strykr runs his hand through his hair, making it stick up in all directions.

"You are anything but the pit." I press my lips to his in a long kiss. "But you are my fighter. You taught me there are things worth fighting for. And to me, that's you."

"Sweet mate," he murmurs, his dark eyes studying me as he gently slides a clawed hand around the back of my neck and into my hair. "I don't deserve you."

"We deserve each other," I say firmly.

"Kat?" His hand drops away from me, and he shifts me off his lap, turning to the enormous tray of food he brought in earlier.

"What is it?" I ask, concerned at his sudden movement.

"I have something to ask you." My breath stutters as he swirls in the water to face me. "Will you take my band?"

Strykr holds out a tiny circlet of metal. A bright blue that glints in the light. It looks like the one Bianca wears, only this is even more beautiful.

"It's stunning." I can hardly speak.

"Humans do mate for life don't they?" Strykr asks, voice loaded with concern.

"This one does." I wrap my arms around him. "I will take your band, my love. I want to be with you forever."

Strykr slides the metal over my hand and up my arm until it reaches my bicep. There, it settles, warm and as if it's part of me already.

"What about you?" I ask. "Will you take my band?"

He chuckles. "I'm already bound to you. I was the moment I set eyes on my little prey on the space station." He holds out a larger band, the same color. "But I have this for you anyway. Please take it, take all of me, make me yours, your mate, your forever, and my boundless flight."

I slip the band over his left arm and up over the glistening wet skin until it reaches the same place as mine. Strykr lets out a long, deep breath. "My Kat."

"I am your Kat. I will always be yours for as long as you want me and beyond. You are my star, Strykr. You brought me home."

Epilogue

Kat

"Kat," Strykr groans into the crook of my neck, his hands running over my bare skin and causing goosebumps to shiver over every part of me. "Your scent, by Nisis, your scent, it's enough to drive a Gryn to..."

His hands rove lower, cupping my little bump easily as he presses his mouth to it. As is usual, this time of day, I'm entirely naked. Already stripped for his attentions, each garment removed by him until I'm panting, bare, and spread for him.

"Distraction?" I query with a smile.

Ever since the Gryn doctor, Orvos, confirmed I was pregnant, Strykr has been unable to let me out of his sight, even for an instant.

I would say it makes things awkward, but instead, I've been treated like a queen. And it makes the whole concept of being pregnant so much more fun. We've fallen easily into a routine. Strykr trains every morning with his unit, and I'm waited on hand and foot by them all. Afternoons are spent checking on the progress with the ships, checking how the other humans are settling in, and mating.

Mostly mating. Believe me, I'm not complaining!

Because if there's one thing Strykr likes more than chasing his prey, it's pregnant prey. Since my pregnancy began to show, about three weeks ago because apparently Gryn babies only like to bake for five months, and these babies, Bianca has already told me, are BIG.

All of which means I'm only two months pregnant, and I'm bulging.

Strykr loves it. Worshiping my belly more than makes up for not being able to hunt me down.

"I want to taste you." His mouth moves lower, tongue skirting down between the crease in my thighs, huge hands parting my legs. "Your sweet cunt tastes even better with our youngling inside you."

My hands flail as he descends. I'm grabbing for anything and connect with his wings. He moans at me as I rub the soft feathers.

"You are to be devoured, delicious prey." He swipes his tongue through my folds, one enormous, clawed hand spanning my stomach. He lifts up his head to gaze at me. "And then I'm going to mate you until you scream my name."

I'm already panting. The way he delights in my changing body is a constant turn on.

His head drops again, and this time, his tongue is joined by his fingers, slipping inside me as he sucks my clit between sharp teeth, and my senses explode beneath his touch.

"So beautiful, spread for me," he rumbles, tongue exploring my channel and dipping lower until he's lapping at my sensitive anus. I'm shaking, writhing, and grasping at his feathers as he continues to enjoy me, slurping and moaning as I flood him, time and time again.

"Will you come for me, perfect prey?"

I'm convulsing as he curls his finger deep inside me, the

smooth back of his claw pressing on my g-spot. My eyes squeeze shut until I hear his growl.

"Prey will look at her predator when he pleasures her."

"This prey wants to pleasure her captor."

He's already stroking himself from base to tip, both cocks weeping pre-cum copiously. I know exactly where those are going, and I know exactly how to send him wild. I roll over and prop myself up on all fours, looking over my shoulder at my gorgeous warrior.

His eyes are huge, dark, and glittering as I present him with my rump, my belly hanging low so he can see.

"Mate!" He groans, on the very edge.

"Fill me with your cocks, Strykr. I want to lose my voice with shouting your name."

He roars out. Cocks pressed at my entrance, he separates them, and I stretch around his primary cock as he enters me, rough and hard. His secondary cock slides up and hits my clit with every single ridge and node.

"I cannot...I cannot be gentle, sweet one. I have to take all of you." Strykr groans, sliding his hand around my waist and under my belly where he grasps his secondary cock, pressing it up against my clit as he begins to thrust.

I cry out in pleasure as he pistons into me, one hand grasping at my hip and the other caressing my bump. With each thrust, he goes deeper, and then he slows down.

"By Nisis, you look so glorious wrapped around my cock," he rasps out. When I check over my shoulder, he's staring down at where we are joined.

His words cause another flood of moisture, and he groans out loud. "Strykr!" I moan. "I need to come."

I want his cocks pounding my pussy while he enjoys every inch of me.

"I need to come so hard!"

He pulls me to him, redoubling his efforts, plundering my channel.

"My mate, my mate. You're so delicious, so ripe!"

He suddenly withdraws from me, and I gasp out loud because I'm so close, so very close to an orgasm that will leave me boneless. Then I'm flipped over onto my front, dragged to the edge of the bed as Strykr towers over me, wings wide, stretching almost the full width of our nest.

"I need to see you when I fill you." He groans and slams back inside me, impaling me on his cocks, plundering both of my channels with ease.

He places one huge, clawed hand on my belly, the other on my hip. He gazes down at my body with a look of complete and utter adoration.

"I need to take in all of you, my most perfect mate." He pumps his hips, circling and making sure I feel every node, every ridge. "You are the glory, you are the boundless flight, you are mine." Strykr increases his pace, and his eyes glow with pure lust.

I'm not sure I can take a breath. Everything convulses at once as the orgasm takes me, my body coming undone as he roars out, shaking the very foundations of the eyrie with his joy, his desire, and his ownership of me.

"Mine," I growl back at my handsome mate. "All mine."

Book 2: Jay and Lauren's story, FURY: A Sci-Fi Alien Romance. Read on for a taster!

Sign up to my newsletter for a free super sweet bonus scene where Strykr surprises Kat with his nest. You'll also get sneak peaks, cover reveals, exclusive content and giveaways.

So if you want all of the above, sign up HERE

You can also sign up on my website www.hattiejacks.com

And you can follow me on Bookbub, Amazon or even join my Facebook group - Hattie's Hotties!

FURY: A SCI-FI ALIEN ROMANCE

Lauren

"Hey, you!" The big green lizard creature shouts.

The words are partially garbled by sharp teeth and a heavy accent. But then these are aliens. I'm on an alien planet and somehow—they haven't bothered to explained the process—I can understand them.

"Yes, you!" It repeats. This one is male, over six foot tall. It carries a long silver tube which lights up at the end and burns. Don't ask me how I know.

I point to myself. "Me?"

'Hey, you' indeed! It's come to this, abducted by aliens and I go from 'Professor' to 'hey, you' overnight.

"Come here, female." It snarls.

Oh, yes. And 'female' is the other generous nickname bestowed on me by my alien friends. I walk slowly to where he is standing. Attracting the attention of the lizard aliens, who call themselves 'Drahon', is never a good thing. Or so I've found out in the time I've been their captive.

"Clean this up." He points at a pile of what can only be dung.

"Really?" I stare at him, which is a mistake. Questioning him at all is a mistake. He wields his stun tube and the light glows.

"What the zark else are you here for, female?" He spits, towering over me in an attempt to intimidate, his hand around my neck pinning me against the wall.

I shrink away from the light. They only had to touch me with one of those things once, and I understood the hideous pain it created once it hit my skin.

I shouldn't even be out in the compound on the alien planet, where two moons always hang in the sky and their sun seems a long way away. Dust drifts where it hits the high walls, intended presumably to keep in all their prisoners. I was only using a short cut I've discovered from one side of the interconnected domes to the other, better to speed up the drudge work I now do.

I might be the only human captive of these lizard aliens, but I'm not their only prisoner.

Which is presumably where the dung comes in.

I spot an implement nearby that could be a shovel and hurry over to collect it. The last thing I want is for the Drahon to question why I'm out here in the first place. We get precious little food or rest as it is. Any punishment will result in those limited privileges taken away from me.

"So, where do you want me to put this?" I ask the Drahon who hovers over me disconcertingly. I swing around with the shovel full of evil smelling stuff, and he takes a step back with what seems to be a look of horror on his weird lizard face.

"Over there!" He points to a hole in the ground. "Quickly." He adds.

I deliberate whether I can manage to 'fall over' and get some of it on him, but decide such a small victory would probably not be worth the punishment.

Because when it comes to pain, I'm pretty weak, something the Drahon found out quickly when I'd first arrived. They haven't even bothered collaring me; I'm that easy to control. Doesn't stop my mouth running away with me on occasion, with inevitable consequences.

"That's enough, female. Get back inside." The Drahon snarls at me as I dispose of the last shovel full.

"No, really, it was my pleasure." I mutter under my breath as I dump the shovel and have to go back the way I came.

All of which means I'm now late to clear up after the midday meal. There will be consequences.

I hate what I've become. It's a far cry from my job as a senior locum lecturer in ancient studies, most recently at a prestigious university in the North of England. I might not have been a professor exactly, but it had been a dream of mine to get to that level one day. The job wasn't great. A constant fight for funding with the university board which contained my ex, Mark, the senior professor in History and the man I'd caught fucking his secretary just before we were supposed to go to my mother's funeral.

I didn't shovel dung or clear up after a myriad of lizard aliens. I wasn't constantly threatened with pain, or worse. The one saving grace is apparently the only reason I've not been sold for 'pleasure' as the Drahon put it, is because I'm considered too puny to survive the sexual attentions of other aliens.

I'd hardly consider myself 'puny', certainly by human standards. I'm taller than average with a generous amount up top, down below and everywhere else. Even the significant diet since I've been here hasn't reduced me that much. I suppose I should be grateful for small mercies, especially given the types of aliens I've seen since I've been at the Drahon's mercy.

Yep, if aliens that look like massive walking monitor lizards weren't bad enough, there are *things* with tentacles, claws, more than two eyes, snapping sharp teeth and more. But what is worse are the ones that look humanoid.

Because they are not, and every time I see one, my heart leaps into my throat that I'm not alone in this terrifying new universe.

"Lauren?" A low voice calls to me out of a dark corner. "Where have you been?"

A small body steps out of the shadows.

"I tried to take the shortcut and got caught, sorry, Nari." I say to the little lizard alien.

She's smaller than the Drahon and claims she's a different species, something called a Kijg. Her skin changes color with her mood, unlike the Drahon. Presently she's a deep purple, which means she's worried.

"You're late." Her green eyes dart from side to side. "I did what I could but she noticed."

"Don't worry, I'll deal with *her*." I reply with a boldness that belies the quaking terror within.

Every day I wake up in this hideous new existence, I wish I'd not gone star gazing that night. Out in rural Northumberland, up near the Scottish Borders, where the skies were dark and clear. Where we were excavating some Roman remains, if I'd not left the camp to look for the aurora the weather forecast had said would be in the night sky, the aliens never would have found me.

Instead, I'd be back in the ruins of my existence, hating my ex, hating his new partner, and fighting to have my contract renewed.

It's funny how a crappy life can suddenly seem so much better when viewed through the lens of alien abduction.

Instead, I'm about to go toe-to-toe with the nastiest creature this side of Alpha Centuri, or wherever the hell I am. If I thought dealing with academia and betrayal was bad, they have nothing on Yuliat, the Drahon boss.

"Where is the human?" Her shrill voice rings out further down the corridor.

There's something about me being human that pisses her off. I can't put my finger on it, but somehow, I can't help but emphasize how human I am when I'm around her. Because I want to piss her off more, it's as if I can't help myself.

And I can't. I've never liked bullies, human or alien.

"I'm here." I push Nari behind me. It's not her fault I'm late, and I don't want her punished. "I got asked to clear up some shit outside. We're going to start clearing up in here now."

Yuliat stomps through from the canteen. Nari tells me she used to be a high-powered scientist, with friends in high places. What she's doing here is anyone's guess. Although in the main, it appears all she wants to do is make my life a misery.

Fortunately not only am I already miserable, there's not anywhere to go when I'm already at the bottom, so her attempts generally fail. Which usually pisses her off even more.

My shoulder is grabbed by a three fingered clawed hand as Yuliat leans into me, her eyes glittering nastily as her lips hitch in a grimace that I believe passes for a smile among the Drahon.

"You won't be doing any more cleaning today, human."

"I won't? You are most kind, Yuliat." I reply, knowing that sarcasm is entirely lost on aliens, but it makes me feel better.

"No, you've got a special assignment." She says, leaning closer, almost conspiratorially.

Oh shit. That is not going to be good. At all.

"I don't mind cleaning the canteen." I garble out. "I can do some feed rounds as well." I add, meaning the other prisoners, some of which have disgusting eating habits, and some of which have sharp edges and short tempers.

Occasionally, the Drahon bring them out into the compound and make them fight each other. It's never pretty.

But I'd do anything to avoid doing something 'special'. It's likely to result in bodily injury.

"No." Yuliat looks me up and down. "You're perfect for this assignment. You'll be tending to the Gryn until he recovers."

There's a sharp intake from Nari behind me.

"What's a Gryn?" I ask, and I wish I hadn't because Yuliat's grimace widens.

"You'll find out soon enough." She laughs, increasing her grip on my shoulder and propelling me in front of her towards the prisoner's cells.

Jay

I attempt to growl out a warning at the approaching Drahon male, but my lungs don't want to comply.

"Wake up, Gryn. You're being moved." He snarls at me.

"Vrex off!" I snarl back, swiping out at him, anything to keep the disgusting creatures off me. Their scent alone fills my mouth with bile. It takes a huge amount of effort, but I unfurl my wings and attempt to make myself look as big as possible.

"Zarking Gryn. I hate them." The guard shouts over his shoulder at his friend. They always come in pairs as a bare minimum. Since yesterday, there hasn't been less than four. "All feathers and nasty tempers."

"Like you can talk, Drahon scum." I spit at him as my breath wheezes and every single part of me hurts like a bastid. "Can't say it's been sweetness and light for me either."

He slams me in the side of my head with the less painful end of his stun stick and I fall back onto the floor.

"Hold this piece of trash down." He calls over his shoulder. "Yuliat wants to see him."

There's some grumbling, because I've probably managed

to mark every single Drahon in this place with my claws at least once. But I'm pretty badly banged up, and it only takes three to subdue me.

Some time ago, I'm not entirely sure how long, given everything that's happened since, I stupidly allowed myself to get caught by the Drahon while trying to free my Commander from their clutches.

Instead of staying with my unit, I charged ahead of my fellow warriors, so vrexing sure of myself, so vrexing clever. All that had happened was I ended up trapped in an escape pod with the Drahon after they set the auto-destruct on their ship.

Even now, the idiocy of that move burns within me. Because by now I'm probably light years from Ustokos and my unit. All I want is to get back home. I want to know if my unit are alive, or if the blast I saw as we ascended into space killed them all.

If they're dead, that's on me. The thought fills my mind in every waking moment. It haunts my dreams.

"What's Yuliat want with him?" A Drahon male kneels on my chest, making breathing harder and more painful. "He's zarking untrainable, she won't be able to sell him."

The Drahon have plans for me, or so I've been told. But, to my amusement, it's not been working out for them. The control collar they fitted might shock me, but I don't comply. They repeatedly try to goad me into fighting, but I won't, no matter what they do.

Because I have to get back to my unit. I have to get back to Ustokos and make sure I didn't kill them all. Getting back is all I can think about.

So for the last seven turns, I'd been observing. Keeping up enough resistance to the Drahon so they don't work out what I was doing, but I was working out their weaknesses, their routines.

It was more than enough knowledge for me to escape. And that's what I did. Yesterday.

My problem was I didn't know there was some sort of energy field over the compound. Once I got outside, it seemed easy enough to fly away. Instead, I flew head first into something that disabled me. I hit the ground hard enough to do some damage to my ribs and shoulder, and, what's worse is I've injured my left wing. Something I can't let the Drahon know.

A Gryn warrior has always been ready for the fight, but injured and alone? I'm angrier than I've ever been, despite my flesh being weak. Once I'm back to strength, the Drahon will pay for what they've done.

"Get the vrex off me!" I squirm under the Drahon.

"Want to fight, Gryn?" The guard laughs at me. "I'll fight you and I'll win."

"That sounds like your style, taking on an injured warrior." I reply, unsheathing my claws.

He pulls out one of his stun sticks, the white light glowing at the end and shoves it into my injured ribs. Unable to help myself, I let out a howl of agony, white sheeting my vision.

"Stop that!" A higher pitched voice rings out in my tiny cell. "We need this one alive and well if we're to meet our quota."

I look up from my position on the floor to see a female Drahon. She's slender like most of the Drahon, possibly feminine, but then she's the only female I've seen so far. She is slightly taller than the males and wears a long coat over their usual uniform of a single one-piece white suit.

"Nothing we do makes him comply. This one's been free far too long. He's useless to us if he can't be trained." The Drahon not currently kneeling on a body part says.

"And we need to recoup the costs of the ship you lost."

She stabs a green finger at him. "This is all we've got. We don't have to say he's trained, there are buyers for Gryn regardless. They're rare enough."

She kneels next to me and runs something over me which bleeps, and she frowns.

"I prefer my Gryn compliant though. But a shot of this," she pulls a silver injector from the pocket of her coat, "that should cure his rebellious nature for the time being." Yuliat grins at me, or at least she bares her teeth.

She goes back to studying the small pad in her hand.

"What did you let him do to himself?" She glares at the guard standing at the door. "He's going to need some time to heal, and while he's under the influence, a nursemaid."

"He did that to himself because he zarking escaped. Put two of my cohort in the infirmary, even in that state." The male snaps and one of the other Drahon holding me down thumps me in my ribs. I grunt.

"He's worthless if you kill him, understand?" Yuliat fires out. "And your cohort need more weapons and armor if they can be beaten by a Gryn warrior in this state."

"Where do you want me to put him? He can't stay in here." The male says. "He smashes himself to pieces, even in *this state*."

"He's going to be just fine." Yuliat presses the injector into my neck. I feel a cool sensation against my skin as it hisses the narcotic into my veins.

"That stuff should do the trick, but in any any case, put him in room four. Maybe with a bit of pampering and the right incentives, he might see the sense in complying." She takes my chin in her hand, turning my heavy head to face her.

"See? They're such darlings when they're like this. All soft and dreamy." She croons horribly.

I try to pull my chin from her grip, but I can't. Everything is weak. The female Drahon swims in my vision and I feel nauseous.

Then I feel good.

Really good.

To be continued....

Get your copy of FURY: A Sci-Fi Alien Romance now!

Also by Hattie Jacks

ELITE ROGUE ALIEN WARRIORS SERIES

STORM

FURY

CHAOS

REBEL (Coming soon)

WRATH (Coming soon)

ROGUE ALIEN WARRIORS SERIES

Fierce

Fear

Fire

Fallen

Forever

SCI-FI ROMANCE ANTHOLOGY

Claimed Among The Stars includes:
Fated: A Rogue Alien Warriors Novella

HAALUX EMPIRE SERIES

Taken: Alien Commander's Captive

Crave: Alien General's Obsession
Havoc: Alien Captain's Alliance
Bane: Alien Warrior's Redemption
Traitor: Alien Hunter's Mate

Just who is this Hattie Jacks anyway?

I've been a passionate sci-fi fan since I was a little girl, brought up on a diet of Douglas Adams, Issac Asimov, Star Trek, Star Wars, Doctor Who, Red Dwarf and The Adventure Game.

What? You don't know about The Adventure Game? It's probably a British thing and dates me horribly! Google it. Even better search for it on YouTube. In my defence, there were only three channels back then.

I'm also a sucker for great characters and situations as well as grand romance, because who doesn't like a grand romantic gesture?

So, when I'm not writing steamy stories about smouldering alien males and women with something to prove, you'll find me battling my garden (less English country garden, more The Good Life) or zooming around the countryside on my motorbike.

Check out my website at www.hattiejacks.com!

Printed in Great Britain
by Amazon